THE SEA WITHIN

What Reviewers Say About Missouri Vaun's Work

Chasing Sunset

"*Chasing Sunset* is a fun and enjoyable ride off into the sunset. Colorful characters, laughs and a sweet romance blend together to make a tasty read."—*Aspen Tree Book Reviews*

"This is a lovely summer romance. It has all the elements that you want in this type of novel: beautiful characters, great chemistry, lovely settings, and best of all, a nostalgic road trip across the country."
—*Rainbow Reflections*

"I really liked this one! I found both Finn and Iris to be well fleshed out characters. Both women are trying to figure out their next steps, and that makes them both insecure about where their relationship is going. They have some major communication issues, but I found that, too, realistic. This was a low key read but very enjoyable. Recommended!"
—Rebekah Miller, Librarian (University of Pittsburgh)

"The love story was tender and emotional and the sex was steamy and told so much about how intense their relationship was. I really enjoyed this story. Missouri Vaun has become one of my favourite authors and I'm never disappointed."—*Kitty Kat's Book Review Blog*

Spencer's Cove

"Just when I thought I knew where this story was going and who everyone was, Missouri Vaun took me on a ride that totally exceeded my expectations. ...It was a magical tale and I absolutely adored it. Highly recommended."—*Kitty Kat's Book Reviews*

"The book is great fun. The chemistry between Abby and Foster is practically tangible. ...Anyone who has seen and enjoyed the series *Charmed*, is going to be completely charmed by this rollicking romance."—*reviewer@large*

"Missouri Vaun has this way of taking me into the world she has created and does not let me out until I'm finished the book."—*Les Rêveur*

"I was 100% all in after the first couple of pages and I wanted to call in sick, so I could stay home from work to immerse myself in this story. I've always enjoyed Missouri Vaun's books and I'm impressed with how she moves between genres with such ease. As paranormal stories go, this one left me thinking, 'Hmm, I wish I was part of that world,' and I've never read a book featuring vampires or weres that left me with that feeling. To sum it up, witches rock and Vaun made me a believer."—*Lesbian Review*

Take My Hand

"The chemistry between River and Clay is off the charts and their sex scenes were just plain hot!"—*Les Rêveur*

"The small town charms of *Take My Hand* evoke the heady perfume of pine needles and undergrowth, birdsong, and summer cocktails with friends."—*Omnivore Bibliosaur*

Love at Cooper's Creek

"Blown away...how have I not read a book by Missouri Vaun before. What a beautiful love story which, honestly, I wasn't ready to finish. Kate and Shaw's chemistry was instantaneous and as the reader I could feel it radiating off the page."—*Les Reveur*

"*Love at Cooper's Creek* is a gentle, warm hug of a book."—*Lesbian Review*

"As always another well written book from Missouri Vaun—sweet romance with very little angst, well developed and likeable lead characters and a little family drama to spice things up."—Melina Bickard, Librarian, Waterloo Library (UK)

Crossing the Wide Forever

"*Crossing the Wide Forever* is a near-heroic love story set in an epic time, told with almost lyrical prose. Words on the page will carry the reader, along with the main characters, back into history and into adventure. It's a tale that's easy to read, with enchanting main characters, despicable villains, and supportive friendships, producing a fascinating account of passion and adventure."—*Lambda Literary Review*

Birthright

"The author develops a world that has a medieval feeling, complete with monasteries and vassal farmers, while also being a place and time where a lesbian relationship is just as legitimate and open as a heterosexual one. This kept pleasantly surprising me throughout my reading of the book. The adventure part of the story was fun, including traveling across kingdoms, on "wind-ships" across deserts, and plenty of sword fighting. ...This book is worth reading for its fantasy world alone. In our world, where those in the LGBTQ communities still often face derision, prejudice, and danger for living and loving openly, being immersed in a world where the Queen can openly love another woman is a refreshing break from reality."—Amanda Chapman, Librarian, Davisville Free Library (RI)

"*Birthright* by Missouri Vaun is one of the smoothest reads I've had my hands on in a long time."—*Lesbian Review*

The Time Before Now

"[*The Time Before Now*] is just so good. Vaun's character work in this novel is flawless. She told a compelling story about a person so real you could just about reach out and touch her."—*Lesbian Review*

The Ground Beneath

"One of my favourite things about Missouri Vaun's writing is her ability to write the attraction between two women. Somehow she manages to get that twinkle in the stomach just right and she makes me feel as if I am falling in love with my wife all over again."—*Lesbian Review*

All Things Rise

"The futuristic world that author Missouri Vaun has brought to life is as interesting as it is plausible. The sci-fi aspect, though, is not hard-core which makes for easy reading and understanding of the technology prevalent in the cloud cities. ...[T]he focus was really on the dynamics of the characters especially Cole, Ava and Audrey—whether they were interacting on the ground or above the clouds. From the first page to the last, the writing was just perfect."—*AoBibliosphere*

"This is a lovely little Sci-Fi romance, well worth a read for anyone looking for something different. I will be keeping an eye out for future works by Missouri Vaun."—*Lesbian Review*

"Simply put, this book is easy to love. Everything about it makes for a wonderful read and re-read. I was able to go on a journey with these characters, an emotional, internal journey where I was able to take a look at the fact that while society and technology can change vastly until almost nothing remains the same, there are some fundamentals that never change, like hope, the raw emotion of human nature, and the far reaching search for the person who is able to soothe the fire in our souls with the love in theirs."—*Roses and Whimsy*

Writing as Paige Braddock

Jane's World and the Case of the Mail Order Bride

"This is such a quirky, sweet novel with a cast of memorable characters. It has laugh out loud moments and will leave you feeling charmed."
—*Lesbian Review*

By the Author

All Things Rise

The Time Before Now

The Ground Beneath

Whiskey Sunrise

Valley of Fire

Death by Cocktail Straw

One More Reason to Leave Orlando

Smothered and Covered

Privacy Glass

Birthright

Crossing the Wide Forever

Love at Cooper's Creek

Take My Hand

Proxima Five

Spencer's Cove

Chasing Sunset

The Sea Within

Writing as Paige Braddock:

Jane's World: The Case of the Mail Order Bride

THE SEA WITHIN

by

Missouri Vaun

2020

THE SEA WITHIN
© 2020 By Missouri Vaun. All Rights Reserved.

ISBN 13: 978-1-63555-568-4

This Trade Paperback Original Is Published By
Bold Strokes Books, Inc.
P.O. Box 249
Valley Falls, NY 12185

First Edition: October 2020

CREDITS
Editor: Cindy Cresap
Production Design: Susan Ramundo
Cover Design By Sheri (hindsightgraphics@gmail.com)
Cover Photo By Michael Ryan

Acknowledgments

This story was written months before the pandemic. There are threads in this novel that seem eerily similar to what we're experiencing now, but not quite the same. I fought the urge to go back and add details that one could only know from experiencing the rapid spread of a novel virus, but I didn't. Because this is a story of another time, an imagined future Earth, where humans face still more challenges. Even still, hope remains and even triumphs.

Special thanks go out to Dr. Kristy Miller who helped me figure out what California was like long, long ago. And a big thank you to Jenny for beta reading an early draft and offering great notes about some of the San Francisco Bay Area details. Local librarian Rachel Icaza pointed me in the right direction for some valuable research. To my other beta readers, Alena and Vanessa, thank you for helping make the story stronger. Evelyn, you are so supportive and endlessly offer insights as I craft characters. I'm so lucky to have you in my life.

I also want to thank the team at Bold Strokes Books. Rad, Sandy, Ruth, Carsen, and Cindy, you're an amazing team to work with and I can't say enough about how you've helped me grow as a writer. You guys are the best. Oh…and last, but certainly not least, thank you Michael Ryan for the amazing cover photo.

Dedication

To Evelyn

CHAPTER ONE

Rain pelted Jackson Drake as she ducked under the shallow overhang and waited for the doorman. Actually, the beefy guy was more of a bouncer than a doorman. The Green Club wasn't a dive, but it wasn't exactly sophisticated either. This place had more of a clubby vibe. Darkness had descended a couple of hours earlier and it wasn't much brighter inside. She flashed an ID and handed her soaked overcoat to a willowy young woman at the coat check counter. The woman had to use both hands to manage the weight of the waterlogged overcoat.

Jackson swept her hand across the soft stubble of her close-cropped hair and shook the droplets from her fingers. Damn, she was sick of the weather. Erratic weather had become a constant. She'd taken an oath to protect and defend. That used to mean from foreign threats; now the weather itself was a threat and the military spent most of its time managing climate fallout, including rescues and displaced people.

The Green Club was pretty full for midweek. Jackson paused in the entryway and scanned the room. Most of her friends preferred the ease of apps like AltLuv for hookups, but not Jackson. An app couldn't tell you everything; the subtleties were what mattered to her. The scent of a woman's hair, the casual caress of fingertips along your arm, and the intangible unknowns of possibility. Besides, to utilize an app or a larger VR space like New Life required building a digital profile, something she didn't have the luxury of doing. Virtual reality didn't really work for Jackson. She craved the real thing. The evenings when she ventured out for companionship were rare anyway. When she got to the point where the ache, the loneliness, kept her from sleeping, eating, or became a dangerous distraction, then she knew she had to take action. So, here she was. Out in the *real* world, where anything could happen.

Jackson usually liked to play a game with herself. She'd identify the most beautiful woman in the club and challenge herself to win the woman over for the night. Her success rate hovered very close to one hundred percent.

A small dance floor in the center of the room was packed. It was the only well-lit spot in the club, ringed by small tables and booths around the darker edges of the room. A strobe bounced circles of light across the patrons in random patterns and then, just as quickly, left them in the dark. Jackson waited for her eyes to adjust.

The music was pulsing, and a woman touched her arm as she slid past in the crowded space. Jackson smiled but didn't engage. There were other potential candidates, but she was looking for a certain— something. As she rotated her head to slowly sweep the room, one woman in particular came into focus. Her target was at the bar. Shoulder-length dark hair with girlish curves. Her attire was casually elegant. This candidate required reconnaissance. The woman glanced toward the door and she locked eyes for a moment and lingered before redirecting her gaze.

Promising.

A middle-aged fashion butch in a dark suit occupied the stool next to the woman, but it would only take a moment to remove that obstacle. Jackson crossed the crowded room, ignoring the women who attempted to catch her attention as she wove through them. Her focus was singular.

"You're in my seat." Jackson towered over the dark-suited butch.

"This isn't your—" She rotated, possibly to start something, but then her gaze angled up.

"Do I know you?" Jackson knew she'd never met the woman.

"I don't think so. Listen, I'm sure you can find another seat at the bar."

"But *this* is my seat, and you're in it." She wasn't really in the mood to negotiate. She was aware that the woman seated next to Fashion Butch was watching, but Jackson didn't look in her direction. This wasn't about her—yet.

The butch woman slid from the stool. She opened her mouth to speak.

"Don't forget your drink." It was obvious that it hadn't been her intention to vacate her seat permanently. She'd probably only stood up to face Jackson, albeit from a much lower elevation. But now that short, dark, and clueless was on her feet, Jackson handed her the drink.

The woman scowled as she accepted the glass.

Jackson casually occupied the now vacant stool at the bar as if it had been her seat all along. She waited until the woman walked away and was swallowed up by the crowd before she rotated. The androgynous bartender in a tight-fitting black T-shirt and jeans came over immediately.

"I'll take a whiskey, neat." They started to walk away, and she called after. "Make it a double." The bartender nodded.

She sat, faced forward, and pretended not to care who was seated next to her. To her credit, the beautiful woman she'd homed in on said nothing. After a couple of minutes, the bartender returned with her drink. Jackson placed one palm flat on the glassy surface of the bar as she tasted the liquor. She held it on her tongue and exhaled after swallowing to allow the flavor to fill her senses.

"How did you do that?" The woman's words had a mellow, sexy timbre.

"Do what?" Jackson still didn't turn to look at her beautiful seatmate.

"It took me twenty minutes to get a drink from them."

"I find that hard to believe." Jackson arched an eyebrow and for the first time since taking her seat, made eye contact. The eyes that met hers were hazel, and her expression was soft and warm. Damn, this woman was checking off everything on Jackson's list. And she didn't seem to be swooning over Jackson's aloof, power-butch performance, which made her even more alluring.

"Jackson." She didn't usually give her full name and she wasn't going to now, but she considered it. Something about this woman compelled disclosure, honesty.

"Is Jackson a first or last name?"

"Most people just call me Jackson." A friendly, but vague response.

"Eliza." She air tipped her glass in Jackson's direction. "My friends call me Elle."

Jackson imagined whispering Elle's name in bed. She closed her eyes, picturing the scene, then nonchalantly checked the small metal coin that rested on the bar next to Elle's cocktail napkin. The green side was up. Elle covered the dollar-sized disc with her hand.

Green meant go; that's the way this sex club worked. If someone was looking then the green side was up. If an advance was unwanted all the holder had to do was flip the coin to the red side. Green meant go, red meant no-go. This was an easy system. No harm, no foul, and no awkward conversations. Red meant the exchange was over. But Elle had covered the coin with her hand knowing that Jackson had already seen that it was green side up. What did that mean?

Jackson's coin was still in her pocket. She didn't really need it if they played Elle's. Having a coin meant they'd both paid the entrance fee to be there. The fee meant access to the rooms upstairs, the fee meant you were looking for a companion, or at least curious. This particular Green Club was known to be mostly lesbian, so it was Jackson's favorite. It was a little bit out of the way, but usually worth the trek.

"I was talking to that woman, you know. You interrupted a very interesting conversation." The corner of Elle's mouth curved up.

"I doubt that." Jackson focused on her whiskey.

"God, you're so…has anyone ever told you how arrogant you are?" Elle didn't really sound as if she minded.

"Yeah, I may have heard that a few times." Jackson shrugged.

They sat for several minutes without speaking. The thumping base from the dance floor enveloped them. Jackson could feel the music in her chest like the pulse of a second heartbeat.

"I haven't seen you here before." Jackson tried for neutral.

"Is that the line you're going to lead with?"

"Is it a line if it's the truth?" Jackson relaxed against the bar and half rotated to face Elle. She braced with her foot on the floor.

"What do you want me to say?" Elle seemed momentarily vulnerable, or unsure. "I'm not a regular?"

"I didn't mean anything by the comment." Jackson softened her words. "I only meant that if you'd been here before, I'd have noticed." An equally unoriginal line, but she meant it as a compliment. Was Jackson normally this inarticulate? If so then maybe she should consider talking even less. She regarded Elle over the rim of her glass as she took a sip.

"Thank you, I think." Elle dropped her hand to her lap, revealing the green coin again.

Jackson sensed the scales tip ever so slightly in her favor. Elle's long dark lashes closed for an instant, and when she opened them she gave Jackson a soul destroying, heart stopping smile. Jackson fought the urge not to feel invested in where this was headed. She was beginning to sense the burn from that irresistible spark of attraction, the sort of spark you couldn't snuff out easily. Elle's skin was smooth and smelled of something both earthy and floral, her eyes were warmly appraising, and Jackson couldn't help wondering if she was what Elle was looking for. She hoped so. Some women didn't go for the butch-femme dynamic.

Elle shifted on the stool, turning only a little in her direction. The deep vee of her blouse offered a teasing glimpse of cleavage. She wouldn't have described Elle as athletic, but she definitely looked fit. Jackson figured her for a runner. The pants she was wearing hugged her svelte thighs like leggings, tapered at the ankle above—now that was an interesting detail. Elle had the look of a woman who preferred heels, but she was wearing sensible flats. Maybe it was the soggy weather. Regardless, heels or no heels, Elle was indisputably sexy and Jackson wanted to take this whole encounter upstairs for further exploration.

Elle watched Jackson's confident repositioning. Jackson swiveled to face her, planted one booted foot on the floor, and undressed Elle with her eyes. Her skin warmed and she worried that Jackson might suspect she was a novice at this whole sex club scene. Hadn't she just admitted as much?

She knew about the Green Club because of her friend Jasmine, but she'd never actually paid for a coin, let alone planned to cash it. She usually preferred the safe distance of perusing dating apps.

Yet, here she was, green side up.

She still hadn't decided if her decision to venture to this place was about some search for adventure or just desperation. Her last attempt at a hookup had been sort of a disaster. The woman had seemed safe enough based on her profile, but reality didn't completely match the profile. The misfire of that encounter had kept her off the app for weeks.

It had been just as well that nothing had happened. Who had time to actually date anyway? She was too focused on her research, and any time outside the lab was spent grabbing a few hours of sleep or worrying that her research would never get any traction with the higher-ups.

Stop thinking about work.

If she didn't connect with someone physically, and soon, she feared she was going to lose her mind. Elle desperately wanted someone to rescue her from herself. She wanted someone to get her out of her head.

There it was again. She'd lost herself in her thoughts, while Jackson's blue-gray eyes were laser focused on her breasts. She chose to interpret that as a compliment. But was Jackson her type? Could she even go through with this? Elle would never describe flirtation as one of her top skills. She was too direct. She knew that if she took five minutes to apply eye liner and lipstick, and wore something besides a lab coat, that she could pull off "pretty." At least she knew that much about herself. So, this whole uncomfortableness-with-seduction thing wasn't a lack of confidence in the looks department, but in the experience department, well, that was another story. Elle preferred to know exactly what was happening, the steps that it would take to get there, and the payoff. This whole mating ritual thing was a black hole of unknowns.

"Would you like another drink?"

Elle hadn't even noticed her glass was empty. Her response time slowed as she calculated the effects of more alcohol in her system and the consequences that would have on her ability to make smart choices.

There was no denying that Jackson was roguishly attractive, handsome even. Jackson was close to six feet, with broad shoulders and long legs, the muscles of her thighs strained against the fabric of her slacks. Elle wondered if that sort of physique required chemical enhancement because Jackson was just a little too perfect. She was extremely fit and had the demeanor of someone in law enforcement. Jackson was wearing a dark colored dress shirt, but her brownish-khaki pants and shiny black boots looked like the lower half of a uniform of some sort. Possibly she was on the police force, Homeland Security or—the dark stubble of a crew cut made Elle guess military. Something about Jackson told Elle that she was used to telling lesser ranking personnel what to do. She had no doubt that Jackson was more experienced, and probably great in bed. She oozed sexual confidence.

The trait that gave Elle pause was her arrogance. Jackson seemed so sure that Elle would swoon beneath all the swagger that Elle wanted to reject her advance, assuming she made one, simply on principle.

But the Green Club wasn't a place for principles, it was a place for one thing—sex.

"Since you seem to be the only person this bartender pays attention to, yes, I'll have another gin and tonic." She decided to give this encounter a little more room to breathe.

As before, the bartender scurried over the moment Jackson signaled and their second round was delivered promptly. Around them, the music and the uneven hum of voices seemed to grow louder. The noise was making it hard to think. Elle closed her eyes and pressed her fingers against her temple.

"Headache?" asked Jackson.

"No, just the noise." She glanced over at Jackson. The second drink was kicking in. She rolled her shoulders and straightened on the uncomfortable barstool.

"We could go somewhere quieter." Jackson's words cut through the clamor.

Okay, decision time.

The green coin bounced light from the dance floor strobe as if sending her a signal. But what? Agree or abort? Stop or go? Her hand rested near the coin as she considered flipping it to red.

CHAPTER TWO

Elle studied the mosaic pattern on the carpet floor in an attempt to quiet her nerves as they rode the narrow lift to the third floor. Jackson seemed completely at ease. Given the bartender's attentive, familiar behavior, she assumed Jackson was a regular. Should she feel lucky or offended?

The door swished open and Jackson motioned for her to exit the elevator first. The hallway had low lighting similar to the bar and the décor was minimal, sterile even, except for the fact that each door was painted a deep forest green. Halfway down the hallway from the elevator, Jackson stopped near an unoccupied room. She paused with her hand on the sliding handle. Was she giving Elle a moment to reconsider?

Jackson opened the door; she followed and stood silently as Jackson slid the latch to "Occupied."

It wasn't as if the door was locked. If she wanted to she could stop this at any time. She told herself these things in a very scientific way, as if anything about this scenario was controlled or controllable. That's what made it exciting, right? She'd wanted to get out of her head and feel something, right?

The room was obviously only meant for one purpose. Jackson ripped a plastic band from the wall mounted bed that read "Sterilized." The simple, monochromatic bedding was tucked at the corners with formal precision. Jackson crumpled the plastic and tossed it into the corner. She sat on the edge of the bed and started unlacing her boots. She didn't look at Elle, and that made her wonder if this was some tactic to tip the balance of power, make her uneasy by ignoring her.

She couldn't help noticing Jackson's long fingers and her strong hands as she worked the laces free. Her biceps flexed beneath the dress shirt that pulled taut across her muscled shoulders when she bent over. Elle swallowed and considered the possibility that she was in over her head. Serious second thoughts began to swarm, and she was about to reach for the door when Jackson stood.

"Music, volume low." Jackson spoke to the room.

A nondescript instrumental piece began to play, something you might hear in a soundtrack for a film—strings, and the occasional minor key change.

Jackson slowly swept her palm down Elle's arm. She shivered.

"Kiss me." Jackson placed her other hand at the base of Elle's neck, beneath her hair.

How had she managed that maneuver so stealthily?

Jackson pressed her lips to Elle's. Jackson held her firmly. She yielded, parting her lips until she felt Jackson's tongue tease hers. She rested her palms at Jackson's waist and squeezed lightly with her fingers. She angled her head as Jackson deepened the kiss. Her heart rate ratcheted up. She sensed Jackson's hand move down her ribs to her hip and then, and then...Jackson's hand on her ass pulling her closer. She broke the kiss.

This was happening too fast.

"Wait." The word came out breathy.

"Why?" Jackson kissed her neck and continued to caress with her fingers in very sensitive places. "Your kiss tells me you don't truly want me to stop."

"This was a mistake, I'm sorry." She pushed against Jackson's rock-hard abs, moving out of her embrace. She reached for the latch, but Jackson followed and stood behind her with arms braced on either side, blocking the door.

"Don't go." Jackson spoke very close to her ear, a request rather than a command this time.

"This just isn't who I am. I'm..." She didn't rotate to face Jackson, whose firm body pressed against her back. She exhaled, weighing what course of action to take.

"Look at me." In contrast to the strength of her body language, Jackson's words were soft.

Jackson's palms were still braced, with outstretched arms against the door. The scent of Elle's hair invaded her air space. The smell was lightly floral and familiar. Elle rotated, tucking her hair behind her ear as she slowly looked up to meet Jackson's gaze.

Camille. Memory whispered her name.

Jackson's subconscious had become her enemy. She dropped her arms and took a step back. She stared at Elle, breathing hard. The room began to shrink and then tilt. That movement, the way Elle touched her hair, the expression on her face, the smell of her hair, the way her eyelashes seemed to flutter in slow motion, her vulnerability, the leaving—all of it came crashing down on Jackson. A horrible reminder of what she'd lost.

"Is something wrong?" Elle's expression was somewhere between puzzled and concerned.

Jackson's throat was dry. She took another step back and dropped to the edge of the bed, afraid that if she didn't sit down she might pass out. She stared at the floor because she couldn't look at Elle. Elle knelt in front of her, invading her line of sight. She felt the warmth of Elle's hands on her thighs as she squeezed her eyes shut to block out the room.

"Hey, should I call someone? Are you ill?"

"No." The knot in her throat made her response sound like a hoarse whisper. Jackson pressed the heels of her palms against her eyes.

Elle stroked her face.

"Don't...don't touch me." She batted Elle's hand away.

"Okay, just relax, and breathe."

Elle's tenderness was making it worse—the hurt, the loss, the despair. Tears threatened and one escaped to travel down her cheek. Fuck, she was going to lose it. She swallowed the memories and covered her face with her hands. That was the trouble with memories, they held on and sometimes refused to let go. Even if you tried to train your mind to bury them, to cut them loose.

Maybe she'd made one too many jumps.

Maybe it was starting to mess with her head for real.

She'd discovered that no matter where the Slingshot dropped her off, everything she'd tried to leave behind was still with her. Even in the past, she was unable to truly escape the present.

The problem was she could never outrun the memories. Even if she could travel to a time before *they* existed, before *she* existed, the memories remained. Those remembrances were like cold, echoing, erratic surges of feeling that she had no control over. A scent in the air would remind her of the perfume Camille wore on that day, the day they first met. Sometimes nothing more than the sound of someone laughing, a particular kind of laugh, light and airy, would bring everything rushing back. Even the remoteness of strangers reminded her of the day she'd lost her. The day her life slipped beyond Jackson's reach.

Like an ever-present shadow, the memories remained.

She took several deep breaths and exhaled. The spinning room began to settle, and she remembered she wasn't alone. She sensed the closeness of Elle, the warmth of her body, now quietly seated on the bed next to hers.

"I need to leave." Feeling somewhat stabilized, Jackson pulled on her boots. She loosely tied them and tucked the excess laces into the top.

She stood and walked to the door without turning around. She hesitated and grasped the handle to still her shaking hand.

"I'm sorry." She stepped through the door without looking back.

She took the stairs rather than the lift. The club was like some bizarre alternative reality. Jackson shoved her way through the thick crowd. At the exit, she had to circle back because in her haste she'd forgotten to claim her coat. The shoulders were still soaked and cold when she tugged it on. She held the front closed as she left the club and strode down the covered passageway toward the nearest train station. She left the cover and safety of the enclosure to cross the street. The door made a sucking sound as it sealed behind her to safeguard the air inside. If she walked very far in the open, she'd need a re-breather, but it was a quick crossing to the elevated station platform.

The rain had stopped, but large puddles remained on the crumbling street making it hard to judge where the pavement was broken. Jackson dodged puddles, not knowing how deep the water was or where the concrete had crumbled. A black sedan bearing a military insignia on the door slowed. A train swept past on the track above at the same moment a flood light from the vehicle swept over her position. She simply held up her palm in greeting.

"You want a lift, Captain?"

She recognized the voice as First Lieutenant Nikki West. She approached the car.

"Yeah, thanks, Nik." This was a lucky break. It was too messy to walk, and the train would be crowded and Jackson wasn't in the mood for a crowd. She rounded the car and got in on the passenger side.

"Hey, you okay? You don't look so good." Nik hit the gas.

"Bad day." Jackson slouched in the seat, with the collar of her coat pulled up around her ears. She wanted to disappear. "Would you mind dropping me at my place?"

"Sure."

Jackson was thankful that Nikki knew her well enough to be able to tell she wasn't in the mood for small talk. Nikki didn't ask her any other questions, and Jackson was happy to sit in silence for the ride.

She angled her head and watched the dingy city sweep past. Piles of garbage punctuated several corners. Tent cities invaded abandoned buildings and spilled out onto the surrounding concrete. The tents on the sidewalk sagged from the heavy rain earlier in the evening. Every so many blocks, a working streetlight offered a small oasis against the oppressive darkness. The naked bulb's reflection multiplied by puddles of various sizes in the eroding asphalt. This was a mixed neighborhood; better than some, worse than others. It bordered the more affluent parts of the city, the parts that could afford uninterrupted solar power, piped-in purified air, and water. There were a few buildings near the Green Club that had suffered enough gentrification to have all the modern conveniences, but they were surrounded by the less fortunate.

"Fuck!" Nikki slammed on the brakes. "I didn't even see them—Jeezus."

The seat belt pressed into Jackson's chest. A woman and child crossed in front of the car. Both were hollow-eyed and had clothing several seasons past wearable. The child held a breather to her lips and locked eyes with Jackson as Nikki accelerated again.

So many people had nothing.

Jackson wondered how people continued to have kids given the future was a toss-up. Resentment was palpable in the air for public officials and industry leaders who, for decades, had turned a blind eye as most of the world was swallowed up by the rising sea. Those that weren't wading away from their submerged coastal cities were slowly being smothered by toxic air. In the end, it wasn't that the one percent exploited the working class, or the planet, it was that they just didn't care. They didn't care about anything except the almighty dollar.

Jackson couldn't help but wonder about the long game of that approach. Where do you spend all that money when the world is dead?

The scientific community and anyone who was really paying attention had been warning about climate change for almost a hundred years, at least since the 1970s. But the problem was so big as to be almost ungraspable. The death of the planet? Who could get their head around that?

The general public had mostly decent food and streaming video until mid-century, which made climate collapse seem like alarmist, leftist propaganda. It was easy to ignore the looming doomsday until the oil reserves dried up, Amazon shuttered its warehouses, and New York began to truly sink. The ocean came in and didn't recede. Buildings floated off foundations, wastewater plants failed and contaminated ground water systems; millions were displaced. FEMA was overwhelmed and unable to handle the numbers of those in need.

Industrialized nations wanted to agree that the doomsday thermometer should be set at two degrees, but at that temp, parts of Ethiopia, Maldives, Barbados, and Cambodia were already under water. The coral reefs were all dead by the time the thermometer hit one and a half degrees. The problem was scale. Just to slow things down, huge fundamental changes would have had to happen. Humanity couldn't even agree that the planet was getting hotter. And if it was, some argued that it certainly wasn't humanity's fault. Given all of that noise, how could leaders possibly agree to make changes to slow the warming?

The military had been Jackson's way out. Lucky for her, she had the skills and the disposition to make it work. Her father had pushed her to be tough. He'd probably guessed at the future long before lung cancer claimed him. She closed her eyes and sank onto the headrest.

Her father had been an iron worker, a welder. They'd lived in Southern California in a trailer city on the edge of the ever-expanding desert. She never really knew her mom. Her mother hadn't been around by the time she was old enough to remember things. She'd left her father for another man and promises of a brighter future. At least that was the story she got from her father. Whatever her reason, she never looked back. She obviously didn't have the sort of maternal instincts that might cause someone to worry about her kids.

Jackson's older brother, Kenny, hadn't been as lucky as she had. Maybe it was tougher for guys. He'd gotten sucked into hanging with a rough crowd. Eventually, that led to drugs. He finally got clean and was working on a protein farm in the central valley. That's the word she got from her father. She and Kenny hadn't spoken in a very long time.

Time marked all things, didn't it?

Time disappeared quickly, as swiftly as the reflected city sliding past her window.

Since she'd begun the Slingshot missions, her perception of time had shifted. A day had taken on new meaning. The days sped by and once gone, could never be recaptured. Time was relentless. It ruthlessly bore down on her, on everyone.

Most people had become gifted at the art of forgetting. That was the easiest way to deal with the new reality, to forget how things had once been. But Jackson couldn't forget Camille, and maybe on some level, she didn't want to. She was stranded in her own life, with no hope of rescue.

CHAPTER THREE

Elle stepped through the sliding glass door and approached the main entrance to the multi-level concrete facade of BIOME Industries. Every time she approached this building she couldn't help thinking that it looked as if it belonged in some cold place like Siberia, rather than northern California. But looks weren't everything. What mattered to Elle was the work she was allowed to do here, not the dreary gray concrete architecture of the building. She paused and looked skyward. The temperature was expected to climb by late afternoon.

Several security personnel were clustered around a row of three metal detectors when she entered the building. Elle was running behind, so there was no one in front of her as she approached the guard station. She'd gotten home late and couldn't sleep. Jackson's abrupt departure had looped through her head endlessly without any possible resolution.

"Good morning, Dr. Graham." The security guard took her shoulder bag and waved her through the metal detector.

"Good morning." Elle smiled and then closed her eyes and squeezed the bridge of her nose with her fingers while the guard searched her satchel. In addition to poor sleep, she was also feeling the morning-after effect of too many cocktails.

The guard handed Elle her bag and she took the elevator to the third floor. She deposited her things and went down the hall to get coffee. Ted was in his office as she headed back to her lab, intently studying his computer screen.

Ted Hoffman was her primary collaborator. Usually, he only wore a T-shirt under rumpled oxford shirts, but today he'd worn a tie for some reason. His shaggy brown hair was disheveled, as if he hadn't slept well either. They weren't close enough friends for her to ask how his night had been. Ted was serious, focused, and detached. He was the perfect research partner as far as Elle was concerned. She knew he was married and had a kid, a son, who'd had some very serious health issues, but that was pretty much all she knew. He was one of those emotionally remote guys who didn't share personal details easily. Ted glanced up and smoothed his hair with his fingers when he noticed her.

"What's with the tie?" He probably wouldn't tell her, but she couldn't help asking as she sipped the coffee.

"No reason."

Ted's desk was piled with documents and file folders. He seemed to have a general distrust of technology despite the fact that his work was utterly dependent on computers. He kept many of his most important notations on paper. It wasn't a completely crazy notion to have hard copies. The power grid regularly flickered these days. But Elle had no idea how he ever found anything. His haphazard filing system was far too chaotic for her liking.

Numbers cycled across the screen. He slouched in his chair.

Ted was a paleoclimatolgist. His research required serious computing. He spent hours running simulations, then he'd comb through the data to interpret the output. Basically, Ted spent hours upon hours looking at numbers—thousands upon thousands of lines of code. Those numbers told a story and that was the part that informed Elle's research.

"Have you compiled data yet on the new batch of sediment cores?" he asked.

"I need a few more hours." She turned to leave. "I'll have some results by tomorrow."

A few minutes later, Elle sat with her coffee, waiting for data to populate on her screen.

The low hum of a cooling fan whirred in the background. She set her coffee a safe distance from the container where the core samples were stored. Her research made use of so-called proxy methods as a way to infer information about the past condition and evolution of the world's oceans.

As a paleobotanist, she studied the plant life of the geological past—the deep past. If the history of Earth was packed into a single twenty-four-hour day, then life emerged before sunrise. Photosynthesis evolved sometime around midmorning, and an oxygen-rich atmosphere happened right before lunch. Most of this imaginary day was pretty boring. It wasn't until around nine o'clock in the evening that the first multi-celled beings showed up. This all happened half a billion years before now. She spent most of her time, along with Ted, reconstructing the how and when and at what temperature things happened beyond that point.

Paleobotany was part of the more comprehensive science of paleontology, although, in general practice the latter was concerned mainly with animal remains, and plants received only brief consideration. Perhaps that's why Elle was interested in it. This particular slice of paleontology was less crowded, and as such, there was room to make discoveries.

In some ways, paleobotany was the study of rock formations in which the plants were preserved. Luckily, geology had been of almost equal interest to Elle in college and she could easily have taken that route. In the end though, botany was where her heart resided, plants fascinated her, plants and trees.

Sediment core samples were the focus of her current research. Elle was on a mission to save the seas, and her thesis was that the oceans' savior would be found in the past. That sounded crazy when she voiced it out loud, but inside her head, and on paper, somehow it made sense.

The seas of the planet were in dire need of oxygen, and oxygen came from plants, namely microscopic marine algae known as phytoplankton. Phytoplankton at one time had been the foundation of the aquatic food web, feeding everything from microscopic, animal-like zooplankton to multi-ton whales. Not only were they an integral part of the food chain, they were the rain forests of the ocean, creating more oxygen and absorbing more CO_2 than any other organism cluster on the planet.

But exactly when, and where, to find a population that could save the ocean in this warmer climate? That was the question. And once located, was it possible to reconstruct the organisms from ancient DNA? Or was this entire idea simply science fiction? Someone at BIOME obviously believed in her thesis enough to keep funding her research, so she carried on. In search of a tiny savior of the ocean's future from the past.

Elle's team had extracted core samples from various points in the Pacific Ocean. The total thickness of sediments that had accumulated since the beginning of decipherable geologic time was several miles deep. Unfortunately, there was no single place on earth where the entire sequence was visible. Except, possibly, in the deepest parts of the ocean where deposition had been going on continuously without interruption.

Plant fossils were usually preserved in rocks composed of sediments deposited in water. That's how it worked. Very seldom did a plant get preserved all in one piece with its tissue intact. Elle had to build a species by deciphering its parts.

Sediment cores were very useful in establishing ocean plant life from long ago. Her focus was on the reconstruction of past ecosystems and climates based on the study of microfossils from ocean floor sediments. Cross-referencing with Ted's research, she had identified time periods in the geological past when there were similar rises in ocean temperature. But with far less CO_2.

It was a big puzzle and she was searching for that final piece to complete the scene.

Elle reached for her coffee, now lukewarm. She rocked back in her chair as data compiled on her screen.

Over time, humans had injected massive amounts of CO_2 into the atmosphere. After years of climate change denial, pretty much no one now contested that humans had contributed to rapid warming of the atmosphere. People were slow to catch on. As a species they seemed to have a general distrust of the science behind climate change. Elle struggled to understand. Science wasn't political or emotional, it was simply a conclusion based on study of the facts. She certainly wasn't trying to push some underlying agenda. She was simply trying to make things better—for everyone.

A large portion of the additional CO_2 dissolved in ocean waters, which had resulted in acidification. Adding extra nutrients to coastal oceans, as well as the warmer temps, ultimately lead to a reduction in the overall oxygen content of subsurface ocean water. The looming result—warming, acidification, and anoxia was killing the seas.

Current projections painted a grim picture. If drastic reversal couldn't be achieved, the oceans would be dead in less than a decade. Ten years was a very small window and the clock was ticking.

As a result of decades of public inertia and denial, the Pacific, which she could glimpse from her third-floor lab window, was in the final stages of becoming a vast blue desert.

Her computer pinged. A small alert appeared above the data stream, and she squinted at the message. Elle groaned. The last thing she wanted to do was get called into a surprise meeting with the director. She'd not had nearly enough caffeine for that.

Elle shucked out of her lab coat and reached for the blazer she'd taken off when she first arrived. If she'd had any advance notice about a meeting she might have worn something different. A dress or a skirt perhaps. As it was, she'd worn casual navy blue slacks and a vintage plaid wool blazer over a scoop-necked T-shirt. Her usual attire for a day in the lab. At least it was a clean T-shirt, possibly a bit more form fitting than she would prefer for a meeting with her boss, but maybe that would work in her favor.

The receptionist, whose name escaped her, was seated at the desk in the entryway. She was on the phone and motioned for Elle to wait. After she hung up she glanced in Elle's direction. "I'll let Mr. Allaire know that you're here. One moment please."

She stood in the center of the stark room until the receptionist returned. The woman wore a dark skirt with a white blouse. Her hair was pulled tightly into a bun and her expression was humorless. But who could blame her. The seas were dying and taking the planet down with them. These were serious times.

"Mr. Allaire will see you now." She held the office door open for Elle.

Liam Allaire stood as she entered.

"Hello, Dr. Graham." He extended a hand in her direction. "Please, take a seat."

Elle sat down facing the enormous sleek desk. Elle wondered what sort of person was able to run a huge facility and keep his desk so completely uncluttered. Not that she was messy or unorganized, but every surface in her workspace was covered with orderly stacks of something *in-progress*.

Elle crossed her legs as she waited for Liam to explain why she was here. Liam was handsome, square-jawed, with salt-and-pepper hair cut neatly close. He wore a suit that looked as if it had been custom tailored.

Dr. Liam Allaire had an enviable résumé. Fairly early in his career, he'd been the head of the department of atmospheric science at NASA and after eventually leaving the agency was briefly the director of NOAA. When any science that mattered became privatized, he'd left NOAA and taken over as managing director for BIOME, a for-profit company focused on solving the Earth's current environmental problems. And there were many of them. Any scientist who was serious about getting their research funded wanted to work with BIOME. Elle had been recruited by company headhunters right out of grad school and finished her doctorate while working in the BIOME lab. She felt lucky. This was applied science at its best.

Elle had been seated for less than a minute when the door opened behind her and a man in a military uniform entered.

"I asked Major Riley, head of Space Operations, to join us." Liam motioned for the major to take one of the leather chairs along the wall.

Major Riley was wearing a blue dress uniform with a colorful array of ribbons on his chest. Elle didn't know exactly what they all meant, but she knew they meant he was important. The fact that he was from Space Operations was highly curious. Space Operations, really?

"Major Riley, this is Dr. Eliza Graham, a paleobotanist and the head of our paleoceanography research department."

Major Riley wore his gray hair in a crew cut, his posture was stiff, his shoulders so square they appeared to have sharp edges. He sized Elle up as he took his seat. He had the look of a man whose time was valuable and only doled out in very small, precise servings. The crisp khaki slacks he wore unexpectedly conjured a mental image of Jackson. Elle's mouth was suddenly dry. She cleared her throat and blinked to dislodge the image.

She wasn't sure what the focus of this meeting might be. She'd presented her preliminary findings to the board. That had been two weeks ago and she'd heard nothing since. Maybe today she would learn something, or receive input as to where the team should be directing their research moving forward. She was confused about why a high-ranking military officer was present. Sure, the military sometimes provided security for trips into the field to obtain core samples, but they were still doing tests on the last round of sediment samples and hadn't requested an escort in weeks.

The presentation two weeks earlier to the board had been somber. How do you tell a room full of people that the oceans were going to be dead before the end of the decade? That dead seas meant the Earth was on life support. There'd been no response, everyone simply stared at her. Elle understood how they were feeling. The conclusions she and Ted had presented were too big to grasp. Which is why she'd sampled and resampled sediment from layers of ancient rock and oceanic core samples. She'd checked them against Ted's figures for ocean surface temps and rechecked and checked again.

Climate scientists had been sounding alarms forever, so why was everyone so surprised? Did the policy makers simply assume they could keep doing the same things to the environment and climate systems would reset? The Earth's climate was resilient and long-suffering, but even the planet had limits.

"Are we sure about the date?" The major looked at Elle and then at Liam.

No one spoke. She wasn't even sure to whom he'd directed the question.

"I'm sorry, what date are you referring to?" Elle uncrossed her legs and adjusted her position in the uncomfortable chair. When the major didn't respond she turned to Liam.

"The date from the core samples. You identified a window around one hundred and twenty thousand years ago." Liam casually leaned at the edge of his desk.

"Oh, yes, the last interglacial period took place between one hundred and sixteen thousand and one hundred and twenty-nine thousand years ago." But why would a military officer care about that information? She'd simply been trying to predict what a warmer planet might have been like. And what about the environment might change, and ultimately how that would affect human populations and food supplies if the conditions were duplicated on present-day Earth.

Major Riley stared at her as if she were an errant schoolgirl. She shifted in her chair again in an attempt to improve her posture. He probably had that effect on everyone.

"That's a big window, Dr. Graham." The major rested his palms on his thighs. If it were possible for someone to seem at attention while seated, he gave that impression.

"Please, call me Elle." She paused, glancing from one man to the other. "I'm sorry, I feel like I've missed the first half of a conversation here." Elle hoped the question didn't sound impertinent, but she really hated being in the dark.

"Why is this particular window important?" The major ignored Elle and looked at Liam.

"Earth has gone through periods of cooling and warming for millions of years. We often look for clues hidden in layers of ancient rock and ice to determine what conditions were during different climate periods." Liam was also a scientist so he easily rattled off this information. "The window of time we're talking about is the last time in recent Earth history when global temperatures were as warm as they are currently."

"A hundred and twenty thousand years ago doesn't sound very recent." The statement almost sounded like a joke, but there wasn't a hint of amusement in the major's expression.

Again, Elle wondered why the Space Force cared about this information. She was puzzled. This meeting didn't make sense.

"So, you want to go back to when the planet was warmer. You think you'll find something there to fix our current problems. Is that about the size of it?" The major sounded so matter-of-fact.

"Wait, what are we talking here?" What did he mean by *going back*? Why did they invite her to this meeting if they weren't going to fully explain what the hell they were talking about? "Going back where?"

"Not where, but *when*." That might have been another joke, but the major's expression told her it wasn't.

But it had to be, right?

The monochromatic walls of Liam's office began to feel as if they were closing in. The sparrow-like fluttering of Elle's heart made her lightheaded. Something big was about to happen, her nervous system registered it even if her mind had no comprehension of what it was.

"Elle, all the information I'm about to share with you is highly classified." Liam was somber. "Verbally acknowledge that you understand."

"I understand." She took a breath and tried to focus.

CHAPTER FOUR

Jackson tugged a clean T-shirt over her head for the ride north. She'd grab a uniform shirt once she got on base. Her efficiency apartment looked more like a budget hotel room than a place where someone actually lived. There were no pictures on the wall, no color to speak of. The apartment was sparse and mostly shades of gray. Even the rumpled blanket on the bed was dark charcoal. There was one small window and she'd draped a towel over the curtain rod. Lame.

Her phone buzzed just as she reached for the bike fob, right before she angled for the door.

"Hey, Ren." She cradled the phone on her shoulder.

Camille's sister Renee called Jackson almost once a month, sometimes more often, sometimes less. Ren and Camille had been close, and on some level, Jackson knew Ren's attachment to her was an effort to stay connected to Camille.

"Jackson, you didn't call me back. I was worried." Ren always worried about her.

"Sorry, I had a late night." The truth was, she didn't want to burden Ren with her depression and lack of a life. Ren didn't deserve that. Besides, she was sick of listening to herself talk about it. The whole situation was pathetic.

"I'm going to be in the city in a couple of weeks." Ren paused. "I was hoping we could meet for dinner or something."

"Sure, if I'm in town." Jackson knew she probably wouldn't be.

"Another secret mission?" Ren's question was playful.

"Yeah, something like that." Jackson checked the time. "Listen, Ren, it's nice to hear your voice." That was a lie because her voice simply made her think of Camille's. "But I need to run. I'm gonna be late as it is."

"Okay." Ren sounded disappointed.

"I'm sorry to cut this short." She felt bad now for how often she gave Ren the brush-off.

"It's all right, I understand. Take care of yourself, okay?" Ren was sweet, genuine. "I'll get in touch about that dinner."

"Okay, sounds good. Bye for now."

"Bye."

Jackson slid her phone in her pocket and grabbed her jacket and helmet. Her tiny place was on the fifth floor. She trotted down the stairs to the second floor to the encapsulated breezeway that connected the building to the multistory parking garage. The space for her bike was an extra fee per month, not included in her apartment rental. But there was no way you could leave a bike on the street. It would be picked clean for parts if left in the open.

The windows of the covered connector were smudged and dirty so that you couldn't really see out of them any longer. The air in the tunnel didn't smell so good. When she reached the other end, she knew why. One of the panels had a big hole in it. There were shards of glass on the walkway. She scuffed it to the corner with the side of her boot.

She climbed four flights of stairs in the garage to reach her bike. She unplugged the motorcycle from the charger and stowed the cord in a small compartment behind the seat. She adjusted the re-breather inside the helmet and slipped it on, then popped the shield down. She swung her leg across the bike and braced her feet on either side. For a moment, she closed her eyes and just savored the silent cocoon of the padded helmet.

She'd moved up to San Francisco from Vandenberg Air Force Base a year after losing Camille. She'd needed a change in every way possible. Everything reminded her of her life with Camille, a life that no longer existed. She initially enlisted in the Air Force, but when the opportunity presented itself, she joined the Space Force. And when Space Operations Command relocated to northern California, she gladly migrated with them. Decades earlier, the Air Force barracks had been located in the Presidio, near the Golden Gate Bridge. But the Presidio was mostly under water now. Command had taken over a bunker about thirty miles north of the city. Jackson had quarters on the base, but she'd decided to keep a small efficiency apartment in the city. Sometimes she needed to get away. And there was no way she could have intimate encounters with women on base. Jackson kept her professional life and her personal life thirty miles apart, literally.

Jackson felt a tendril of warm air slither down the front of her jacket as she crossed the bridge riding into a headwind off the Pacific. The inland heat kept the Pacific fog bank at a distance. The ride across the Gate, as always, was invigorating. Her system hummed with adrenaline as it always did before a mission, an addictive mixture of anticipation and fear. Yes, fear.

Jackson was quick to remind her team that fear was their ally. Fear made you sharply aware of danger, and that awareness could be the one thing that kept you alive. The soldier who told her they had no fear was a soldier not to be trusted. Everyone was afraid of something. It was what you did with the fear that mattered. Bravery was nothing more than facing your fear and putting it behind you. Calling it by name and then harnessing the power of it.

Around her, traffic climbed the Marin Headlands grade, and cars were populated by passengers looking at devices. Tablets and phones added an eerie glow to the interiors of the self-driving autos. Jackson rarely used the AI driving functionality of her motorcycle. Where was the fun in that? An AI driver rarely lane split even though it was still legal. She saw an opening and hit the gas, weaving between two cars.

Jackson sped through the tunnel. She could hear the roar of traffic bounce off the curved concrete walls even through the padding of her helmet. She let the bike gain speed as she cruised down the grade at the foot of Mount Tamalpais. The California coast was rugged and inhospitable in some spots despite the city's expansion. Narrow houses crowded the hillsides and filled every inch of space all the way to the shore of the San Francisco Bay, which was higher than it used to be. Miles of beachfront property had been reclaimed by the rising sea.

A proximity alarm sounded inside her helmet. She instantly braked and a car swerved in front of her, barely missing her front tire. The car rammed into the vehicle in the next lane. Metal scraped metal as the two collided. It was the sort of sound that pierced your chest like a jagged sharp object and then sickeningly splintered to settle into your stomach. It was the sound large things made when they crushed small things. And for an instant, just a micro-flash, Jackson considered letting go. Relaxing her grip, releasing the brake, and just letting go. She'd be swept up with the carnage and it would all be over—the pain, the hurt, the longing.

But something snapped her out of it. Some glimmer in the deepest recesses of her mind, like a single candle in a dark cavern. Jackson slowed and wove her way to the shoulder. For several minutes she focused on taking long, slow breaths.

The forward motion of the two mangled vehicles had stopped. Like water in a river avoiding a large rock, traffic flowed around the two cars. They'd come to rest in an embrace of crumpled, heated metal.

A police drone appeared and hovered over the accident scene and then a second. A siren whined in the distance. AI-driven vehicles altered course to avoid the wreck based on proximity warnings and instantaneous satellite traffic updates. The accuracy of the auto-drivers was perfect, despite the limited visibility coming out of the tunnel. In these conditions AI was a much better driver than most humans.

The flashing red and blue lights of a squad car emerged over the crest of the hill, followed by an ambulance. Jackson straddled the bike on the shoulder and stared as the white-suited emergency personnel arrived on the scene. The white medical suits sent her mind to dark places.

The triggered memory took her back to that day.

It was May and the air had been dry and hot. Technicians wore white Tyvek suits and medical masks as they grasped the corners of the black body bag. The memory of the sound of that long zipper echoed inside her head. The scuff of boots on concrete. Two forensic doctors examined more bodies, to be put in more bags. One of those bodies belonged to Camille.

Camille.

The whole area had been quarantined.

Jackson never got close enough to say good-bye.

Someone was calling to her now. The man's voice tugged her back to the present. One of the officers who'd just arrived strode toward her with his hand raised. She took off her helmet.

"You can't park there." He dropped his hand when she held up her military ID.

"I saw the accident. I just want to make sure everyone is okay."
He stopped within arm's reach, and she peered around him for a better
look. "I can make a statement if you need any additional witnesses."

He held her wallet up to take a closer look.

"So, what are you guys doing up there?" Sometimes her military
ID triggered questions.

"You know, secret stuff." She shrugged as if she had no idea.
"They don't really tell me much."

"Yeah, us grunts never know what's going on, do we?"

"Knowledge is power." There was so much hidden truth in that
statement.

"You said it. And we've got none of it." He handed Jackson her
wallet.

"Do you need a witness statement from me?" She hoped the
answer was no.

"Thank you, but I don't think it will be necessary." He rested his
hands on his utility belt. Law enforcement no longer carried guns in the
traditional sense, but he had a rather intimidating looking Taser. And
a breather tethered to his shoulder. He put the mask over his face and
took a few hits before continuing. "One of the people involved is taking
full responsibility for the crash."

"What happened?"

"Some guy from the BIOME lab...he said the AI driver failed."
The officer frowned.

"How often does that happen?" She already knew the answer.

"Never."

Jackson nodded, replaced her helmet, and cranked the bike. She
watched the crew work the scene as she fastened the chin strap. It
was unheard of for an auto-driver to fail. And there were safeguards
and backup contingencies in place in case they did. A satellite uplink
would immediately take command of the car. If this guy's AI system
truly malfunctioned, then it meant that multiple systems had failed
simultaneously. That seemed like a long shot. The guy was probably
driving a hacked system or—Well, thankfully, it wasn't her problem to
figure out. If she didn't make up some time she was going to be late.
And she wanted to finish her duty roster and get back to the city early,
if possible.

Forty minutes north of San Francisco, she turned down a two-lane road and stopped at the security checkpoint. The checkpoint was a gated entrance through a nondescript, ten-foot concrete barrier. The fortified wall was surrounded by open fields of dry grass and the charred remains of coastal oaks from the last big fire, the previous October. The guard on duty waved her through after checking her ID and cross-referencing it with a retinal scan. Jackson parked in the lot near the entrance to the substation, an underground science and training facility. The rain had stopped, but the scent of damp concrete hung, with a whiff of gasoline, in the air. The base had a certain smell that you could never quite escape. The scent of machines and fuel and anticipation.

A light-duty transport passed her in the sleek steel tunnel from the entrance as she strode toward her office. She spotted Nikki West standing near the door, trying to look casual. Nikki was a soldier, on duty, off duty, even in her sleep. That's probably why Jackson liked her so much. She knew Nikki was serious. Nikki paid attention and didn't take chances. She was always there to watch her back.

Nikki was five foot six with a muscular build, leaning toward stout, but there wasn't an ounce of fat on her compact body. Her dark hair was pulled back from her face into a controlled braid and bun. Her light brown skin was flawless. Guys hit on her while simultaneously being completely intimidated by her. Jackson didn't fault them. Nikki was a tough woman; she didn't suffer fools lightly, demanded honesty from those close to her, and was a loyal friend. Nikki was into women, but she took male attention in stride. She sort of had no choice. Men outnumbered women in the Space Force by ten to one. Nikki was Jackson's number one draft pick for all the missions she led.

"Captain." Nikki greeted Jackson with a nod.

"Good morning, Lieutenant." They weren't mission active yet. This wasn't exactly military operations anyway; this was a different sort of thing, a mix of civilian and military specialists. Nikki followed Jackson into her office. She set her helmet on the corner of her desk and unzipped her leather jacket. "Thanks for the lift last night."

"No problem. The National Guard squad was light so I picked up an extra shift. You were the highlight of my night." Nikki immediately realized how the statement sounded. "That came out wrong—"

"Oh, so I wasn't the highlight of your night?" Jackson quirked an eyebrow and tried not to smile.

Nikki cleared her throat. "I thought you might have details on the next mission."

"Not yet, but I'm expecting to get the call any time." She touched a keypad to wake her computer and glanced up. "Don't worry. Yours is the first number I'll call when I get the word."

That's assuming she was in control of the roster. Sometimes it wasn't her call to make depending on which departments were involved and who was funding the jump.

CHAPTER FIVE

Elle checked the readout on the treadmill. Almost there. Her heart rate was steady and she'd finished three miles. The run had been good. Her head was spinning with unanswered questions, and the cardio workout hadn't helped her sort through any of the clues she'd gotten in the meeting she'd had with the director. She was to report to a briefing in the morning, at Liam's request. If Major Riley was running the meeting, then she expected more cryptic comments leaving her with more questions than answers.

The atmosphere had too much carbon and the seas were too warm. Pretty much everyone who was paying attention knew that. And that's basically what they'd discussed today during the meeting. Liam knew all of this data so she had to assume the back and forth was for Major Riley's benefit. Billions of dollars had been spent to find a solution for extracting carbon from the atmosphere. Spraying particles into the atmosphere, not unlike a volcanic eruption, would deflect solar radiation and cool the climate for a few years, but would have to be done perpetually to fully solve the problem and would do nothing to curb ocean acidification. The vast swath of particles continually pumped into the air would disrupt rainfall. Which would be a disastrous side effect for a planet already short on fresh drinking water.

The seas were the only engine large enough to repair the damage. That was basically Elle's thesis in a nutshell.

Between 1950 and 2090, scientists had measured almost a complete die-off of phytoplankton. The greenies had been so focused on saving the rainforest that they neglected the largest group of carbon scrubbers on the planet—phytoplankton.

Ted had been studying ice cores from Antarctica and she'd cross-referenced them with marine sediments from ocean basins to develop an accurate portrait of Earth's temperature at certain points in time. They'd discovered a temperature jump that took place over several thousand years, where this time, the warming had happened in barely over a century.

Elle was breathing hard when she stepped off the treadmill and reached for a towel. Running helped her think. She checked her phone, plenty of time for a quick shower.

What little information Liam had given her made it sound like she'd be busier than usual the next few weeks. If she wanted to see her friends, she needed to make plans to see them now. This wasn't a new thing, and luckily her best friend, Jasmine, understood. Sometimes she'd be away collecting samples or surveying a dig for a month at a time. Friendships were hard enough to maintain with a demanding job, so no wonder a dating relationship was nearly impossible.

Jasmine had suggested a restaurant a few blocks away that they both liked, although Elle hadn't been there in months for some reason. It wasn't even that far from her place. One stop on the train or a fifteen-minute walk. The afternoon had been warm, and the temp was still comfortable when she left the apartment building so Elle decided to walk.

The blocks between her place and the restaurant were an eclectic mix of business and residential. Sometimes both existed in the same building, with a shop or eatery on the first floor and housing on the second and third. Most of the structures in this part of San Francisco were over two hundred years old, brick structures and Victorians built after the big quake. There were small encampments in any open spaces that existed between buildings, makeshift shelters for those who couldn't afford housing. Even in spaces as narrow as six feet, tents and cobbled together shacks of discarded cardboard and plastic were often erected overnight. The makeshift habitats sometimes were wedged right up against the enclosed pedestrian passageways, long narrow covered sidewalks that offered protection from both weather extremes and poor air quality. Giant air scrubbers created a low humming vibration that you could both hear and feel as you passed through the grubby glass and plexiglass corridors.

There were gaps in the passageways, so at the end of certain blocks you had to traverse sections of the street in the open. Elle had a portable breather in the bag, but she didn't think she'd need it for this short trek.

As she exited the automatic door, she sidestepped a middle-aged guy sitting on a flattened piece of cardboard. She wasn't sure if he was asleep or awake. It was hard not to engage or make eye contact with people living on the street. But she'd had bad encounters in the past, so these days, she avoided interactions when possible. Children were her weakness though, and most of the time she couldn't help offering a child food or clothing, sometimes a blanket. There just wasn't enough work. Automation and peak oil had taken more than sixty percent of lower and middle-class jobs, and social services failed to keep up. Layer on top of that the communities displaced from sea level rise and cities just couldn't accommodate everyone.

Elle wondered on rare occasions, when she was feeling pessimistic, if the problems were so big that no one and nothing could solve them. She chided herself. She could only focus on the issues she could improve. Big problems got solved by chipping away at them with small actions.

"In a hurry?" A shaggy bearded man stepped out of a shadowed doorway. Elle hadn't seen him and had to step off the sidewalk to keep from bumping into him.

Elle didn't answer him. She made eye contact for an instant. His demeanor seemed a little aggressive although he made no move to follow her as she passed. After another twenty feet she was inside the next corridor, breathing better air.

The tension in her shoulders didn't ease until she'd put two blocks between herself and the man.

Jasmine was already at the restaurant when she arrived. Her short dark curls framed her slender face, cut in such a way as to accentuate her elegant cheekbones. Jasmine smiled when she saw Elle. Her brown skin contrasted warmly against an emerald green blouse. Jasmine was a full-time ER nurse and a part-time yoga instructor. She was enviably fit. Elle had tried yoga, but she could never quiet her mind. For her, the treadmill was a better fit.

"Is this table okay?" Jasmine stood and gave her a one-armed hug. "There was only one other spot, but it was right up front near the door."

That would have put them right by the passageway exit, too much foot traffic and too much noise.

"No, this is good." Elle slipped out of her light jacket and took a seat. The café was packed. The dull hum of voices surrounded them.

After a few minutes, a waiter took their order.

"You're not getting a drink?"

Jasmine had ordered a mineral water.

"I have to go straight to the hospital after this." Jasmine grimaced. "Night shift."

"We could have rescheduled."

"No, I wanted to see you. Besides, I needed to eat and so do you." She touched her glass to Elle's when their drinks arrived.

"I'm sorry it's been so hard to connect lately." The waiter brought a small wooden tray with tiny portions of pickled veggies, olives, and sweet peppers. "You know how it is."

"Yes, I need to hear all about that." Elle tasted her cocktail. It was pink and had a decidedly strawberry flavor. She couldn't taste the alcohol at all, so she'd probably end up drinking it too fast.

"Well, let's see. There was Steven. That date lasted all of twelve minutes."

"Oh, wow, you're practically engaged," Elle teased her.

"Ha ha, very funny."

"How does a date last twelve minutes?"

"We chatted over the app, then decided to meet for drinks." Jasmine paused as the waiter delivered two steaming bowls of Thai peanut noodle soup. "The first few minutes went okay. He was cute and funny. Then I asked him where he grew up and he said hell. And then clarified that he'd meant Arizona."

Hell was an accurate description of Arizona. No one had been able to consistently live there for probably twenty years. Too damn hot.

"What happened then?" Elle stirred her soup with chopsticks.

"I thought he was joking, you know, because Arizona *is* sort of like hell, right?"

"Yes, absolutely."

Heat became lethal for anything that breathes at one hundred and fifteen degrees. The sun assaulted you. The air would be thick and hazy.

The heat radiated up from the concrete. Trains became convection ovens. Planes couldn't get enough lift in the thin, hot air. Power lines sagged, buzzed, and transformers overloaded, popped, and exploded.

"Well, he wasn't joking. And when I agreed with him that Arizona was a hell-scape he got all offended and started arguing with me."

"What a jerk."

"Yeah, he just kept getting louder and louder. No matter what I said." Jasmine put up her hands in mock surrender. "I finally asked him to leave and then I waited in the bar for over an hour before I left to make sure he wasn't waiting outside to follow me home."

"Creepy."

"Yeah, luckily, I bumped into Dane. He walked me back to my place."

Dane was a mutual friend that they'd both known since college. He was a nice guy, but more friend material than hookup material.

"I'm so sorry that happened."

"Oh, God, it was such a disaster."

Elle shook her head, sympathetic to Jasmine's plight. She held a few noodles aloft to allow them to cool. Threads of steam rose and then disappeared.

"At least it was only a twelve-minute disaster."

"Truth." Jasmine air toasted with her water glass. "Okay, your turn. Did anything interesting happen at the Green Club the other night?"

Elle exhaled and shook her head.

"I thought so, but then…well, it just didn't go anywhere." Elle studied her soup. "It was weird. We actually got as far as one of the upstairs rooms and we kissed…" She paused.

"And?"

"And then something changed. It was like a switch got flipped and the woman just left." Elle sampled more of her dessert cocktail. "It was a completely awful experience. I really hate trying to meet—anyone."

Jasmine covered Elle's hand with hers.

"Don't let one weird, random experience derail everything, Elle. It's good that you put yourself out there. I have no idea what her problem was, but I'm sure it had nothing to do with you." Jasmine quirked an eyebrow. "Have you seen you?"

"Any and all ego stroking is welcome, thank you." Elle smiled around a mouthful of noodles. "In the meantime, I'll just live vicariously through you. Tell me another story while I get a second one of these pink, whatever this is." She held her glass aloft until she got the waiter's attention.

"I think it's called a Cotton Candy Dream Date." Jasmine laughed.

"Whatever it is, it's delicious."

"Let's see, my new neighbor's name is Kevin. I've been working up to asking him out. He's tall, blond, and he has great abs."

"Hmm, he sounds delicious too."

They both laughed.

"I'm really happy you have a yummy distraction. You've got such a stressful job I don't know how you do it." Elle couldn't imagine working as an ER nurse. Going in every day with no idea of what trauma you might encounter. Somehow, Jasmine was able to compartmentalize and leave her work behind at the end of each day. Elle was sure the yoga and meditation were what kept Jasmine sane.

"Everyone has stress in their life. It's our modern condition, right?"

"I guess." Elle was swiftly finishing beverage number two. "My core samples are pretty high maintenance. I might go as far as to say they're needy."

Jasmine laughed.

"You and your rocks."

"The way you say that makes it sound sort of sexy." Elle tipped her head from side to side playfully.

Jasmine laughed with a mouth full of noodles, which made her sputter. She fanned herself. "Don't make me laugh when I have a mouthful of soup."

Elle decided not to have a third drink and instead switched to bottled water. There was a bit of a line at the front. The restaurant had gotten much more crowded. People clustered in small groups as they waited for tables. After an hour and a half, they decided to give theirs up. It was hard to linger with a hungry audience looking on. Jasmine's shift started soon anyway. Elle stood to put on her jacket and a familiar profile caught her attention. She stopped mid-movement, one sleeve dangling limply from her arm.

"What is it?" Jasmine tried to track Elle's gaze.

"*Green Club* is at the bar." She was fairly certain that Jackson hadn't seen her. The table where they'd been sitting adjoined a booth with a high back, making her position invisible from the bar. Plus, Jackson had her back to the room. She seemed very focused on whatever she was drinking.

"You mean, from…"

"Yeah, the other night." Elle took one more sip of water. "You go ahead, I might just say hello on my way out."

"Okay, good luck." Jasmine hugged her. "And be careful, but have some fun."

"Yes, Mother."

Elle was standing near Jackson and still she didn't look up. The bar was as crowded as the rest of the place. A guy cut in front of Elle to order a drink, which gave her a moment to search in her purse for the green token. She was sure she still had it.

Found it.

Maybe it was the Cotton Candy Dream Date talking, but she was feeling brave despite the I-like-to-drink-alone vibe Jackson was giving off. She squeezed closer to where Jackson was seated and placed the token, green side up, on the bar. Jackson glanced at the coin and then turned, almost in slow motion. It was obvious that she was surprised to see Elle, but her expression was impossible to decipher—a good surprise or a bad one? Elle had the distinct impression that Jackson was very practiced at masking her feelings.

"You know, this isn't that sort of place." Jackson cocked one eyebrow.

Elle's liquid-infused bravery wavered for an instant, but she rallied.

"I never got the chance to use the token. I thought my credit might still be good." That made Jackson smile and Elle relaxed a little.

Another person tried to squeeze between them to get a drink, but Jackson blocked him with her arm. Elle moved into the small open space Jackson had created. Someone bumped her and she put her palm on Jackson's thigh to catch herself.

"Sorry, this place is getting crowded."

Jackson relished the warmth that radiated from Elle's hand on her thigh. She didn't mind the contact at all, and if it took a crowd to bring Elle closer, then bring on the masses. She stood and offered Elle her stool.

Elle shook her head. "I've been sitting for a while."

"Can I buy you a drink?" Jackson sat back down and swiveled so that Elle had no choice in the tight, limited space near the bar except to stand between her legs.

"Maybe just a soda. I've already hit my limit."

"That sounds promising." She waved the bartender over so that she could order a soft drink for Elle. Damn, Elle was even prettier than she remembered. This was an unexpected second chance. Should she start this encounter by apologizing? Maybe they could both pretend their previous encounter at the club hadn't happened.

"I was here with a friend having dinner and I saw you. Are you… are you getting any food?"

"No, just a drink." Jackson needed to deal with the elephant in the room so that they could move forward. She swallowed. "Listen, I need to apologize about the other night."

"It's okay, really." Elle sipped the soda without making eye contact.

The green token was still on the bar. Elle reached for it, possibly having second thoughts.

"Maybe I should hang on to this." Jackson covered the token before Elle could remove it.

Elle shifted her stance, brushing the inside of Jackson's thigh. The fleeting contact sent sparks to her crotch.

The lights over the bar blinked and then everything went dark for a few seconds. Red emergency lighting flickered on, casting the café with an eerie underworld ambience. A wind advisory had been issued, and the power grid had probably gone offline to prevent fires. Although, that seemed more like corporate bullshit since there'd practically been a downpour the night before, so she figured they were way below an orange flag warning. But maybe the rain had been localized and the hills were still dry. At any rate, a power outage presented other opportunities.

"The grid is probably down for the rest of the night."

"Damn. I walked here from my place." Elle glanced around the café. Patrons were slowly closing tabs and leaving.

"Why don't I walk you home." Jackson downed the last swig of her bourbon and stood up, not really waiting for an answer.

"Um, okay, if it's not out of your way." Was Elle nervous? Elle had seemed so confident when she'd first approached Jackson at the bar.

"Hey, I'm just offering to walk you home. No strings." Jackson smiled. Depending on how long the walk would take, she had a little time to make her play for at least a few strings. "You can even hold on to this if it makes you feel better." She offered the green token to Elle.

Elle smiled. Her fingertips softly feathered against Jackson's palm as she reclaimed the coin. She followed Elle to the door and into the pedestrian passageway. Elle was wearing a summer weight dress, some clingy fabric that highlighted the sensuous curve of her hips. She had a casual denim jacket on over the dress and a scarf of some glittery, sheer material—more for looks than warmth. The wind picked up, and Elle clutched the front of the jacket together as they crossed the open street for the next segment of covered sidewalk.

"I was expecting to be home before it got chilly." Elle crossed her arms, hugging herself.

"Who can tell these days." The daily weather swings could give you whiplash. It was best to just prepare for anything. Layering was the only way to deal with it.

Elle glanced over at Jackson as they walked. Jackson kept a respectable amount of space between them, and Elle wondered if she should interpret that in some way or if Jackson was simply being polite. Jackson kept her hands in her jacket pockets at they continued down the pedestrian passageway toward her apartment.

The sidewalk tunnels were crowded and dimly lit. People used tiny key fob sized flashlights as they headed home from work, or off to work, or just shopped. The small corner market had a generator that created an oasis of light. They passed through and kept going. A power outage used to be an opportunity to watch the stars but had become the time when other things happened. A siren sounded far away. The distant siren reminded her to be cautious.

Something about Jackson's quiet confidence made her feel safe.

"It's only another block or so." Elle maintained the cordial distance as they walked.

Jackson figured this night was going to end with a coin toss. She suspected things could go either way, hot or cold, and Elle was giving her no clues. Or maybe she just couldn't read the signs any longer. That was a discouraging thought.

The pedestrian traffic thinned as they entered the next block. This section of the street looked a little iffy, with some tent housing in the narrow spaces between the mid-rises.

"We should cross the street at this exit." Elle glanced over her shoulder as she pushed the door release.

"Is something wrong?" Jackson felt suddenly protective.

"It's probably nothing. Earlier, when I walked to dinner, some guy tried to engage." Elle started to cross the street. "I don't really want to run into him. He seemed a little...off."

"Do you see him?" Jackson stopped walking. "Point him out to me."

"What?" Elle was a few steps ahead and turned to look at her. "Why?"

"Point him out to me."

"Maybe he's not even there...oh, wait, I think I see him." Elle was searching the shadows between the buildings across the street where someone was standing on the sidewalk looking in their direction.

"Wait here." Jackson strode across to where the man was standing in the red glow of emergency lights in the nearest building.

Elle hugged herself as she watched Jackson. The man visibly stiffened as Jackson got closer. Did he know her? Like the first time Elle had seen Jackson, she was wearing a light jacket over a dark shirt, with slacks and boots that looked like the lower half of a uniform. And now she was confronting some strange man as if this was something she did all the time. This had to mean Jackson was in some branch of law enforcement, right?

The exchange was brief. Jackson stood in the street with her hands braced on her hips as the man gathered his belongings and shuffled down the sidewalk away from Elle's apartment. A few pedestrians and one small electric vehicle wove past where Jackson stood. She didn't return to Elle until the man reached the corner and turned out of sight.

"What did you say to him?" Elle crossed to Jackson, since her apartment was on that side of the street.

"I gave him enough units of credit for tonight and directions for a shelter a few blocks away." Jackson fell in step with Elle as they transitioned from the street to the sidewalk. "He won't be back."

"How can you be so sure?" She studied Jackson's face for a clue.

"I know the type. He'll find somewhere else to camp, trust me."

It seemed the conversation was over. Whatever it was Jackson had said to the man she wasn't going to share.

"Thank you." Elle wasn't sure what else to say.

"You're welcome." Jackson looked so serious, despite the smile. Within only a few more steps, they were in front of her apartment. If she hadn't been certain about inviting Jackson in, the hero display in the street had made the decision for her. Elle took Jackson's hand and they entered the mid-rise building through a security door. Elle's place was on the second floor. Low-wattage emergency lights gave the stairway a spooky amber glow. The air between them seemed to have warmed since Jackson came to her rescue. Elle was anxious to be rid of her denim jacket and scarf.

CHAPTER SIX

Jackson followed Elle into the apartment. The living space wasn't large, but unlike Jackson's, it was cozy. Camille had always been the one to make a place seem like home, and without Camille, Jackson had let her place lapse into something between threadbare and barely functional.

"Would you like a drink?" Elle retrieved a glass and waited for her answer.

"Sure."

The main living space contained both a sitting area and a small kitchen separated by an island ringed with stools. Jackson ambled toward one of the stools, taking in details of the room as she moved. There was a grouping of small framed photos over a long narrow cabinet. A vase of blown glass and other small decorative objects were on top of the cabinet—interesting stones, a feather, and a seashell. She couldn't see details in the framed pieces without being obvious, so she didn't look closely. The sofa was little more than a love seat, piled with brightly colored pillows. There were a few larger throw pillows on the floor near the sofa. Jackson envisioned an intimate social gathering with someone sitting on the couch while others lounged on the pillows. There was one door off the main room, probably the bedroom and bath. The door was partially closed so she didn't get a look inside. Jackson had tried to gather as much information about Elle as possible, without looking as if she were, as she simply crossed the room.

"Ice?"

"Two, thanks." She watched as Elle dropped ice into glasses and poured two fingers of bourbon.

"Sorry, I don't have something else to offer you. I'm not sure what you were drinking before, but maybe you're okay with this." Elle handed her a glass.

"It was bourbon. So, thanks. This is great." She sipped and savored the warmth of the liquor in her throat.

Elle rounded the counter and motioned for them to sit. Instead of sitting down, Jackson took a moment to study the pictures. There were several images of plants—a close-up of an interesting leaf, a yellow flower, a twisted tree stripped of foliage against a blue sky, and off to the side, an older photo in which Elle looked younger as she stood with someone who was maybe her sister.

"Nice photos." She sipped the drink as she slowly swiveled. Elle was watching her from the sofa as if she were on a witness stand, as if Elle were trying to decide whether she could be trusted or not.

"Thank you." Elle continued to study her. "What did you really say to that guy on the street?"

"Why do you ask?"

"It seemed as if he knew you…as if maybe there was more to that conversation than you shared."

Elle was smart. Something about the way she noticed details. Jackson had picked up on it the first night they'd met. Smart women were a big turn-on.

"I've done sweeps through this neighborhood before with the National Guard." The National Guard was spread so thin that sometimes for larger initiatives they had to enlist the help of other branches of the military. She paused and took a drink before continuing. "I told him if I saw him on this block again I'd kick his ass. Then I gave him the credits and directions to the shelter."

"Would you really do that?"

"What?"

"Kick his ass."

"If provoked, absolutely."

A shiver ran up Elle's arms. Jackson was like a tightly coiled spring, ready to bolt for the door again, or—she wasn't sure. But intensity pulsed off Jackson. The muscle along her jaw kept flexing and she still hadn't joined Elle on the sofa. Maybe this had been a bad idea. Jackson obviously had some unresolved thing going on that had nothing to do with her.

Elle had one other idea about how to change the tone of the evening. If that didn't work, then she was going to finish the drink and end this, whatever *this* was.

"You seem tense." Elle tested the waters. "Why don't you come sit and I'll rub your shoulders."

Jackson stoically faced her, as if Elle had just challenged her to a duel and all that remained was to select a weapon of choice.

Elle placed a large throw pillow on the floor between her feet.

"If you sit here, I can rub your shoulders while you finish your drink." She patted the cushion with her hand. "It's the least I can do since you came to my rescue out there on the street."

"Really, it was nothing."

Jackson hesitated but finally took a seat on the floor pillow with her back to Elle. Her broad shoulders brushed against the inside of Elle's knees. She slid the hem of her dress up a little in order to spread her thighs to make room for Jackson. Before Elle even touched her, she could see that Jackson was tense. Her well-defined lats strained against the lightweight jacket she was wearing as she partially turned her head to look at Elle.

"Here, I'll help you out of your coat." She gently tugged the jacket from Jackson's shoulders. "Better?"

Jackson nodded. She tilted her head from one side to the other as if trying to loosen the muscles in her neck. Elle's impression that Jackson was in law enforcement of some kind had been on point. Jackson's clothing and her physical strength supported that assumption. And the display in the street earlier seemed to further confirm her conclusion. It wasn't necessarily a problem. Elle had had experience with women in law enforcement in the past. Sometimes they saw the world as too black-and-white for her taste. Everything was about right or wrong, with little room for shades of gray. As a scientist, Elle searched for absolutes, but in terms of the human experience, absolutes were rare. Most of life existed in the gray middle.

She slid her fingers across Jackson's tense trapezius and deltoid muscles, then returned her fingers to her traps and began to squeeze. The muscles under her hands barely gave way to the pressure. Jackson was one big knot of stress.

"Let me know if this is too much." Elle's hands weren't strong enough. She began to use her elbow on different pressure points along Jackson's shoulders.

"No, that's good." Jackson exhaled. She draped her arms over Elle's knees and began to relax against her.

"So, do you work out like seven days a week, or what?" It was impossible not to ask. Jackson had the physique of an elite athlete.

"Yeah, most weeks." Jackson's words were muffled. She was finally beginning to truly unwind a little.

"Well, it shows."

Elle moved from Jackson's shoulders to the vertical muscles at the back of her neck, working her fingers slowly up into the soft stubble of Jackson's crew cut. She'd been massaging Jackson's shoulders and neck for several minutes when she had the urge to expand her exploration. She reached around Jackson's neck, brushed her lips against Jackson's cheek, and unfastened the buttons of Jackson's shirt.

Jackson moaned softly when Elle's fingers slipped past her collarbones to rub the tight muscles of her upper chest. She was careful not to drop lower now that she knew Jackson wasn't wearing a bra. She returned her fingers to Jackson's shoulders but as she did, she lightly kissed the outside edge of her ear. Simply caressing Jackson's shoulders was turning her on, and so far, this encounter had only been one-sided so she wasn't sure what Jackson might be feeling.

She was rubbing her fingers up the back of Jackson's head when she bent forward, moving out of Elle's reach. Was that too much? Maybe she shouldn't have unbuttoned Jackson's shirt. Jackson sat forward for a moment and Elle waited to see what might happen next.

Jackson felt the intense need to touch Elle. She rotated, braced on her knees, to face Elle. Her heart was jackhammering in her chest and her crotch and all Elle had done was rub her shoulders. Something about this woman triggered a response she hadn't felt in a long time. Despite the fact that this *feeling*, whatever it was, scared the shit out of her, she wasn't going to run this time. She braced her palms on her thighs, flexed her arms, and took Elle in. The hem of Elle's dress had worked halfway up her thighs. Far enough so that from this angle, she could see the dark fabric of her satin underwear. Elle's face was flushed. She hadn't shifted her position or covered herself, even though she had to know that Jackson could see up her dress from this position on her knees.

She didn't take her eyes off Elle's as she slowly unfastened the remaining buttons of her shirt. She tugged the tail of it free from her trousers and let it drape open. Then she slid her palms up Elle's creamy thighs. Still on her knees, she positioned herself between Elle's legs and kissed her. Elle cupped her face with her hands as Jackson deepened the kiss. Her hands were under Elle's dress now. She hooked Elle's underwear with her fingers and started to pull them off.

"Is this okay?" She whispered the question against Elle's lips.

"Yes." Elle's response was breathy.

Jackson tipped back enough to slide the undergarment off, along with Elle's pumps. She shucked out of her shirt and reclaimed her position between Elle's legs. This time, she slid Elle forward so that her sex was pressed against her abs. Her stomach muscles twitched when they made contact with Elle's wet center. She wanted to fuck Elle right now, right here. She pressed into Elle, sweeping her palm across Elle's breast as she kissed her hard. Elle's fingernails skimmed her shoulders. She was definitely sending Jackson signs that she was into this. Elle found the hard point of Jackson's nipple with her fingers and squeezed.

"How about this? Is this okay?" She broke the kiss and looked at Elle. Her fingers were between Elle's legs. She teased at Elle's entrance with her fingertip.

Elle nodded.

"Say it. Say that you want it." It was all Jackson could do not to slide inside.

"I want it." Elle held her face. "I want you, Jackson."

Something about the way she said Jackson's name. Sensations she'd forgotten washed over her bringing a surge of emotion. She moved her hand and rocked back on her knees. What the hell was she doing? She blinked. She was breathing hard.

"No, don't pull away." Elle slid forward.

Elle wasn't going to let Jackson escape so easily this time. Jackson regarded her as if she were seeing Elle for the first time, as if she were seeing a ghost. Elle put her arms around Jackson's neck and held her, forcing her face against Elle's chest. Then she stood and led Jackson by the hand to the bedroom.

At the side of the bed, she shimmied her dress over her head and then removed her bra. Jackson stood still and watched as Elle undressed herself and then began to unfasten Jackson's belt and trousers. She dropped to her knees and unlaced Jackson's boots. Jackson seemed to come out of whatever trance she'd slipped into. She kicked off her boots and drew Elle up and into her arms. Elle slipped her hands into the back of Jackson's trousers and pushed her underwear and pants over her hips at the same time. She backed to the bed and tugged Jackson along with her.

Jackson's body was like something she'd conjured in a dream. Every muscle taut and toned, like some Greek warrior goddess. She was enveloped by strong arms, and Jackson's muscled thigh was between her legs as Jackson settled her weight on top of Elle. Warmth radiated from Jackson's body.

Elle took Jackson's hand and placed it between her legs. She wanted Jackson to fuck her in the worst way. They'd almost done it on the sofa, but some switch had flipped for Jackson. Elle could see it, she could feel it. But they'd gone too far and Elle wasn't going to let Jackson escape so quickly this time. She needed this.

Jackson's mouth was on her breast as she slipped her fingers inside. Elle opened her legs and arched against Jackson's hand as she thrust inside her. She grasped Jackson's forearm as she rocked beneath her.

She was too close, too fast.

Elle tried to slow down, but she couldn't. Jackson was inside her and she was hungry for it, starved in fact. There was no *going slow* option.

"Just…just…ah, yes…that's it." Her entire body shivered as the wave of the orgasm crested, she was coming way too fast. She hadn't had sex in so long that she'd come too quickly—in a fevered rush.

Jackson stilled her movements but stayed inside as she feathered kisses down Elle's neck. Elle's limbs were limp. She sank into the pillow, breathless. Jackson's weight on top of her was the only thing keeping her grounded.

Jackson could feel Elle's heartbeat against her fingertips. She caressed slowly until Elle squeezed her forearm, a signal to move her hand. Reluctantly, she slid her fingers out, repositioning her palm on the curve of Elle's hip.

Elle's dark brown hair cascaded across the pillow. The pale skin of her neck and chest was flushed with a blush color that rose to her cheeks. Her eyes were closed. She licked her lips and brushed damp tendrils off her forehead as Jackson braced on one elbow for a better view. The soft curves of Elle's body pressed gently against her. She lightly trailed her fingers up Elle's torso, committing the sensuous topography to memory. The gentle roundness of Elle's breasts, the slight contour of her stomach, and her toned legs; Elle was gorgeous. It took a few moments for her to realize Elle was studying her. She had lain quietly allowing Jackson to caress her, to take her in. She stopped the exploration and rested her hand on Elle's stomach.

This felt so real, too real. She wasn't ready for this, not by a long shot.

A tsunami of emotion pounded over Jackson, causing a lump to lodge in her throat. It wasn't that she hadn't been with other women since Camille. She had. But she never felt anything when she'd been with them. Being with them had only confirmed what she'd lost and convinced her that she'd never feel the same with anyone again. This, being with Elle, felt different, different enough to be scary.

Elle pressed her hand against Jackson's shoulder, rolling her onto her back. Then she began to place light kisses down Jackson's chest and her stomach until she reached the apex of her thighs. Elle slid down farther and lightly pressed her palms against Jackson's legs to open them. Elle started to kiss her there, exploring with her tongue.

"Don't go inside." Jackson spoke through clenched teeth. She sank her fingers into Elle's hair. She wanted to be sure Elle had heard her. Elle was doing things with her mouth that threatened to breach Jackson's carefully constructed defenses. She'd only ever let one woman close enough to—close enough to slip inside.

Elle seemed okay with the request.

Elle teased and sucked until her muscles began to twitch with the need for release. Once again, she filled her fingers with Elle's hair. She was losing herself and needed to hang on. She stiffened beneath Elle as her orgasm climbed, until she toppled over the razor-sharp edge. She was falling now and fighting the impulse to let go. Letting go wasn't an option. Letting go was more vulnerability than she was willing to share with a woman she didn't really know.

Elle relaxed on top of her, with her cheek against Jackson's stomach.

Was she asleep? Jackson stroked Elle's hair and tried to regain her composure, reconstructing her defenses as she stared at the ceiling. They were naked on top of the sheet and cool air from the ceiling fan made her skin tingle. Or was that a result of Elle's skin against hers?

She felt weird and exposed—and emotional. She hoped Elle was asleep because if they did much more she might just lose it. She covered her face with her hands. What the fuck was her problem?

When she moved her hands, she saw that Elle was watching her again. She was still lying across Jackson's stomach, but her eyes were open now and her head angled upward. Thankfully, she didn't say anything or ask Jackson what was wrong.

Elle pulled the sheet up to cover them and slid up so that her head rested in the hollow space of Jackson's shoulder.

"Can you stay for a little while?" Elle kissed her on the cheek.

"Sure." She could barely get the response out around the lump in her throat.

Elle snuggled against her and she became acutely aware of every point of contact between their bodies. She was still incredibly turned on but fought the impulse to make love to Elle. Make love? Where did that come from? How did she get from a simple fuck to making love? She needed to leave.

Beside her, Elle's breathing was slow and steady. If she wasn't asleep then she wasn't far from it. Jackson gently dislodged her shoulder and started to quietly gather her clothes. She dressed in the living room with the plan of letting herself out and never looking back.

CHAPTER SEVEN

Elle sensed Jackson's departure long before she got out of bed. She let Jackson think she was asleep so that she could slip away without having some awkward conversation about when they'd see each other again, or if. Clearly, Jackson had some wounds that hadn't healed. Some woman had really done a number on her.

When she heard the door click shut, she rolled onto her back and exhaled. Damn, Jackson was as good in bed as she'd expected. Why were the hot ones always so messed up? Whatever. She wasn't going to beat herself up for not being able to figure it out. It seemed to her that they'd both enjoyed the sex and now she could drift off to a blissful night, replaying Jackson's touch on an infinite loop in her head.

Suddenly thirsty, she walked to the kitchen for a glass of water without getting dressed. She rotated after filling a glass, resting her lower back against the cool edge of the counter as she drank. A dark figure was seated on the sofa; she jumped and almost choked on the water. Jackson stood and walked toward her. She was partially dressed, with her trousers on but no shoes, and her dress shirt hung open, still unbuttoned.

Elle was taken by complete surprise; she'd been certain Jackson had gone.

Jackson towered over her, took the glass from her hand, and then drew Elle to her. Elle's fingers brushed across the ripples of Jackson's abs. Jackson kissed her while her fingers applied slight pressure at the base of Elle's neck, under her hair. Jackson's other hand squeezed her breast and then moved farther down. She held on to Jackson's neck as she felt herself hoisted up. She wrapped her legs around Jackson's waist. Jackson's hands were under her ass pressing her against Jackson's stomach.

"I thought you'd gone," Elle whispered, between kisses.

"I was about to leave, but…" She didn't finish the statement. She kissed Elle instead.

This was a surprise. She'd planned to drift quietly off to the afterglow of sex, but it seemed Jackson had other ideas. Part of Elle was excited that she'd been wrong about Jackson running for the door, but another part of her was sounding alarms because she'd been wrong. Unpredictability made Elle a little uncomfortable.

Jackson carried Elle back to the bedroom. She laid Elle on the bed then rocked back on her knees to unfasten her pants. In her haste to be between Elle's legs, she shoved them down but not all the way off. Once she was lying next to Elle, Jackson kicked them free.

"What made you change your mind?" Elle needed to know.

"About what?"

"About leaving."

"You're beautiful." Jackson's gaze was intense. "How's that for a reason?"

Elle wasn't convinced but appreciated the compliment.

"Is there something you'd like? Is there something I can do for you?" She felt she'd already received a lot from Jackson. It seemed as if the balance was unequal.

"Yeah, this." Jackson braced Elle's thighs against her shoulders and caressed her clit with her tongue. She angled her head up just for a moment. "I couldn't leave without tasting you."

Jackson started again to caress Elle's sex with her tongue. The torment was exquisite. Elle fisted the sheet on either side. Jackson's tongue slid inside and then Jackson's mouth was on her, but her fingers were there too. Jackson was driving her higher and higher. She feared she might spontaneously burst into flames.

They'd had sex earlier, but this was different. The intensity of Jackson's focus had ratcheted up, times ten. Elle was at her mercy and she was coming fast.

She raised up, trying to pull Jackson's face toward hers. She wanted to feel Jackson's weight on top of her when she came. Jackson obliged, reading Elle's need without her uttering a word.

Jackson was rocking on top of her, bracing her thigh against Elle's sex. Elle clung to Jackson's shoulders. Jackson was applying pressure in just the right amount in just the right place. She was coming undone.

Elle cried out, dug her nails into Jackson's ass, and shuddered—the muscles in her legs jerked with release and she slumped back onto the pillow. She wanted to say something, to cry out, but Jackson kissed her, deeply, swallowing the words.

Elle was spent. Jackson's head was against her breast, her breathing now slow and even. Her arm was draped across Elle's midsection. The sheet partially covered them to waist height. Elle caressed Jackson's shoulder lightly and then let her palm come to rest on Jackson's head. She rotated just enough to press her lips against Jackson's forehead.

"Rest now," she whispered. Jackson didn't stir.

Elle was content to hold Jackson until she herself drifted off. She didn't have a lot of experience with one-night stands, but this didn't feel like one. There had been an intensity, an intimacy to their lovemaking that had taken her breath away. She wondered if that had been partly what scared Jackson off and at the same time compelled her to stay.

Eventually, sleep seeped in from the edges of her mind. Tomorrow was a big day. With Jackson spooned close, she let sleep pull her under.

CHAPTER EIGHT

As promised, the sleek black car with a US Space Force insignia on the door was parked at the curb promptly at eight. Elle climbed into the back seat and settled in for the forty-minute drive north to the substation. The humorless driver was in uniform and other than saying good morning, hadn't uttered a word. Liam had instructed her that the driver would pick her up and deliver her to an installation north of the city where she'd get the rest of the story about this secret mission. It all sounded like something out of a comic book, all cloak-and-dagger, secret society—the stuff of mystery novels. The part of her personality that didn't handle unknowns well threatened to revolt, but her curiosity was too strong. She had to know. And in order to know she was going to have to venture out of her comfort zone.

She sank into the seat and watched the city speed by the window. It was a luxury to have a driver and not have to ride the train. She could get used to this sort of treatment. Maybe secret societies were worth investigating.

Elle tried to picture where Jackson was this morning. She'd woken alone, satisfied, and just the least bit foggy from the enjoyable lack of sleep the night before.

She wasn't surprised that Jackson left in the wee hours of the morning without saying good-bye. But she was a little disappointed Jackson hadn't at least left a note or something. Would they see each other again? It would all be on Jackson's terms now. She had no idea how to reach Jackson, but Jackson knew where she lived. The power balance of that was too one-sided. Maybe she should have thought that through a bit more before inviting Jackson up for a drink.

Elle was tired and must have dozed for part of the drive because their arrival seemed too quick. She had to show the security guard her ID before the driver was allowed to proceed. He parked near the entrance of what looked like a tunnel. A very serious woman greeted her when she exited the car.

"Good morning, Dr. Graham. I'm Nikki West and I'm here to escort you to the briefing."

"Thank you."

Nikki was pretty and intimidating at the same time. This amused Elle and she wondered if she could ever pull off that same combination. Nikki also gave off a definite lesbian vibe, but maybe that was simply the uniform talking. Nikki motioned for Elle to take a seat in something that looked like a modified golf cart, army green with a roll cage. How far were they going? The base must be much larger than it appeared from the entrance. Elle held on to the side bar as Nikki hit the gas. They turned sharply and descended into the sleek, smooth sided tunnel.

Jackson closed her laptop and checked the time on her oversized diving watch. She had ten minutes before the briefing started and she was in desperate need of more coffee. There was just enough time for her to swing by the mess hall and pick up a black coffee to-go.

She stood and stretched, feeling stiff from lack of sleep. She'd left Elle's place around three thirty planning to get some shut-eye before reporting to base, but she couldn't quiet her mind enough to actually doze off. The mess hall was buzzing when she entered, offering background white noise for her thoughts.

Why had she stayed?

Her fingers had been curled around the door latch. She'd opened the door but then froze, released the handle, and the door had clicked shut on its own. Jackson had felt momentarily shaken and dropped to the sofa, seated quietly in the dark until Elle appeared, like a gorgeous ghost.

Replaying the sight of Elle, naked, in the kitchen stirred her insides. She closed her eyes and swallowed. *Fuck.* She definitely wanted to see

Elle again. She should have left a note or something. What an ass. She knew where Elle lived. She'd make it up to her by sending flowers.

She sampled the coffee and then topped it off before grabbing a lid. The exchange reader pinged as she swept her ID across the surface to pay for the beverage. The corridor was crowded but much quieter than the cafeteria. Soldiers in uniform, civilian engineers, and random support staff wearing orange coveralls wove around her. She was lost in her own thoughts.

A soldier saluted when she presented herself at the door. She returned the salute and waited for the retinal scan to verify her identity. The door lock clicked and the soldier opened it for her.

"Thank you." She took the last open seat at the oval table without surveying the room.

"I think everyone is present. I'd like to personally welcome you to Space Operations Command." Major Riley spoke from his chair near the center of the table. "Let's take a moment to introduce the team. From our side, this is First Lieutenant Steve Milloy, first lieutenant and pilot Ken Wallace, and commanding officer for this mission, Captain Jackson Drake."

Jackson scanned the table for the first time. Something about hearing her name dragged her brain from the fog she'd been lost in all morning.

She almost choked on her coffee.

Seated at the far end of the long oval table was Elle. She was sure her surprise mirrored the expression on Elle's face as they locked gazes. *What the fuck?*

"Thank you, Major." Liam Allaire sat across from Major Riley at the center of the table. "Some of you I know." He glanced in Jackson's direction. "For those of you I haven't met, I'm Dr. Liam Allaire, director of BIOME Industries. I'd like to introduce paleoclimatologist Dr. Ted Hoffman. And paleobotanist Dr. Eliza Graham. And two members of the BIOME security team, Cliff Harris and Ed Nunez."

Holy shit. She couldn't take her eyes off Elle.

This was a mission briefing. What the hell was Elle doing here? The coffee roiled in her stomach. She set the cup on the table and dropped her hand to her lap to still the shaking.

"Dr. Allaire, would you kick off the meeting?" Major Riley adjusted in his seat. His forearms rested on the table. He was casually at attention at all times.

Liam got to his feet, allowing his fingers to keep light contact with some notes on paper in front of him.

"Just to recap where we are, let me begin with this." He glanced around the room. "By 2099, the oceans will become too hot for phytoplankton to photosynthesize. Between 1950 and now, we've seen almost a complete die-off."

That was pretty depressing. That meant they were only ten years from a complete die-off.

"Traditionally, environmental advocates have focused on climate. But climate and the health of our oceans are related. Tiny phytoplankton float in the ocean unnoticed, yet they once constituted half the organic matter on Earth and they provided two-thirds of the earth's oxygen." Liam glanced at Elle. "Thanks to the research of our team, I think we have a real chance to repair some damage here."

Elle was making every effort to mask her shock at seeing Jackson enter the room for this briefing. She was rattled by Jackson's presence and was completely unable to read Jackson's face. She was wearing a sharply pressed khaki uniform and her cool expression gave nothing away. How the hell had they ended up at this meeting together? *Captain Jackson Drake.* She silently repeated Jackson's full name a few times. The fact that Jackson was in the meeting wasn't even the strangest part of this. She scanned the group seated around the table.

She was in a room full of professionals, scientists, and military personnel discussing time travel. *Time travel!*

Liam had briefed her prior to the meeting and she was still trying to come to terms with the possibilities of such an insane revelation. And yet, on some level she wasn't surprised.

In some ways, time travel made perfect sense. One of the only ways to understand the current crisis was in the context of deep time. In the realms of the distant geological past. Current generations were being plunged into deep time, like it or not, by the once-in-a-million-year environmental changes currently taking place all over the globe.

Climate change deniers had some damaging, unrealistic, and downright stupid views of the planet's deep past as an essentially static state of affairs. But it was almost impossible to understand what was happening in the present without understanding its context in the past.

"The Pacific Ocean covers one-third of the surface of the entire planet and holds half the world's water." Liam rotated to make eye contact with everyone seated around the table. "We're in the best location for finding the species we need to reseed the ocean, if your team can get us to the right window of time."

"If you can give us the date, we can get you there." Ken Wallace, the pilot, chimed in. He was cocky for sure. "Once we opened the gateway, probing it was the easy part. It was as though we had always been living in a closed room and someone opened a window."

She doubted that was completely true. It couldn't possibly be that easy. Elle wasn't a physicist so she wasn't sure she was following the science, but she'd hold some of her questions for a smaller group setting. For now, she focused on listening intently to every scrap of information being shared.

"For the newcomers in this room, what I'm about to share with you is classified." The major was serious, his expression stern. "In layman's terms, we were looking for travel faster than light and accidentally discovered that we could go around the law of relativity and create a gateway, a wormhole that would allow us to fold spacetime."

"Forgive me, but have you actually done other missions prior to this one?" Elle didn't want to disrespect the group, but she had to ask. This seemed like a giant leap. Regardless of the top-secret status, she found it hard to believe that the military had been able to keep this operation secret.

Major Riley pressed a com button in the center of the table. "Gary, can you bring in the sample?"

The room fell silent for a few minutes. A middle-aged man in a white lab coat entered with a container about the size of shoe box with glass on three sides, and a screen on the fourth side. The major motioned for Gary to place the container near where Elle was seated. She sat back as he placed the square container in front of her. The minute Gary stepped back, she and Ted leaned forward for a closer look. She blinked in disbelief.

"Is that—? Are those—?"

"Honeybees." Major Riley answered as if that was the most obvious thing in the world.

"But honeybees are extinct." She looked at Liam. Pollination had to be done by hand, or by machine.

"We retrieved them from a time prior to extinction." Major Riley poured a glass of water for himself and took a sip.

The room was quiet for a few minutes except for the low buzz from the bees.

"Physical evaluations begin this morning at ten-hundred." Major Riley stood. "All of you will need to remain here at the facility until you've been cleared for the mission or relieved of duty to return to your homes."

"Major, do you mind if we keep the room for a few minutes?" Liam stood. He must have sensed the multiple questions queuing up in Elle's head.

"Not a problem. Take your time."

She watched Jackson file out of the room with the others without even a backward glance. The urge to follow was almost too great, but she'd deal with that later, for now she needed answers from Liam. He waited until the door closed before taking his seat. He swiveled to face Elle and Ted.

"Harris, Nunez, would you mind giving us a few moments?" The two men in dark suits nodded and exited. Elle had only just met them, and her first impression was that they looked like very serious Secret Service agents.

She was a scientist and not used to all this, whatever this was. It all felt almost comical. Also, Elle had no idea that Ted was attending this briefing. He'd not mentioned it and now, given the secrecy surrounding this place, she understood why.

"I'm sure both of you have lots of questions, but if you give this a little time, you'll get answers." Liam was trying to put them at ease.

"I was unaware that we'd be kept here once we arrived. I didn't pack any clothes or…" Elle let the statement trail off.

"I'm sorry. I wasn't able to tell you much, and if you'd known you would be staying here for a few days you'd have felt compelled to talk to someone about what you were doing." Liam poured himself a glass of water. "They will provide clothing and other personal items." He took a few sips of water before continuing. "Listen, you'll both have to pass the physical before they approve you for the mission."

"Why?" Research didn't normally require physical tests of stamina.

"Apparently, this device, the passage is a little rough." Liam was serious. "They call it the Slingshot."

"I see." Elle was trying to process things but needed more time. "What if we don't pass the physical?"

"Then you can't make the trip. Ted knows the *when* and you know the species. I selected you both for this to ensure success. I was doubling the chances of success by selecting two candidates."

"What else can you tell us about the device—this Slingshot." Ted had been silent. Why did he seem so much more resigned to all of this than Elle? "Time travel has always been theoretical, but I assume that's what we're talking about here."

"You're correct. Black holes bend time, but we could never get past the event horizon, a boundary past which nothing can return." Liam paused. "However, we also knew that, in theory, a naked singularity could exist." Liam was talking as if the science behind what he was explaining was easy to grasp, but Elle was struggling to synthesize the information. Also, the way he kept saying *we* signaled that he'd known about this long before today. "In principle, such singularities could be created by compressing very light particles such as neutrinos sufficiently quickly. The trick was to arrange neutrino emitters spherically, aim them at one central point, and ramp up their beam. Such a singularity would not need to be massive in order to work."

"But wouldn't the singularity create excessive gravitational pull?" asked Ted.

"Yes, but they have equipment in place to offset the increased gravity." Liam stood, a clear sign that this conversation was coming to a close. "You'll be here for at least forty-eight hours. I'm sure you'll get better answers from the crew than you will from me."

"How dangerous is this, Liam?" Elle couldn't stop the question.

"I won't lie to you, Elle. This is a risky venture, but given where we are, what choice do we have?"

She nodded. He was right. And if someone was going to have to do this, then it might as well be her. She knew the species they needed to reseed the seas. They probably only had one shot to get this right.

A woman in a khaki uniform similar to Jackson's greeted them as they exited the briefing room. She explained that she would escort them to quarters where they could relax prior to physical evaluations and lunch. Elle's head was spinning, but she tried to pay attention to the route they were taking so that she could keep her bearings.

"Someone will be by shortly to make sure you have all the clothing and any other personal hygiene items you might need for your stay with us," the woman explained politely as she stood to the side to allow Elle to enter a dorm room type space.

"Thank you." Elle remained in the doorway and watched Ted follow the woman to the next room.

She sat on the edge of the bed and surveyed the space. The room was sterile but not altogether unpleasant. It was clean and the bed had been made with close attention paid to the corners. She'd never mastered that sort of bed making. She placed her palm on the covering to test its softness—none. And the blanket felt scratchy.

Elle sighed. What had she gotten herself into?

CHAPTER NINE

Jackson trailed Major Riley to his office. She was wrought up. Seeing Elle in a mission briefing was the absolute last thing she'd expected, or wanted.

"Sir, might I have a word?"

He nodded and signaled for her to enter. She closed the door as he took a seat behind the large desk. She waited for an invitation to sit.

"As you were, Captain." He motioned toward the chair facing the desk. "Please, sit."

"Permission to speak freely, sir."

"Permission granted."

"I'll get to the point. I have concerns about this mission team." Jackson tried to remain calm.

"Explain."

"We've never taken non-military personnel through the gateway. It's physically challenging even when someone has had the training."

"That's not my call." The major entwined his fingers as he leaned forward with elbows braced on the desk. "Look, I'd prefer a military operation same as you, but BIOME is footing the bill for this ride and they think their people are the only way to guarantee that specimens are properly identified for transport."

"Okay, I get that." Jackson was frustrated and trying not to show it. "I know we aren't scientists, but we've done other species extractions with success."

"We've never done deep time like this. And this isn't like catching honeybees. These phytoplankton are microscopic. What if you brought back a jug of ocean water with nothing in it? Then what?" His point was valid. If she was going to get Elle off this mission she'd have to regroup and try a different approach.

"What sort of time are we talking about here?" She didn't remember an exact number from the briefing, but in her defense, she was a little distracted.

"One hundred twenty thousand years before today."

"That's a big number." She decided to table that for now. "What about the two other suits in the briefing?"

"Private security."

"Since when?"

"Since BIOME decided to fund the mission. They insisted on their own security detail." The major frowned. "Listen, I don't like it any more than you do, but it was a deal breaker. We didn't really have a choice."

"So, who on my team is staying behind?" There'd been seven candidates in the briefing and the Slingshot only had gravity tubes for six.

"It'll likely be Milloy, but I asked him to sit in as an alternate in case one of the other candidates doesn't make the cut."

"I understand." Jackson stood. "Thank you for hearing me out."

This conversation wasn't making her feel any more settled or at ease. She was ready for it to be over.

"You're dismissed."

"Yes, sir." She stood up.

"Jackson."

Her hand was on the door; she turned to face him.

"You're the best I've got. Mission success will be on your shoulders. I'm counting on you to see this through."

"Yes, sir."

Once in the hallway, she took a deep breath instead of doing what she wanted to do, which was punch the nearest wall. She needed to find Elle and have a frank discussion about what was involved. Elle needed a reality check. There was no way that Elle understood what she was getting into. She headed back down the corridor toward the briefing room. It was empty. She figured Elle and Ted were in the quarters for recruits and trainees so she walked in that direction.

Elle was standing in the hallway with Ted when Jackson approached. He looked familiar to her, but she couldn't quite place where she might have seen him prior to the earlier meeting. He was a serious nerd, not the sort of fellow who normally ran in her circles. He looked as if he'd be winded climbing a flight of stairs.

Good luck passing the physical.

Elle looked up as she approached.

"Dr. Graham, I'm glad I found you. Do you have a moment?"

"Yes." Elle hesitated and looked back. "Ted, I'll catch up with you later."

"Are you sure?" Ted seemed distrustful or nervous, or both.

You should be. Because you've got no idea what you've signed up for. But that was his problem. Jackson's main concern was Elle.

"Yeah, I'm sure." Elle smiled thinly. "I'll find you later."

He nodded and turned toward the mess hall.

There was a moment of awkwardness before Elle spoke.

"I'm glad you found me. I was hoping to speak with you too."

"Do you mind walking to my office? It's a little more private."

"Lead the way."

Jackson was quiet as they walked through the corridor in the opposite direction from the cafeteria. It took several minutes to reach her office. Several minutes of painful, electrically charged silence. Possibly the longest short walk she'd ever endured. Trying to keep herself in check when all she really wanted to so was sweep Elle up in her arms and kiss her, was testing her will.

She closed the door to her office but neither of them took a seat.

"Jackson, I hope you know I'm as surprised to see you as you are to see me."

That was stating the obvious.

"Why don't you sit down?"

"I don't feel like sitting down." Elle's words sounded soft, almost like a plea.

Jackson couldn't stand the distance any longer. She reached for Elle, drew her close, and kissed her. Realizing where she was, Jackson broke the kiss just long enough to lock the door. The last thing she needed was someone walking in on them.

Damn, Elle was so incredibly kissable. Her lips were warm and soft as she covered Jackson's mouth with hers. Jackson was getting so turned on. She wanted to press Elle against the desk and touch her, make love to her. Elle's hand was on her ass applying pressure, her other hand was at the base of Jackson's neck. They fumbled toward the desk. Jackson braced one arm at the edge of the wide surface to steady herself.

"I'm sorry, I shouldn't have done that." Jackson was breathing hard and her libido was humming. "That wasn't why I asked you to come to my office."

"I'm okay with this." Elle kissed her lightly. "You left this morning without a note, or anything. I thought maybe—"

"That had nothing to do with you or how I felt about last night."

"I'm glad to hear that." Elle slid her palms down Jackson's arms and tilted her adorable face as she coyly looked up at Jackson. "Because I was sort of hoping I'd see you again. Although, admittedly under different circumstances." Elle surveyed the bland office interior.

Jackson began to see the room from Elle's perspective. It was completely without character. This could be anyone's office. She released Elle and took a step back. She hadn't meant to derail a conversation, but Elle had been far too tempting.

"Can we just talk?" Jackson motioned for Elle to take a chair and she rotated a second office chair to face Elle's.

Elle sat down and waited for her to say something. Elle was wearing black dress pants and heels. Her ivory blouse was open at the collar revealing a tempting view of her neck and pronounced collar bones, and that hollow space between that Jackson wanted to trace with her fingertip.

Why was Elle so damn calm? She cleared her throat, rubbed her fingers across the stubble on top of her head briskly a few times, and exhaled. Where to begin?

"You shouldn't do this." Okay, maybe that wasn't the most subtle way to start the conversation.

"Shouldn't do what?" Elle seemed genuinely confused.

"This mission. You should walk away from this. It's too hard."

"I know we don't know each other, I mean, really know each other, but I'm not going to walk away from something just because it's difficult." Elle sounded annoyed.

"Look, I'm not trying to be patronizing and I hope it doesn't sound like I am." Jackson paused to regroup. "All I'm trying to say is that this is very dangerous and I don't want to be responsible for your safety. The fact that we've slept together…well, I think it might compromise the mission."

"Really?" Elle smiled, which annoyed Jackson. This wasn't funny. "You can't be serious. Are you saying that you won't be able to control yourself or act in a professional manner if I'm part of the team?"

"Yes, I mean no, that's not what I'm saying." Elle was getting her all flustered. "I can be as professional as you can." Now she sounded like a fifth grader. *Fuck.* This wasn't going at all as she'd rehearsed it out in her head. "Let's start over."

"Okaaay, I'm listening."

Elle ran her tongue across her lips and Jackson tried not to notice. "I'm serious. *This* is serious." Jackson was exasperated.

"I'm sorry. I'm still trying to get my head around all of this and whether or not any of it could possibly be true. Time travel? We're having serious conversations about time travel. So, forgive me for taking a moment to consider the absurdity of it all." She cocked her head and looked at the ceiling. "Although, time isn't as linear as we imagine is it? And it takes more than a second for my brain to process the words you are uttering, so by the time I figure out what you've said, it's no longer *now* anyway is it?"

"What?" Did Elle just run circles around her?

"What we think of the present, right now, by the time our brain processes the input it's no longer the present."

Jackson shook her head. Science nerds were so hard to talk to.

Elle continued as if she expected Jackson to be keeping up. "And here you are—what *are* you anyway? What is your role in all of this?"

"I'm the mission commander."

"And as the mission commander you're asking me to walk away from possibly the greatest scientific moment of my entire professional career?"

"I simply want you to know what you're getting into. This is dangerous."

"Can you tell me more about how the, what did Liam call it…the slingshot. Can you tell me more about how it works?"

Jackson sank back in her chair, settling in for an even bigger discussion.

"Do you understand how a black hole works?"

"Yes, in theory."

"A wormhole acts in some ways like a black hole, compressing time and space." She motioned with her hands, moving them together as if she was squeezing the air.

"Are you a physicist?"

"No, I studied engineering." That was true, although, not completely. She had a general curiosity about physics, specifically how that applied to flight. Hell, she'd aspired to be an astronaut before the ISS went bust and exoplanet exploration was abandoned. The Slingshot was probably as close as she would get to space now.

"This whole installation was basically designed as a super collider. A particle accelerator. This was supposed to solve part of the energy shortfall. Fusion could have provided an unlimited power source for all kinds of things." Jackson made an arc in the air. "I mean, there were lots of energy projects abandoned for this because the payoff was going to be huge. But they couldn't secure the funding to finish key aspects of the project." Jackson rubbed her forehead, picturing how it had all gone down. "Politics, the recession, and public insistence on controlled spending brought things to a standstill. It was a big mess, so the private sector stepped in thinking there was money to be made in the long term." Jackson took a deep breath. She was probably oversharing, but all the science behind what they were doing got her wound up. "Is this too much?"

"No, I'm following." Elle was completely focused on Jackson, uncomfortably so.

Jackson shifted in her chair beneath Elle's intense gaze. She tried to regain the thread of what she'd been talking about, but it wasn't easy. Elle was insanely distracting. One more reason for her not to be on this team.

"Okay, so the project's scale ended up being twenty times bigger than anything physicists had ever managed before. There were cultural differences between the scientific side of the accelerator's management and the military-industrial culture imposed by the Department of Energy. Anyway, all of this led to conflicts, endless audits, and lack of trust. And the project was basically dead in the water until about ten years ago, when it was repurposed by the Space Force as a command center."

"This is why I ended up at BIOME. The private sector has less red tape in some ways and more funding. I mean, ultimately, they just want to make money and in order to do that, they know they need to move projects forward." Elle adjusted her position. She seemed more relaxed now that Jackson was just talking about science rather than trying to tell her what she should and shouldn't do. "That is, as long as the research you're doing actually makes them money."

"So, you and Ted Hoffman both work for BIOME?"

"Yes, he's my research partner. And you...are you in the Army?"

"I was in the Air Force prior to joining the Space Force, both branches report to the Secretary of the Air Force."

"You still didn't really explain the time travel."

Jackson had been giving Elle lots of backstory, the approved narrative, but not the entire story.

"The discovery that a gateway, a wormhole, could be created happened by accident when they were trying to solve the problem of faster than light travel."

"That's what Liam, Dr. Allaire, said, but how did they know that's what they'd discovered?"

"An unmanned drone disappeared and when it returned it was clear from the onboard sensors that it had experienced time differently than anyone thought possible." Jackson was getting into territory she wasn't comfortable discussing with someone who might or might not end up on the team. She needed to wrap this up and get to the point. "Look, it sort of doesn't matter how we got here. But this is where we are and I have concerns about your safety if you choose to participate in this jump."

"Why are you so concerned?"

"The Slingshot imposes serious—"

"Why do you call it the Slingshot?"

"What?"

"People keep calling it the Slingshot."

"Oh." Jackson regrouped. Whatever point she'd been about to make had gotten completely derailed by Elle's question. "The acronym for the ship is SLST—Singularity Lift System Transport. But when you pass through the gateway it feels like you're being shot into space by a slingshot, and SLST...I dunno, we just started calling it the Slingshot."

"Okay, I get it."

"Listen, what I was trying to explain to you is that traveling through the gateway, the wormhole, imposes serious g-forces. You'll feel like your bones are being crushed even with the gravity tube to offset the stress on your body." Jackson paused. "And then there's the return trip."

"Jackson, I appreciate your concern, but I've dedicated my life to finding solutions for our current environmental crisis. If there's any glimmer of hope that I can actually affect real transformation by participating in this venture, then there's nothing you can say to dissuade me." Elle was firm, bordering on defiant.

"What are you saying?"

"I'm saying you can't tell me not to go. And that you shouldn't have even tried." Elle stood to leave. "Listen, I appreciate that you probably think you're looking out for me here, Captain, but I can handle myself."

That was obvious. And Jackson could tell she'd pissed her off.

Elle strode out of her office without looking back.

Jackson sat looking at the open door. Now what was she going to do?

CHAPTER TEN

Elle lay on the narrow bunk and stared at the ceiling. She hadn't seen Jackson since their earlier, somewhat heated discussion. She'd gotten a tour of the facility, been given three changes of clothing, and done one heart rate test on the treadmill which she'd passed. Luckily, she was pretty fit. She wasn't very happy about the clothing though. T-shirts, camouflage cargo pants, and boots. Not really her style.

The discussion she'd had with Jackson made her even more determined to be part of this mission than she might otherwise have been.

It was true that she didn't like to be told what she could or couldn't do. But additionally, she wasn't sure she trusted anyone else to see this through. She was the one who, working with Ted, had identified the date and the species. This was her discovery. The thought of traveling back in time to primeval Earth did scare the shit out of her, but this wasn't the Slingshot's first mission. Clearly, the team knew what they were doing since they'd done previous jumps. Right? She wondered if Jackson had been part of those missions too.

And what about Jackson? Elle had assumed she was simply a handsomely chiseled specimen of female strength. Now it turned out she was also some borderline genius engineer who could explain wormholes in plain English. Jackson was smart, and unfortunately that just made her more alluring. Captivating or not, Jackson wasn't going to keep her from participating in this mission.

The reality was that the oceans were so close to complete and utter collapse that she couldn't look away or wait for someone else to do this work for her. The public had put up such resistance to the ever-worsening truths about rising temperatures, climate denial had even become a political platform, leaving earth in a terminal condition.

World leaders warned of food shortages that never really came. If they had, maybe that would have captured the public's attention. Instead, enhanced food production during the green revolution had made things worse. Enhanced food production meant fewer people starved, and as a result, those people gave birth to more people who needed to eat. By 2050, most of the planet was devoted to growing or grazing food for humans, while other animals just disappeared. Seemingly oblivious, humanity just kept pressing on.

By the time she was in grad school, refined models had revised earlier predictions of how quickly the ice would melt and how fast and how high CO_2 levels and seas would rise. Earlier models had failed to predict the effect of vast amounts of methane entering the atmosphere from thawing permafrost. The warm climate fueled fierce storms, wildfires, species die-offs, and drug resistant viruses. Superbugs spread through refugee encampments and inner cities, killing thousands.

To call where they currently were *environmental upheaval* was an understatement.

Humanity was learning the hard way that the world's ecosystems were infinitely intricate. The scientific community now knew it had been almost impossible to truly predict how two degrees would change everything, let alone a three-degree jump.

Huge swaths of California burned, successive monstrous hurricanes devastated Texas, Florida, and Louisiana. Cyclone bombs exploded in the heartland, and thousand-year floods recurred every two years. Ice shelves fractured and refugees poured in from East and North Africa and the Middle East where temps now regularly reached one hundred and thirty degrees. At two degrees of warming, more than one hundred and fifty million people had died from air pollution alone.

Elle and many of her generation knew the awful truth. Human beings, in general, were responsible for ecological degradation of multiple planetary systems. The Earth's current condition was a direct result of the power struggle between human beings and all kinds of geophysical forces.

This was a grim, apocalyptic train of thought. She rolled onto her side and closed her eyes. Sometimes it was painful to know so much.

There was no way she wasn't going on this mission. She sat at the edge of the bed after she slipped her shoes on. If there was even the slightest chance that her research might in some way stave off environmental collapse, then she had to face any fear to make that happen, with or without Jackson's support.

Elle stepped out of her room and almost bumped into Ted. He was sweaty, breathing hard, and frankly, not looking so good.

"Hey, are you okay?" Elle was worried. He looked paler than usual.

"Yeah, cardio test…just a little winded."

Winded? He looked like he was a quick minute from toppling over.

"You're probably like me."

"In what way?" He looked nervous about what she might say.

"I thought being a science nerd was code for 'I don't do sports.'" She was trying to lighten his mood.

"Oh, yeah, same here." He wiped his face with one end of a towel draped around his neck.

The truth was, Elle had always enjoyed running, just not as part of a team. And not for winning or keeping score, but simply for the fun of it. Plus, it helped her think. Many problems got solved on her daily treadmill jog.

"Hey, have you talked much with the two security guys?"

"Not really." Ted shook his head.

"They haven't talked with me either. It just seems weird that we didn't really meet with them at all, doesn't it?" Harris and Nunez kept to themselves. They were a unit of two in a team of six.

"Maybe." He sounded unconcerned. "I think I'm going to take a break." He angled toward his room. He obviously wasn't in the mood to chat, but that wasn't anything unusual.

"Sure." She watched him slog to his quarters. "I'll see you later."

He didn't look back or acknowledge her words. Something seemed off with Ted. More than just too much cardio. Maybe he was worried about his kid. It had to be hard to spend even a few hours away from your child if he was truly ill.

Elle took a step without looking and almost bumped into Nunez. He was so solidly stout it was like running into a brick wall.

"Oh, sorry." She apologized but then instantly had the thought that he'd intentionally stepped into her path for some reason.

Harris and Nunez were supposed to be her security team, but they'd been distant during evaluations. The two men were the opposite of security in her opinion. Personally, they made her feel uneasy rather than safe. She assumed they were really only there to provide security for the acquisition of samples and not the people involved in that extraction, because their bedside manner was less than zero.

"You nervous about the mission?" he asked, as if he cared. His demeanor said he didn't.

"Not really." And if she was, she certainly wouldn't admit it to him.

"Yeah, what's to worry about if you know what you're doing, right?"

Was he trying to piss her off? She decided to give him the benefit of the doubt. Maybe she just wasn't used to his type of humor.

"Yeah, right." She smiled, stepped around him, and headed toward her next test session, balance and agility.

She looked back before she exited the corridor to see that he was still watching her.

CHAPTER ELEVEN

For about thirty seconds, Jackson considered pulling herself out of the team. She couldn't control Elle; the only thing she could control was herself.

Jackson knew she had to accept command. She was the only person she trusted to keep Elle safe. She was determined to distance herself from Elle, for the sake of the mission, and for the sake of her own heart. That would be difficult, but not impossible. She'd had a lot of experience controlling her emotions. This was just one more test of her resolve. And besides, the last thing she wanted was to fall for another woman willing to sacrifice herself to save the world. That was something she just couldn't handle again.

They were halfway through day two of readiness evaluations and training. It was Jackson's turn to talk about the strain of time travel. So far everyone had passed the physical and medical tests that cleared them for the rigors of travel through the gateway. She made notes on a white board as Ted, Elle, Harris, and Nunez filed in and took their seats. Having made two previous jumps, Milloy and Wallace already knew this stuff so they weren't required to attend. Chairs scuffed on the tile floor behind her.

Harris and Nunez hardly spoke. Jackson still couldn't get a read on them. Both men seemed generally fit and capable, but a little too siloed for her to feel comfortable counting on them as part of a cohesive unit. There were too many damn unknowns on this ride. Elle seemed to take all the rigorous testing in stride. Jackson knew from close, personal inspection that Elle was in great physical condition. Ted on the other hand, was thin and awkward, bordering on uncoordinated, and she was frankly surprised he'd passed the testing so far.

"We're going to spend a few minutes talking about g-forces." Jackson underlined a number on the board with the broad-tipped marker. "The typical human body can withstand about five g's. Jet pilots and astronauts undergo intensive g-force training that acclimates their bodies for up to nine g's. Any higher than that and the pilot loses consciousness."

Elle was listening with a completely neutral expression. Maybe Elle had also decided distance was the best approach for their current situation.

"Have any of you had any previous g-force training?" She didn't want to assume without asking.

No one raised their hand.

"For lower ranges, pilots normally wear a g-suit, an anti-gravity garment that inflates to prevent blood from pooling in the feet and legs. For the Slingshot we use pressurized gravity tubes in addition to the suits."

"How many g's are we talking about here?" Asked Harris.

"Let's just say, that passage in the SLST craft pulls g's at greater than ten."

Elle's eyes widened, but that was the only change in her expression. If Jackson had hoped to scare her off, it hadn't worked so far.

"If you'll follow me, I'll walk you through the crew cabin in the simulator so that you can see what the g-tube looks like."

Elle's pulse sped up as they entered the simulator. This was serious astronaut stuff and way out of her comfort zone. She watched as Jackson demonstrated the functionality of the g-tube on Ted. It looked like something from a science fiction movie. The sort of sleep tank used for long distance space flight. But this would be different. The time in the tube would purportedly seem like only seconds and when they landed they'd have traveled into Earth's long ago past.

"Technicians will make sure you are properly set up in the grav tube before we ignite the drive." Jackson made eye contact with her for the first time. "Without this tube, the g-force of traveling through the wormhole would kill you."

Jackson handed over the rest of the demonstration to a technician who walked the group through other details about the simulator. Elle was listening, but she couldn't help looking over at Jackson. What was she thinking? Jackson stood, eyes forward, with her arms across her chest. She was like a statue, impossible to read.

After another twenty minutes of questions from the group and answers from the technician, they were released for lunch.

Elle lingered in the corridor as the others went for food. Jackson finally appeared in the doorway after a few long minutes.

"Hi." She greeted Jackson as if she hadn't just been in close proximity to her for the better part of the morning.

"Hi." Jackson wasn't expecting the ambush. Elle had given her no room to escape.

"I'm glad I caught you. Do you have a minute?"

"Sure." Jackson glanced around and then motioned for Elle to step back inside the simulator.

If it was possible, Jackson looked even hotter than usual in a snug fitting black T-shirt and camouflage cargo pants. Somehow, Jackson made the military issue clothing look sexy.

"Why do you guys wear camouflage?" The question just popped out.

"Excuse me?" Jackson was caught off guard.

"I thought this was the US Space Force. Are you anticipating the need to blend in with some as yet undiscovered *space jungle*?"

"We wear the same uniforms as our joint counterparts, since we'll be working with them, on the ground." Jackson clearly wasn't amused by her attempt at humor. "Is that what you wanted to ask me about? The US Space Force dress code?"

"No."

Elle decided to get right to the point.

"Are you still concerned about my participation in this mission?"

This was a small team and it was going to be super awkward if they couldn't find a way to move forward and get past their discomfort with each other. That's assuming Jackson still felt anything for her. She'd been so arrogantly aloof since their initial discussion in Jackson's office that Elle was beginning to wonder if she was the only one who had any feelings about the night they'd spent together.

"No." But she didn't sound sure. "You've passed the physical benchmarks. And from what I hear, you're the resident expert on phytoplankton."

Of course, she'd passed. Every time fatigue threatened to pull her under she heard Jackson's voice telling her she wasn't tough enough to do the mission. Her competitive nature spurred her on.

"You really know how to make a girl feel special," Elle muttered, half to herself, glancing toward the exit.

Everyone else had already headed toward the cafeteria for a break. Elle started to walk away too. She wasn't going to beg Jackson for her approval.

She'd only taken a few strides when Jackson spoke.

"Can you just hang on for a second?" All the bravado was gone. Jackson's question sounded like a genuine request.

"Okay." Reluctantly, Elle retraced her steps.

"Listen, I know it might seem like I'm being a hard-ass here, but as commander it's my job to make sure that not only does the mission succeed but that everyone gets back safely."

"I understand."

"It can't be perceived that I'm showing any kind of favoritism to you or cutting you any slack."

"I get it."

"Do you?" Jackson sounded frustrated.

"Yes, I do." Elle was getting frustrated too. "I'm as serious about this as you are."

She wanted to reach for Jackson, to stroke her face, to comfort her and tell her that everything was going to be okay. But she didn't know that it would be. They seemed to be having a hard time understanding each other. In truth, the short time they'd spent together before joining the mission hadn't really been focused on communication, at least not the verbal kind. So, what did she expect.

"I'm going to join the others for lunch." Elle smiled thinly and walked away.

She didn't look back to see if Jackson followed her. In her heart, she knew Jackson hadn't. Why would she? She'd made it pretty clear that the only thing she wanted from Elle was professional distance.

CHAPTER TWELVE

Jackson stood in the crew quarters of the simulator for a few minutes before stepping out into the corridor. She needed lunch too. She'd had too much coffee and not enough food this morning. At least that was how she explained the knot in her stomach that just wouldn't seem to unwind.

The mess hall was busy and crowded. She was shuffling down the line with a tray making food selections as if she had an appetite when Nikki spoke beside her.

"Mind if I join you?"

"Please."

"Mission readiness protocols going that well, huh?" Nikki playfully bumped her arm with her elbow.

They carried the food trays to a table at the fringe of the crowd. Elle was probably seated somewhere in the large space, but Jackson didn't look for her. In fact, she made a point not to. She and Nikki chose seats across from each other. Jackson had her back to the room.

"Hey, I'm sorry you're not on the roster for this one." That was the understatement of the year. Ken Wallace was okay, she liked him as a friend, but he was a little too cocky sometimes. Nikki was solid, level-headed, and a strong team player.

"I know it wasn't your call. I heard from Wallace that I got squeezed out by two private security suits."

"Yeah, definitely not my decision either." Jackson chewed a mouthful of food. "That decision was made way above my pay grade."

They sat quietly for a few minutes as they both ate. Clinking silverware and the dull murmur of voices surrounded her.

"So, who's the hottie?" Nikki was looking past Jackson's shoulder.

Without thinking, Jackson turned to see that Elle was sitting only two tables away talking with Ted.

"I was her escort to the briefing on the first day."

"Then you know who she is." Jackson didn't feel like talking about Elle.

"Yeah, some super scientist who just happens to also be gorgeous." Nikki scowled. "What's up? I thought she'd totally be your type."

"We met once at the Green Club." She might as well tell Nikki at least part of the story or Nikki would keep pestering her about it.

"Oh."

"Yeah."

"So, she *is* your type."

"Yeah."

"And she's part of your team for this ride?"

"Yeah." Jackson moved food around with her fork, not looking up.

"It sucks to be you."

"Yeah."

"You could always just…I don't know…talk to her."

"I have talked to her." Jackson glared at Nikki.

"Okay, okay, don't get defensive." Nikki held up her hands in mock surrender.

"I'm not defensive." Jackson scowled.

"If you say so." The corner of Nikki's mouth tipped up in a half smile, the smug smile of victory.

"Are you gonna eat that?" Wallace was already reaching for the unfinished half of a square of cornbread as he slid into the chair next to Nikki.

"Not anymore." She glared at him. The cornbread was already in his mouth.

"Thwank yew," he said, crumbs flying.

"Get your own lunch, man." Jackson was trying to come to Nikki's defense.

"The line's too long." He dusted the crumbs from his fingers. "I'll give the herd a minute to thin out and then I'll grab something." He braced his elbows on the table. "So, what are we talking about?"

"Jackson's issues with communication," Nikki volunteered.

"I thought maybe you were talking about me." He grinned.

"How does anyone put up with you?" Jackson's question was playful.

"I have no idea." He smiled as he nibbled a French fry he'd just swiped from her plate.

CHAPTER THIRTEEN

The last round of tests required that Elle fast for the night. She'd grabbed a quick meal after mobility and reflex testing the previous evening but was supposed to fast until the next morning so that the lab could take samples for blood work. They were going to run tests for risk factors and pathogens.

By nine, her blood samples had been drawn and Elle was starving. Her head pounded. She was in dire need of coffee. She was on her second cup when Liam surprised her in the cafeteria. Although she shouldn't have been surprised. He was very invested in the success of this mission, so really, she should have expected him to be hovering about every day. She was almost more surprised that she hadn't seen more of him.

"May I join you?" His manicured hand rested on the back of the chair across from hers.

"Please do. Would you like a coffee?"

"No, I'm good." He surveyed the room and then turned back. His dark suit made him stand out amid the military garb and coveralls. "I wanted to check in with you and see how everything was going."

"Things are going well." Had he heard something about her tests that she wasn't aware of? Something about his demeanor reminded her of her parents when they had to deliver bad news and were avoiding it.

"Great. That's great." He was restless. His eyes kept darting around the room. "I thought I'd check in with Ted also. Have you seen him?"

"Not since this morning." She took a sip of coffee, considering whether to share her observations or not. "He seems...depressed."

It wasn't as if Ted was a super upbeat sort of guy, but he was definitely more melancholy than usual.

"I had a status update meeting with Major Riley and I just thought I'd check in with you both. I'll see if I can track Ted down." He stood up.

"He might be in his quarters. We both had bloodwork done this morning. He might have gone to rest afterward." She wasn't sure where Ted was, but that was her best guess.

"Thanks." He turned to leave but looked back. "And good luck."

"Thank you."

Something about that encounter was off. Liam was normally warmer and more conversational. He'd definitely been distracted, or bothered by something.

Elle was suddenly feeling fatigued. Maybe she should follow her own suggestion and go lie down for a little while. Having blood drawn always made her a little woozy. The food and coffee would only get her so far. She wasn't sleeping that great. Her brain wouldn't shut down at night. She'd replay every encounter with Jackson throughout the day and try to solve the puzzle of what any of it meant. So far only sleeplessness. She'd gotten no closer to answers.

She took the long route back to her quarters passing by the observation level above the Slingshot. They'd been inside the simulator a couple of times, but she'd only seen the actual vessel from a distance. It sort of looked like a gleaming silver football. The core of the craft was an oval that was surrounded by a series of external rings. From what she could glean, the ship was propelled by two different rotations; the core of this ship rotated and the rings also spun independently. This was what helped the ship achieve gateway speed.

The aircraft was suspended in a long cavern, a huge tunnel, with a circumference of about seventeen miles. The tunnel was actually constructed above ground so that when the Slingshot breached the gateway it would arrive in the open air, in the same position where it launched, the only change would be the time stamp.

It was a hard concept to grasp.

They would travel faster than light but go nowhere. They would end up in the exact same location, simply at another point on the timeline.

The observation window was probably fifty feet away from the actual ship, which currently was surrounded by technicians in white coveralls prepping the craft with all the materials they would need for the journey, which might last as long as five days. And the gear required to retrieve and transport specimens.

Watching the hive of activity beneath the window was making Elle feel more tired, and a little nervous. She walked back to her quarters to try to rest. The last presentation for the team was hers. She needed to mentally prepare.

CHAPTER FOURTEEN

The final day before departure was all about the science of the expedition. Until now, Elle and Ted had quietly suffered days of rigorous evaluation to ensure that they could physically endure the journey through the gateway. Now, finally, it was Elle's turn at the front of the class. In advance of the presentation, she'd written several notes on the white board. She turned to face the group. There were only six crew members now. Steve Milloy had gotten bumped when Elle, Ted, and the security team passed all the physical exams and were certified mission ready.

Elle had been tasked with briefing the team about what to expect when they arrived at the destination. All that she could give them was an educated guess. There would undoubtedly be things about primordial Earth that no amount of modern research could tell them. But she did know some things and was happy to share that knowledge with the group.

Jackson sat near the back of the room like a reluctant student. Elle tried not to take it personally.

"Okay, I'll give you guys a brief overview." Elle was confident and relaxed, this was her comfort zone. "On the western edge of the North American plate, much of present-day California did not exist or was underwater until the Mesozoic era. There is some evidence of glaciation about thirty thousand years ago. This region largely escaped Pleistocene glaciation events." She pointed toward the central coast of California on a map next to the white board. "Although, the biota was certainly affected by climatic variability during this time. The large valley between the Sierra Nevada and the Coast ranges was once a great inland sea."

Ken Wallace held up his hand.

"You have a question?"

"What does glaciation mean? Like, glaciers?"

"Yes, sorry, it simply means a glacial period or that an area was covered by an ice sheet." Elle had to remind herself that she wasn't talking to a group of her peers. "Any other questions?"

Wallace raised his hand again.

"What's biota?"

"Oh, biota is an umbrella word for the animal and plant life of a habitat." She paused. "Other questions?"

It wasn't her intention to talk over anyone's head. Every profession had terminology that was specific to the field. She'd make an effort to simplify her word choices.

"By the late Pleistocene era, sea level changes were less than twenty-five meters to over one hundred twenty-five meters and resulted in flooding and draining cycles of bays and estuaries, in fact, at one point, San Francisco Bay was completely empty."

"Pleistocene weather cycles have been well studied. There were over twenty glacial cycles during that period that averaged sixty thousand years, with ten-thousand-year periods of warming. Sea levels periodically dropped by one hundred and twenty meters, providing a connection between Siberia and Alaska via the Bering Land Bridge. Although, humanoid species of that era were only just beginning to venture from Africa."

"So, what exactly will it be like when we arrive?" Jackson sounded genuinely curious. She was sitting forward in her chair as if she were actually paying attention.

This bolstered Elle's confidence.

"Dr. Hoffman and I have analyzed published data on over a hundred sea surface temperature records during the last interglacial period, taken from eighty-five marine sediment core sites. That temperature jump, the one we're looking for, took place over several thousand years. This time, what we're experiencing now, happened in barely a century." She couldn't help bringing it all home to their current problem. "The temperature will feel similar, maybe slightly warmer. And we should see many more animal species than we have today."

"Like what?" Wallace asked.

"Sinclair owls with nearly a five-meter wingspan, gulls, and pelicans—lots of birds. Many more bird species than we have today." Elle tilted her head and looked at the ceiling, recalling the list. "Let's see…we should see bison, deer, and king snakes. and dire wolves and possibly saber-toothed cats."

"Wow." Wallace whistled.

"And conifers, lots of conifers." Elle was pleased. This seemed to be going well. "Any other questions?"

No one raised a hand or spoke.

"Thank you, Dr. Graham." Jackson joined her at the front of the room. "All of you have been given mission docs that outline our strategy, but just to talk through the plan briefly, we set down ten clicks from the Pacific shoreline. We establish base camp near the beach and spend twenty-four hours retrieving samples. We'll be utilizing ATVs for transport of equipment and personnel between the Slingshot and base camp."

When Jackson was in command mode she was pretty damn intimidating. Elle receded into the background even though she was only standing a few feet away. Jackson's presence filled the space. She held everyone's attention without even trying.

"Does anyone have any questions?" Jackson paused. No one spoke. "Start time is zero-eight-hundred tomorrow. I recommend everyone get some rest so you're mission ready in the morning. Those of you for whom this is your first junket on the Slingshot, you're only allowed to bring one standard duffel of personal gear on board, so pack smartly. Bring layers for any type of weather and extra socks."

Jackson looked at Elle for the first time since she'd taken the floor. "Do you have anything else to add, Dr. Graham?"

"No." She looked at Ted. "Do you have anything to add, Dr. Hoffman?"

Part of the research was his, but he always preferred it when Elle took charge of presentations. He wasn't very confident as a speaker in front of a group.

"I don't have anything to add," he responded.

"There's one last detail to take care of." Jackson surveyed the group. "As you leave, report to the infirmary to receive your PTD."

"No one said anything about PTDs." Nunez wasn't happy.

"I'm sorry, what's a PTD?" Elle had no idea what they were talking about.

"A personal tracking device. No one sets foot on the Slingshot without one." Jackson was firm. "No one wants to get lost and left behind in an uncharted wilderness. Trust me on that one."

"Okay, everyone. We'll begin our grand adventure tomorrow. Have a good night." Jackson clapped Wallace on the shoulder as she filed out behind him and the others.

Ted hung back. He waited until they were alone before he said anything.

"I guess this is it." He shoved his hands in his pockets. He'd been unusually quiet since they'd arrived on base. Even more quiet than normal. Elle figured he had more at stake. She was alone. He was leaving behind a wife and a child.

"Yes, this is it. How are you feeling?"

He shrugged.

"Who knows what we'll find when we get there."

That seemed oddly defeatist.

"I hope we'll find what we're looking for."

He nodded and shuffled toward the door.

Elle waited for Harris to leave and then she was next up to meet with the medical technician. The serious looking woman in a white lab coat and scrubs motioned for her to sit. She settled nervously into an uncomfortable vinyl chair next to a square rolling tray of tools and meds. The technician sat on a squeaky rolling chair. In contrast to her serious demeanor, she playfully scooted from one spot to another without getting up, like a kid playing with her father's office chair.

"This will only sting a little." She held something that looked like an injection gun. Not a gun really, but it had a trigger and a syringe looking chamber.

"That's what they always say." Elle hated shots.

The technician smiled for the first time but didn't make eye contact. She was probing the tender underside of Elle's wrist with her gloved fingers.

"Okay, I'm going to inject this tiny locator device, just under the skin."

"How does it work?"

"There's a tracking device on the ship and also a handheld unit will read the signal."

"What's the range?"

"Infinite, unless you climb into a heavy steel box one hundred feet underground."

That was comforting, sort of.

"Is it easy to remove when we return?"

The woman made eye contact. "It's a simple extraction."

A simple extraction. The words echoed inside her head. Every so often the past few days, Elle experienced moments of near panic. The reality of what they were about to attempt would present itself through some statement or action, and with crystal clarity, she was faced with the enormity of it all. A rush of adrenaline would follow, her heart rate would soar, and then a shiver would travel up her arms. She tried her best to hide her fear. If any of the others felt the same, they didn't share it with anyone.

She felt a stinging pinch on her wrist. The technician had injected the tiny device while she'd been distracted.

"All done." The technician placed the device on the table.

"Thank you." Elle rubbed her wrist. She could feel the tiny hard capsule beneath her skin.

There was some comfort in knowing that of all the myriad of things that could possibly go wrong on this expedition, getting lost wasn't going to be one of them. One less thing to worry about.

CHAPTER FIFTEEN

Jackson wanted to check ship preparations, sort of her own version of a pre-flight checklist. Her gear was packed so she dropped the small duffel bag on the floor next to her bed and headed toward the staging area. Flight support technicians and engineers in white coveralls swarmed around the Slingshot.

"Good evening, Commander," Saro Eiseley, the chief engineer for the SLST program greeted her as she approached.

"Hello, Saro. I'm just checking in." Saro Eiseley was as good-looking as she was smart. Jackson wasn't sure exactly how the program had been able to recruit such a talented engineer as Saro, especially since she had no military background and a general distrust of government. Both those details assured Jackson that she'd always get an honest report from Saro, because she didn't suck up or play nice just to get ahead.

"We're mission ready within the hour." Saro ran her fingers through her short dark hair, sweeping it off her forehead. Her olive skin contrasted warmly against the white coveralls. Her green eyes were laser focused on something just past where Jackson had come to a stop. "Hey, Lopez and Walsh! Get that case off the platform...now!" She shook her head. "Make that mission ready within an hour and ten."

"You're tough." She wondered if she worked under Saro if she'd measure up. Possibly not. This was what you wanted from a chief engineer though, perfection. Or as close to perfection as was humanly possible. There were enough other variables that couldn't be anticipated once an aircraft got under way. Eliminating as many variables as possible before the figurative moment of wheels up could mean the difference between success and failure, injury or death. The Slingshot didn't actually have wheels. The curved underside of the ship was cradled by a platform that dropped away as the ship started to rise and gain speed.

"I heard you have sort of a green crew for this tour." Saro was scanning a readout on a tablet, checking things off. She spoke without looking up.

"They'll be okay." Jackson tried to sound confident. "We've got a non-military science detail from BIOME on this ride."

"Yeah, I met Dr. Graham." Saro arched an eyebrow. "Wow. She's smart, among other things."

Why was Elle talking to Saro? She pumped the brakes on getting annoyed. She had to remind herself that civilians played by different rules when it came to chain of command.

"She had questions about the transport containers and how much water you could bring back with the samples." Saro answered her unasked question.

"We're all good then? She was happy with the setup?"

"Yeah, we're good."

"Okay, well, I'm going to check in with the team before lights out. I'll see you tomorrow."

"Have a good night, Commander." One of the technicians walked up just as they finished talking. Saro followed the technician over to take a look at a digital readout screen near one of the ship's sensors.

Jackson rode the elevator back down to the dormitory level. The civilian quarters were on the opposite side of the cafeteria. People milled about as they finished dinner. Others loitered in the corridor chatting or with towels, heading to the gym or indoor pool.

She was on her way to see Ted first, but he ended up passing her in the hallway before she actually reached his room. He was lost in thought and didn't even see her. Seeing him from a few yards away with his head down, rubbing his temple with his fingers, she finally remembered where she'd seen him. He was the guy from BIOME who'd been in the accident north of the city. The accident that had been attributed to an AI failure.

"Ted."

He passed her and looked back when he heard his name.

"Yeah, sorry. I didn't see you, Captain." He walked back to where she stood in the center of the wide corridor.

"I'm making the rounds, checking in with everyone."

He nodded but didn't say anything.

"Are you okay?" He didn't look okay. He looked very distracted, which bothered her.

"I'm fine, thank you." He blinked rapidly. "We report to the ship at eight o'clock, right?"

"Yes." She decided she had to ask about the crash. "I think I've seen you before."

"Oh, really?"

"Yeah. Were you in an auto accident just north of the city a few days ago?"

His eyes widened and he glanced over his shoulder. Why did that question make him so nervous?

"Yes, that was me."

He seemed so unnerved by the question, why?

"I'm glad you're okay."

"Yeah, I was lucky. No one got hurt." He motioned with his thumb toward the cafeteria. "I was just going to get something to drink before they close up."

"Sure." She watched him back away. "Get some rest." He looked as if he needed it.

"I will. Thanks."

Ted was a puzzle. He was super quiet and kept to himself. She wondered if Elle and Ted were actually close or if they were simply lab partners, with no personal connection. He seemed like a hard guy to warm up to.

Jackson continued down the hallway until she reached the rooms adjacent to Ted's where Harris and Nunez were, across the hall from each other. Both doors were open; she checked with Nunez first. He was seated at the foot of his bunk cleaning a handgun.

"Hey, if you guys are bringing firearms onboard they have to be cleared by the engineers and stowed in special casing. Do that tonight. We don't want any departure delays tomorrow." She stood in the doorway with her arms across her chest.

"We'll walk them over tonight before lights out." Nunez spoke without looking up from his task.

When she pivoted, she saw that Harris was standing in the doorway behind her with his shoulder braced against the doorframe.

"Is there anything we need to discuss, gentlemen?" She took a step back and addressed them both, looking from one to the other as she posed the question.

"Meaning?" Harris asked. His tone was as neutral as his stance.

"I'm just making sure there aren't any side agendas I should be aware of." These guys were on board to provide additional security for the science team, so she'd assumed they'd bring their own weapons, but during the entire training they'd really kept to themselves. There was something about these two guys that Jackson didn't like. She couldn't put her finger on it, but she'd done enough tours to be able to read people in all sorts of situations, good and bad. The fact that she couldn't read these two bothered her.

"We're just along for the ride." Nunez spoke from his bunk.

"Okay, well, get some rest. Tomorrow is a big day."

Jackson only had one more stop to make. Her last stop. To find out how Elle was doing. She was disappointed to discover her quarters empty. She really wanted to see Elle once more before liftoff.

Chapter Sixteen

Elle was packed and ready but couldn't relax. It was too early to try to sleep anyway. She strolled leisurely to the cafeteria hoping for a decaf coffee, or hot tea, or something. She was on edge and restless, like the way you felt the night before a big exam. Except this was going to be the test of a lifetime.

The large room was sparsely inhabited when she arrived. She was at the coffee station, filling a cup with hot water for tea, when she saw a familiar face. Nikki West, the woman who'd escorted her the day she'd first arrived. They'd bumped into each other a couple of times since that first day. Nikki always said hello. Elle liked Nikki's straightforward manner. Under different circumstances, given more of an opportunity, she felt sure they'd have been friends.

"Dr. Graham, nice to see you." Nikki added sugar to the coffee she'd just poured.

"Please, call me Elle." She was genuinely happy to see her.

"And call me Nikki." Nikki smiled as she sampled her drink. "Be careful, mine is really hot."

"Thanks for the warning." Elle scanned the room trying to decide if she wanted to sit or take the tea back to her depressingly bare sleeping quarters.

"Tomorrow's the day, right?" Nikki asked.

"Yes, tomorrow morning." Elle took a breath. "Is it normal to be this nervous?"

"Absolutely." Nikki motioned toward the nearest table. "Do you want to sit?"

"You know what I'd really like? I'd like to see the sky or the ocean. I've literally been in this building for days. Is there any way to get outside for a little while?"

"There is." Nikki smiled. "There's an insulated rooftop deck. Come on, I'll join you."

Elle was almost giddy. Breaking free from this windowless underground facility with a hot cup of tea and someone with friend potential—this felt almost normal. She'd been dying to talk to Jasmine and fill her in on everything, but she couldn't. Maybe she and Nikki could have a real conversation.

They rode the elevator to the top level, an area of the building Elle hadn't visited, and then she followed Nikki through a series of doors that finally opened onto a rooftop deck, enclosed under a glass dome. Not a deck in the proper sense. It wasn't as if there were lounge chairs or anything. It all felt very military with a short buffer of concrete block along the edge of a large space. The glass dome was dingy from pollution in spots, but someone had made an effort to clean a ring of windows at eye level to offer a view of the surrounding area. When she leaned her elbows on the short wall she could see the Pacific Ocean in the distance and the sun dipping very close to the horizon. If she'd known this was available she'd have been up here every night.

"Thank you. This is perfect." A large venting fan kicked on pulling AC into the domed room. The chilled air cut through her thin T-shirt. She hugged herself, cradling the tea in one hand.

"Here, take this." Nikki began to remove the burnt orange micro-fleece vest she was wearing.

"No, I'm fine...you'll be cold without it."

"I have on more layers than you. Seriously, take it." Nikki was wearing a tan uniform shirt with a white T-shirt underneath. She held the vest out to Elle.

"Okay, if you insist." Elle set down her tea to slip it on. "Thank you."

"It looks good on you."

"I'm happy to have a little splash of color to offset these camouflage pants." Elle looked down at her clothing. "I don't know how anyone looks good in these."

"Trust me, you wear them well." The edge of Nikki's mouth tweaked up into a half smile.

"I don't believe you, but thanks." She appreciated the compliment even if it wasn't true.

They were quiet, enjoying the view. The sun dipped farther, painting the sky in hues of pink and orange. Elle zipped the vest up partway. Her arms were cool, but at least her core was warm.

"I know it's not easy and involves a whole mind-over-matter sort of thing, but don't be nervous." Nikki watched the horizon as she sipped her tea. "Jackson is the mission commander. She's sharp. She knows what she's doing. She's very good at what she does."

"Do you know her well?" Elle couldn't help asking.

"Yeah, she and I have run ops together and I've done jumps with her too."

"Jumps?"

"That's what we call the Slingshot missions…jumps."

"Oh, yes, right. Is it as bad as they say?" Elle wondered if Jackson had exaggerated in an attempt to scare her off.

"Yeah, it'll kick your ass for sure. But you've got a good team, you'll be fine." Nikki sounded so confident that the tension in Elle's shoulders began to ease a little.

Elle was dying to ask more about Jackson. She didn't want to take advantage of Nikki's friendship with Jackson, but she was at a loss. And it wasn't as if Jackson was sharing anything on her own. They were stiff and formal with each other when anyone else was around, punctuated with moments of—*something*—when they were alone. Elle just wasn't sure if the something she was feeling was completely one-sided.

As it turned out, she didn't have to ask. Nikki just started talking.

"Jackson is a great person. She's just had a rough few years." Nikki looked over at Elle. "She didn't used to be this way."

Elle hung on every word committing the words to memory so she could return to them later and examine each one.

"What happened?"

"Her wife died about five years ago."

"Oh, I'm so sorry, I had no idea." They had never talked about personal history, and since they'd ended up here, there'd been no time to talk about anything except the mission.

"Camille was a doctor. Do you remember the outbreak in the tent city on the outskirts of Los Angeles?"

Elle nodded. She remembered it well. Thousands of people died.

"Camille was part of the CDC team that went in to try and stop the spread of the virus, but also to search for patient zero. Unfortunately, she got sick and…" She trailed off. "Jackson never even got the chance to say good-bye."

"That's heartbreaking." She began to see Jackson differently. This new information helped make sense of some of Jackson's behaviors. Now even some of what she'd said to Elle the first day she'd arrived on base made much more sense. "Nikki, thank you for telling me. I really appreciate it."

"I wish you knew her the way I did, before all this happened."

Me too, thought Elle. But maybe there was still hope.

As usual, before a mission, Jackson was all wound up. She'd done a half hour on the treadmill after making the rounds. Then she'd taken a hot shower, but she was still restless. Maybe a little time on the roof would improve her mood. The sun would be just about to set and the view would be great. It was good to savor the little things when you didn't know if you'd get to come back. There was always the chance with any mission that it would be your last. If that was the case, would she regret the way she'd handled things with Elle?

Maybe.

Probably.

Jackson pushed through the door to the roof and abruptly stopped when she saw Nikki talking to Elle. A surge of jealously came from nowhere. That was ridiculous. Where did that come from? It wasn't as if she and Elle were a couple. She considered leaving before they saw her.

"Hi, Jackson." Elle gave a little wave.

Too late. Elle spotted her before she could escape. It was just as well, since she'd wanted to see Elle anyway.

"Hi." Jackson took a swig from her water bottle. She was glad she had something to hold on to, something to do with her hands.

"Hey, your timing is good." Nikki smiled broadly. "I was just leaving."

"You were?" Jackson was suspicious. "I didn't mean to interrupt."

"No, you're good. You two stay and enjoy the sunset. I've got things...lots of things...to do." She was totally making that up. She grinned and Jackson knew she'd just been set up.

"Oh, here, take your vest." Elle unzipped the front, to reveal the form hugging T-shirt underneath.

"No, you keep it." Nikki waved her off. "You might need it. Besides, that color looks better on you anyway."

"Thanks, Nikki." Elle followed Nikki's retreat with her eyes. "Have a good night."

"You too," Nikki called back just before she stepped through the door.

Jackson took another swig of water. She stood beside Elle with her elbows braced on the barrier, watching the sun set. The air between them sort of crackled, but Jackson wasn't sure just yet what to do about it. She'd made it pretty clear that she wasn't interested in anything, hadn't she? Was that what she really wanted?

After a moment or two, Elle spoke.

"Well, here we are." She sipped her tea without looking at Jackson.

"Yes, here we are."

"Should we declare a truce and agree to be friends?" There was resignation in Elle's question and Jackson knew it was her fault.

"Why a truce?"

"Because...well, I don't really know what's going on with us and I think there are bigger challenges ahead. I just thought if we agreed to be friends that possibly we could move forward." She turned toward Jackson. She seemed sincere. "You know, for the sake of the mission. For the sake of the greater good and all that."

"Sure." Why was the thought of Elle as a friend so disappointing? The intensity of Elle's gaze made Jackson all warm inside.

"I like Nikki."

Jackson sputtered as she tried to swallow a gulp of water.

"Yeah, Nikki's great." Her words came out raspy. What exactly did she mean by *like*?

"It's obvious she thinks very highly of you."

"Don't believe everything she says." Jackson watched the horizon and tried to sound like she didn't care, like she wasn't dying to know what Elle and Nikki had been talking about. All chummy and alone on the roof together at sunset.

Elle couldn't decide if Jackson was annoyed with her, or stressed about the mission, or what. Jackson was clearly on edge. And even though at first she'd seemed happy to see Elle, now she was thinking that might not have been the case. Jackson was incredibly hard to read. And now that she knew Jackson had lost her wife, the shadow she occasionally saw in Jackson's eyes made sense. It was the shadow of loss and heartbreak.

"Do you think we can save the ocean?" Elle sipped the last of her tea and watched the sun fall below the Pacific horizon.

"I think there are things we can do to improve the situation. But the end is probably inevitable." Jackson was somber. "I don't believe that science and technology will necessarily create a better world."

"You know you're talking to a scientist right now, right?" Elle turned toward Jackson, who continued to study the horizon.

"Science and technology guarantee only one thing." Jackson ignored Elle's attempt at levity. "That humanity will become more powerful. If history has taught us anything it's that humans don't use power wisely."

"Not in every instance." Elle was searching her memory to think of an example to counter Jackson's dark interpretation of civilization but coming up blank.

"In almost every instance. Layer on top of that one of the most powerful forces in human history—stupidity. Never underestimate human stupidity. When you combine the limitless resource of human stupidity with new technological powers, then you've got a recipe for disaster for sure."

"Whoa, that's a dark thought." Elle arched her eyebrows. "Aren't you like the champion of the cause here?"

"I'm a janitor...I clean up other people's messes." Jackson took a swig from her water bottle. "Humans have buried the Earth with a shitstorm of greed and selfishness and..." Jackson swallowed and looked away. "Sorry, I shouldn't be saying these things to you."

"If that's the way you feel then why are you here?" Elle sincerely wanted to know. She believed they could make a difference and she wanted—needed—Jackson to believe it too.

"I'm not doing it for myself." Jackson looked at her. Even in the waning light, Elle could see tears gathering along Jackson's lashes. "I'm doing it for someone else."

"Who?" Elle thought she already knew, but she wanted to hear Jackson say it.

"My wife, Camille." Jackson rubbed her eyes with the heels of her hands and straightened. She clearly wasn't comfortable with emotional displays. Elle had known that after their very first encounter at the Green Club.

Elle waited for Jackson to continue.

"She was a doctor…and she died. Camille thought she could save the world, but she couldn't. She couldn't even save herself." Jackson sniffed and looked down at her feet, then back up at Elle.

They locked gazes and Elle sensed the churning sea of emotion in Jackson's eyes, just under the surface, fighting to break free.

"Then let's do this mission for Camille." Elle touched Jackson's arm.

Jackson looked down at Elle's fingers. A tear trailed down her cheek. She squeezed her eyes shut. Elle gently wrapped her arms around Jackson and held her.

"It's okay to feel this," Elle whispered. She kissed Jackson's cheek, damp with tears.

"I'm sick of feeling it." Jackson's words were muffled.

Elle squeezed a little tighter. Jackson's breathing sounded more normal. She wiped at the tears with the hem of her T-shirt, exposing her muscled midriff.

"I'm sorry." Jackson sniffed. She looked away.

"Jackson, It's okay, really." Elle touched her shoulder. "Look at me." Jackson turned in her direction.

"You're going to be okay."

"Maybe…someday." Jackson didn't sound as if she believed it.

They faced the Pacific, standing side by side until the last tendril of pink was swallowed by purple darkness. Jackson seemed calmer, almost lighter somehow. Elle sensed it, even though there was no physical contact between them.

"I think I'm going to turn in and at least *try* to get some sleep."

Jackson nodded. Elle started toward the door. She sensed Jackson was following her. She reached for the door, but Jackson got there first. She held the door for Elle.

"Thank you." Elle lightly brushed against Jackson as she slipped past.

She didn't actually see sparks in the air, but she felt them.

She stood facing Jackson, looking up into her piercing gaze. The door whooshed quietly closed and neither of them moved. The entry was dark except for the moon's glow seeping through the small rectangular window in the metal door.

She had the strongest urge to kiss Jackson. But hadn't she just suggested they only be friends?

They rode the elevator in silence down to the dormitory level. The hallway was empty when the doors opened. They stood and looked at each other. It almost seemed as if they were seeing each other for the first time.

"Good night, Jackson."

"Good night." Jackson's words had warmth and just the slightest hint of invitation.

Jackson smiled, a genuine smile. Something was different between them. Elle could sense the possibility of it, and it was going to make it hard for her to sleep. Jackson had shared something of herself, something real. Jackson had taken the first step of letting her in. She turned and walked toward her room, her steps cushioned by a spring of optimism.

CHAPTER SEVENTEEN

Mission launch was less than a half hour away. Chills ran up Elle's arms. She wasn't cold; the flight suit was warm. It was just nerves. And she hoped the nerves didn't make her toss what little breakfast she'd choked down. The six-member team had assembled on the platform attached to the SLST craft and Jackson was talking. Elle tried to focus on Jackson and calm her churning stomach.

"The technicians will close the gravity tube from the outside and the latch will automatically release once the landing sequence has been initiated." She paused. "Nothing we've done during training can fully prepare you for the entry experience. But I promise you, you will survive it. Try to remain calm until your system resets itself."

Jackson was in serious command mode. She'd said good morning to Elle, but that was all. Since arriving on the flight deck, everyone had been distracted with a flurry of readiness tasks. Just getting the flight suit on had been a challenge with her shaking hands. Jackson paced in front of the team. Technicians in white coveralls ringed the small group waiting for the final word. Saro, the engineer she'd spoken with about the transport tanks, stood a few feet away from Jackson.

"I know some of you might be feeling uneasy or afraid at the moment. There's no shame in fear." Jackson stopped pacing and turned to the group with her fists braced on her hips. "It's what you do with that fear that counts. The person able to push through that fear for the good of the team...for the success of the mission...that's what counts."

Jackson was quiet for a moment, letting her words sink in.

"Are we ready?" Jackson glanced at Saro.

"We're ready, Commander." Saro nodded.

"Okay, team." Jackson faced the group. "Let's go make history."

Everyone moved toward their assigned gravity tubes. Elle climbed into the gleaming bed and lay down. She was so scared she was having a hard time catching her breath. She closed her eyes. The clicking sounds of the technician affixing tubes to the flight suit sounded loudly inside her head. She clenched her fingers over and over inside the cumbersome gloves attached to the cuffed sleeves of the suit.

"Elle?"

The warm timbre of Jackson's voice was like a dream. She opened her eyes. Jackson was leaning over, above her. She smiled and Elle immediately felt calmer.

"Hi." Elle took a deep breath.

"You're gonna be okay."

Elle nodded, grateful that Jackson had taken a moment to say something to her before launch. Her fragile nervous system needed a little bit of favoritism right now.

"Let's go save the world." Jackson's grin was playful. As if they were about to ride a roller coaster, rather than hurtle themselves through a wormhole into deep time.

"I'm ready." Elle tried to sound like she meant it.

"I know you are." Jackson patted the technician on the shoulder and disappeared from view.

"Here you go." The technician held a mouthguard near her lips. "Just so that you don't bite your tongue during reentry."

Jeezus. How rough was this ride going to be?

"I'm closing the hatch now." The technician spoke to her again. His relaxed manner almost put her at ease—almost.

She nodded, unable to speak around the plastic mouthguard.

The hatch seal made a suction sound. Elle had the impulse to adjust the padded helmet she was wearing, but the tube was too small for her to raise her arm. She closed her eyes and focused on taking slow, even breaths. Lights blinked off and she had the sensation of being in a noise depravation tank. She'd only done that once, and the confined, dark space had sort of freaked her out. This was different because there was noise, although muffled, and the bed of the tube vibrated as the engine fired up.

This was trusting technology on a whole other level.

She'd live or die and would have no control over either.

Don't throw up. Don't throw up.

The vibration increased. And then intensified. More. More. More. *Fuck.*

She tried to clench her fingers but found she was unable to move them as they were pressed against the bed of the tube. The vibration was so intense that if the suit weren't attached and strapped down at the feet, waist, and shoulder, she'd have bumped the glass window of the hatch with her face.

The actual flight would only last minutes. Although, as it was explained to her, it wasn't a *flight* in the truest sense. They would be inside the tunnel, spinning at a supersonic velocity. Once the ship achieved the proper momentum, the time travel part would be almost instantaneous. She kept reminding herself that she only had to survive this bone-jarring turbulence for a few minutes.

Her body weighed a thousand pounds, and without oxygen being forced into her lungs from the mask she feared she'd have been unable to breathe. Every muscle felt as if it were being separated from her bones. If she could have gathered enough breath, she was sure she'd have screamed. But there would have been no one to hear her. No one to come to her rescue.

And then it happened.

Nothingness.

Weightlessness.

Extreme fear.

Was she asleep or awake?

Her mind struggled to make sense of what she was seeing. The brightest threads of something that looked like a veil. They sparkled like mica, gold-white on silver-white, and in one place a rigid shaft of metallic radiant brightness pierced the shroud. Then a second shaft of light cut across her field of vision, and drew near, as if to travel with her. Tiny glowing threads sprang out of the lit shaft the way small curved lines are drawn into an ever more intricate pattern. Dizziness threated to overwhelm her. This was too much to take in. She braced her mind, closing it for its own protection.

How much time had passed? She was unsure.

She blinked, becoming aware that the hatch of her gravity tube was open.

The small of her back ached. When she moved, bending her back, shifting her knees, everything whirled hazily. The tethers that had constrained her had released and she was free to sit up but not sure she was able to do so. Her head felt twice its normal size as she tilted it from side to side. She had the strangest sense that her limbs had detached and reattached without her control. Then, with a kind of sliding or shunting like the falling into alignment of a weighted curtain, the interior of the ship came into focus and remained still.

Elle attempted to climb out of the tube but then realized she was very near fainting. She'd swung her legs over the lip of the bed, but sank back for a moment, allowing her head to catch up with the fact that she was sitting up. Something was between her teeth. Oh yes, right, the guard thingy. She tugged it from her mouth and tossed it onto the bed.

There was movement in the space around her as other members of the team began to stir.

"Don't try to stand right away." Jackson was at her side. She held a metal pan out to her, but why?

"What...oh..." She grabbed the pan an instant before throwing up.

Jackson handed her a towel. She pressed it to her face for a minute.

"Sorry," she mumbled into the cloth.

"Don't worry about it." Jackson rubbed her back. "It happens to almost everyone the first time."

Across from her, Ted heaved into a trash receptacle attached to the wall.

How was Jackson so steady on her feet? Her flight suit was unzipped to reveal a dark T-shirt underneath. She seemed so relaxed, so in control. She left Elle to check on Ted.

They'd arrived. She wasn't sure exactly of their position yet, but the SLST craft was definitely no longer in motion. She now knew why they called it the Slingshot. She felt as if she'd been shot through the air into a brick wall. Every muscle ached.

"Drink plenty of water today." Jackson had materialized in front of her again.

She stood quietly while Jackson dislodged the gloves from the suit and tossed them onto the bed behind her. She nodded.

"Thank you." Her words were raspy.

She walked to the small galley and retrieved a cup for water. She refilled it twice before sitting down. Everyone was already seated behind her. She took a seat next to Ted. The two security guys, Nunez and Harris, looked hungover. Nunez rested his face in his hands.

Not such a tough guy now, huh? It seemed the Slingshot was a great equalizer.

Only Jackson and Wallace seemed to show little effect of travel through the gateway. Everyone else looked as if they'd been on a forty-eight-hour rager that they now regretted.

"Okay, everyone. Take some time to hydrate and get some food into your system." Jackson held a digital tablet in her hand. "Wallace and I will prep the ATVs. Nunez, Harris, as soon as you're ready we'll need your help to load the gear." She paused. "Elle, you and Ted will need to verify that we have everything we need to secure samples."

"Okay." Ted spoke for both of them.

"We'll set out in two hours for base camp." Jackson said something to Wallace that Elle couldn't make out, and then they left the galley.

The SLST had enough food and water for five days, but the goal was to extract samples and initiate their return in seventy-two hours. She couldn't imagine how her body would feel making that trip a second time, but she'd try not to focus on that. There were other things to worry about at the moment. She hoped like hell her research was accurate. This was definitely going to be the ultimate field test.

CHAPTER EIGHTEEN

The first thing Jackson noticed was the air. The air was so clear and clean. She'd never experienced anything like this. And then the next thing she noticed was the silence. But then the longer she listened the more she heard different sounds than she was used to. Wallace was close by; he stowed a small case in the back of the forward ATV. There were two light alloy framed all-terrain vehicles and two trailers, now both loaded with gear and supplies. The tires for the ATVs were enormous, offering as much ground clearance as possible.

"How's does everything look?" Jackson tilted her face skyward. She'd been asking about the gear, but a strange call from a bird she didn't recognize caught her attention.

This was the world without humans. It was odd to be a stranger on your own planet.

"Everything's loaded," Wallace called to Nunez and Harris. "You guys ready to depart?"

Jackson walked back to the ship. Elle appeared at the rear hatch before she got there.

"It's time to go." Jackson held her hand out to Elle. "Is the science team ready to head out?"

"Yes, we're ready." She accepted Jackson's offered hand. "Thank you. I still feel a bit unstable."

"That will pass soon."

"This is so utterly strange." Elle surveyed the area around the ship. "What?"

"If I take a step, I will be stepping into the past and the present simultaneously. Will the future know?"

"I think you should save the existential questions for when we get back. Trying to think through the timeline will make you feel lightheaded." Jackson didn't release her hand right away. The warm contact felt good.

"The day was the first finished work of God. If we have the technology to change the order of the days, what does that make us?" Elle searched Jackson's face.

"Adventurous time travelers." She placed her hand under Elle's elbow. "Come on, Professor, let's take a little drive to the beach."

Ted followed on their heels. Jackson split the team into two groups. Ted, Nunez, and Wallace in the lead ATV. Harris, Elle, and Jackson in the second ATV. Jackson had said she wouldn't play favorites, but at some point after touchdown, she'd changed her mind. There was no way she was letting Elle out of her sight for the duration of this operation.

According to the ship's coordinates, they'd hit the target landing site. The ship was at the edge of a wooded area, nestled amid rolling grassy hills. Basically, they were in the same place they'd departed from, only at a different point on the timeline. This was what the modern location should look like, the present-day location. Except that in the present, the clumpy native grasses had been overrun by some invasive species that fueled wildfires. The terrain around the SLST command center had been ravaged by fire repeatedly, until all the gnarled coastal oaks were blackened skeletal remains. The vast contrast in how time had shaped the same location was hard to get your head around.

The trek to the coast was going to be slow as the all-terrain vehicles had to maneuver through and around dense conifers—redwoods and other pines—the largest trees she'd ever seen. The forest floor was blanketed with pine needles and large ferns. The air was cool and damp and only intermittently did the sun breach the canopy and reach the ground.

Wallace was a genius at navigation. Despite the winding route, she knew he'd hit their westward coordinates for base camp. The plan was to set up camp about a half mile from the beach. Close enough to retrieve samples, but sheltered by the tree line before it transitioned to the coastal grass and shrub cover that she expected to find. Camping at the edge of the grove would limit their exposure to coastal winds, rain, and the likelihood of rogue waves during high tide. If the coastline was anything like modern topography, then they'd have to be careful with extraction and might have to do it on foot. The ATVs might not be a safe way to access the beach if the cliffs were too steep and rocky.

It was her job to get Elle and Ted where they needed to be to gather samples. Based on the science briefing, she knew that phytoplankton lived at the top of the water column, only as far down as sunlight could penetrate. What had Elle called it? The euphotic zone. At any rate, they wouldn't have to navigate deep water to extract samples. That was good news. If they'd had to bring diving gear something might have needed to be left behind. The Slingshot could only carry so much weight and that balance was delicate. They would be transporting fifteen gallons of sea water, hopefully loaded with plenty of microscopic aquatic hitchhikers.

That seemed like simple math at first glance, with a gallon of water weighing about eight point three pounds. But the density of water was affected by changes in temperature and atmospheric pressure. Each container would have to be weighed to verify its true weight at time of departure. Nothing was as easy as it seemed initially.

"Have you ever heard so many birds?" Elle sat next to Jackson in the passenger seat. She was scanning the limbs above them.

"No, I don't think I have." Jackson had to focus on steering, no time for sightseeing. The trailer bounced over an extended root giving the ATV a small jolt.

"And the air. It smells amazing." Elle sounded almost giddy. "I swear the air is so clean that you can actually identify the scent of individual plant species."

"Well, you might be able to do that. All I smell is pine trees." Jackson glanced over briefly and smiled.

"That's a Douglas fir mixed in with the redwoods over there. And golden chinquapins, Pacific wax myrtles and redwood sorrel." Elle was like a nerdy kid in a botany-flavored candy shop. "This moist, shaded habitat is probably excellent for Pacific giant salamanders. I hope we see one. Although, I suspect this engine noise is scaring everything away."

"That's probably for the best. I'd prefer *not* to see a short-faced bear if it's all the same to you." Jackson remembered the mention of them from Elle's presentation.

"So, you were just pretending not to pay attention?" Elle's rhetorical question was playful.

It was so hard not to flirt with Elle. She was so damn cute when she was excited about all the flora and fauna of this deep time habitat. Jackson decided that in order to avoid flirtation, it might be best to include Harris in the banter.

"What about you, Harris? You smell anything?"

"Just smells like the woods to me."

Damn, he was a humorless fellow. He and Nunez were so bland that she'd had to create word associations to remember which was which. Harris usually wore a hat, a tan trucker style. "H" for Hat and Harris. His brown hair was a bit long, not quite up to military standards, and his sideburns were on the bushy side. She figured he was an ex-jock. He had the build of a wide receiver. He never volunteered any details about himself, but she'd have guessed he played football at some point.

Nunez's head was shaved and he wore a closely trimmed goatee. He had a much thicker build. His neck was as wide as his jawline. He reminded her of a guy she knew from Nevada City. Nevada City, with an "N" equaled Nunez.

Neither of these guys would be a first-round draft pick in her book, but maybe private corporate security had different standards. It didn't really matter unless they didn't pull their weight. She wasn't here to make friends. She was here to do a job and they'd better do the same.

The drive to base camp took almost two hours. Only rarely were they able to travel as fast as ten miles per hour, most of the time they had to drive much slower.

Elle climbed out of the vehicle as soon as it stopped. She watched Jackson dismount easily from the driver's seat. Jackson made everything look easy, and she seemed completely unfazed by their passage through the gateway. Elle inhaled deeply and arched her back. She was stiff and she'd felt a little woozy the entire drive. She needed to walk around and stand on solid ground. She followed Jackson to the trailer at the back of the ATV.

"Find a nice flat spot for this." Jackson handed her one of the tent bags.

Thankfully, it had already been decided that as one of the only two women on this expedition, Elle would get to share a tent with Jackson. That news made her feel happy and nervous at the same time. So far, the "friend truce" was working, but now they were going to share sleeping accommodations for at least two nights, possibly three. Close quarters would test the limits of the truce from Elle's perspective. Although, camping with four guys in close proximity, regardless of any moonlit romantic potential, was a genuine buzzkill.

The site for base camp was just at the edge of the tree line, just before the sea cliff. The surf provided constant background noise now that they were closer.

Elle tugged items from the nylon bag and examined them. She hadn't set up a tent in years, but it was coming back to her. Wallace's tent was already up several feet away. He glanced over and smiled. He walked in her direction.

"Need some help?"

"I wouldn't turn it down." She shook out the tent, trying to sort out the orientation.

Wallace was moving sticks and debris from the tent space. He took two of the corners and helped her position it so that the door faced toward the west, toward the coast. She tossed a few stones to the side to further clear the area. With Wallace's help, the tent was upright within minutes.

"Thank you." Elle stepped back to inspect their work. "I guess my outdoorsman skills are a bit rusty. I haven't camped in a long time."

She'd only ever done camping with her grandparents and that had been under a protective dome, with piped in air and water. Not quite the same as this at all.

"Don't worry, you'll be fine." Wallace returned to the ATV to help Jackson offload one of the large food containers. It looked sort of like an oversized cooler, except that it wasn't for keeping things cold, it was designed as a bear safe, to keep animals from getting into their food supply. All the provisions were freeze dried and didn't require refrigeration. She wondered if that sort of hermetically sealed snack would even appeal to an animal. It wasn't even that appealing to humans.

"Listen up. Nunez set up a latrine area fifty yards or so in that direction. He flagged it and left a shovel." Jackson spoke to the group. "And remember, this is an extreme *leave no trace* expedition. We pack it in, we pack it out. Pay attention, people. We don't want some archeologist finding a bottle cap in the future."

"Wait, did someone pack beer and forget to tell me?" Wallace looked hopeful.

"What do you think, genius?" Jackson's question was sarcastically rhetorical.

"No beer." Wallace stuck his lower lip out in a mock pout.

"Aw, man, no kegger by the campfire tonight." That was the first joke Harris had uttered since she'd met him.

Everyone stopped what they were doing and faced him as if he'd suddenly sprouted a second head.

"What? I like beer." He shrugged.

Elle pictured an archeologist of the future finding some remnant left behind from this expedition, in a place where no humans should have inhabited at this moment on the timeline. That would be a disaster. She returned to the vehicle for two sleeping bags. She stowed them in the tent, along with her small duffel of fresh clothing. She wasn't sure what else to do. Everything seemed to be coming together.

Harris was digging a shallow firepit and clearing dry debris that could be used for kindling.

She left the soft murmur of voices behind her as she walked in the direction of the sea. The campsite Jackson had chosen was, she estimated, almost a half mile from the surf. It took a few minutes to reach the crest of the cliff overlooking the beach below. The terrain between camp and the cliff transitioned from mature forest to a grassy, rolling landscape with intermittent clumps of scrub oak that resembled shrubs more than trees. The shoreline had the same dramatic cliff exposures as modern times. Rotating north to south, she could see scalloped bays, vast estuaries, and expansive dunes. The wave energy off the Pacific Ocean was fairly high causing severe sea-cliff recession even in this era.

Beneath her position, waves crashed loudly against two monolith rocks jutting up from the surf. Elle took a deep, cleansing breath, as she faced the seemingly infinite Pacific. The ocean was a place of paradoxes. Home to the great white shark and the blue whale. A two-thousand-pound killer of the seas and the largest gentle giant that ever lived.

Simultaneously, microscopic creatures as numerous as the stars existed in the amount of seawater she could scoop up in both hands. The ocean's ecosystems made it simultaneously mesmerizingly beautiful, dangerous, and astoundingly complex. This version of the Pacific was no blue desert. This Pacific was infinitely alive.

"Strange isn't it?" Jackson was standing beside her, facing west.

"What?"

"This sea is beautiful. How could we have managed to kill something so enormous and so integral to our survival?"

"It is hard to come to terms with that realization." The air had cooled, Elle hugged herself. It was still early in the day, but she sensed a change in the weather. It was much cooler than she'd expected. The heatless sun was a white circle behind the far off fog bank.

"We might get rain, or it might just be cloud cover heading our way." Jackson scanned the sky. "I can't really tell."

The air definitely contained a lot of moisture. She wasn't looking forward to camping in a rainstorm.

"Want to grab some food before we hike to the beach?" Jackson asked.

"Sure." In all the excitement, she'd forgotten about lunch, but now that Jackson had mentioned it she realized she was hungry.

Her stomach was still a little unstable. Elle wasn't in the mood for a big meal. She decided on an energy bar and water, something with protein to give her enough of a boost to navigate the steep descent to the beach, and then the climb back. Her legs ached as if she'd run miles, but she assumed it was simply residual jetlag, or spacelag—if that was even a thing, from the gateway. Jackson had suggested that she and Ted make the hike without equipment until they could figure out the best route to the water. Then the team could help them ferry whatever they needed.

First order of business would be to set up the field microscope and take a look at some water samples. She and Ted could gather selections from various shallow areas and test them in camp before taking the containment equipment down. It would be best to verify that this site would give them viable phytoplankton specimens before spending a lot of time and energy lugging containers to the beach.

CHAPTER NINETEEN

Jackson could see the fatigue of a very long, strenuous day weighing on the team. By five o'clock, she ordered everyone to return to camp to rest, eat, and prepare for the next day. Heavy cloud cover moved in around four, threatening rain, but as yet, had not delivered on that promise. That didn't mean the night would remain dry. The scent of rain was definitely in the air. But maybe that was simply the dampness of the fog. This weather was all new to Jackson.

It took all afternoon to sort out the best route from base camp to the waterline. The entire team had worked to plot and carve the best path for the climb down and back. Jackson had determined that they'd have to do the extraction on foot, by hand. The ATVs, although light, were too wide and too large to safely make the trip.

"Here, let me help you with that." Jackson took the ration heater for the MRE meal pack from Elle and ripped it open. She'd watched Elle struggle with it for a few minutes.

"Thank you. My hand strength seems to have evaporated."

"You just need to rest and recharge." Jackson handed over the meal pack. "Frankly, I'm impressed you're still standing after all we've done today."

Elle smiled at the compliment.

Jackson checked the position of the others because she didn't want to be overheard.

"Listen, I'm sorry I said you wouldn't be able do this mission." Jackson regretted what she'd said, even if she'd done it with the best intentions. "I'm happy to admit I was wrong."

"Apology accepted." Elle tucked a loose strand of hair behind her ear and grinned.

God, even exhausted and wearing Space Force fatigues, she was still beautiful. Jackson swallowed. This *friend* thing was going to be complicated.

"I definitely think I'm fatigued. I can't remember next steps here." Elle peered inside the packet and scrunched her nose.

"You need to add water and give it a minute to heat up. Then drop this meal pack in and close it." Jackson handed her the ration pack.

"Right, wait for the chemical reaction." It was coming back to Elle now.

The ration heater contained finely powdered magnesium metal, alloyed with a small amount of iron, and table salt. This mixture only required a small amount of water to create a reaction that would bring the water to boiling temperature fairly fast.

"Cooking without fire. A miracle of science." Jackson grinned and then pivoted. "Hey, Wallace, how's it going?"

"The solar generator isn't quite there yet." He frowned. "I don't think it's gotten enough sun to recharge since lunch. We'll have to do this old school."

"It'll have to be headlamps and campfire tonight then." Jackson nodded.

"I'll start a fire." Nunez began to toss dry limbs onto the firepit that Harris had dug earlier.

Jackson had planned to have a nighttime fire for safety reasons anyway, to ward off unwanted visitors from the animal kingdom.

"How did the samples look?" Elle had set up a microscope and mini-lab on the tailgate of one of the ATVs and Jackson wondered what she'd found.

"Oh, they looked great." Elle's expression brightened. "We're going to get plenty of specimens. The slides were very active with organisms."

"Good. That's good news."

This expedition had almost gone too well so far. The tiny hairs at the back of her neck kept tingling, from what, she didn't know. Best to pay attention. A mission could go sideways in an instant. More than half her team was green in her eyes, so who knew how they'd react in a crisis.

Dinner was finished and the group had scattered. Wallace was securing the vehicles and trailers for the night. Nunez and Harris had gathered more wood and piled it next to the fire. Ted was seated nearby, staring at the flame. He seemed lost in thought. Elle was nowhere in sight.

"Hey, Ted, have you seen Elle?" He blinked rapidly a few times as if her question had dislodged him from a trance. He looked around. "Um, I'm not sure. She might have gone for a walk."

"A walk?" Jackson scanned the surrounding area. "And you didn't go with her?"

"I—"

"I thought I said that we would all use the buddy system, except for trips to the latrine." She was pissed.

"What's the problem?" Wallace was at her side.

"Elle went for a walk." Jackson looked down at Ted, still seated by the fire. "Which way did she go?"

"Um, that way, I think." Ted pointed north, the opposite direction of the latrine, but she wasn't confident about his powers of observation at the moment. She knew he was probably exhausted so she tried to cut him some slack. But, dammit, that's how accidents happened, that's how people got hurt.

"Christ on a cracker." Wallace seemed as frustrated by this development as she was.

Harris and Nunez joined them by the fire.

"Hey, you two dropped the ball here." Weren't these guys on board to act as security for the science team? Wasn't that why Nikki hadn't made the roster? It wasn't Ted's job. He was half the science team. *What the fuck?*

"I don't see the problem?" Nunez's question was almost a challenge.

"The problem is that an unarmed civilian, our lead scientist, walked away from base camp into an uncharted wilderness and it'll be dark soon." Did she have to break out a chalkboard and draw a diagram to explain it to these guys? "Every member of this team is integral to the mission's success." In her mind, some more than others, but she was being generous. "If we lose the chief scientist because she wondered off, how's that gonna work out for us?"

"We'll look for her." Harris nodded at Nunez and turned to leave.

"No, *I'll* go." There was at least one hour of good daylight left. Jackson pointed at Ted. "You stay here with your security detail." She couldn't help the sarcasm.

Jackson booted up the location tracking device. It took a moment for the GPS grid to populate the screen. She eliminated everyone who was still at base camp and homed in on Elle's PTD signal, a small blue dot on the gray-green screen. Ted was right, Elle was north of their location. She retrieved a sidearm and clipped the holster to her belt. She decided right then and there to keep the gun handy. Something about this expedition wasn't feeling right. The weight of the semi-automatic pistol was comforting as she strode off in search of Elle.

❖

Elle took slow and deliberate steps as she wove among the trees. Coastal redwoods were the tallest trees in the world. She'd read that some had reached as high as four hundred feet and survived for over two thousand years. Even in modern times, her time, a rare few remained. But nothing like this grove near base camp. These trees seemed almost from another epoch. In truth, this species had lived at the time of the dinosaur, sixty-five million years ago. They had real staying power. They were sentinels of geologic time. Like the mythic titans of ancient Greece.

She took a long, slow stride, trailing her fingertips along the rough bark as she passed. The reddish-brown skin of the tree was soft and rough at the same time. Trying to glimpse the crown of the tree made her dizzy.

These giants thrived along the coast of northern California where the cool fog from the ocean brought moisture for growth, while at the same time blocking the evaporating rays of the sun. The condensed fog would slowly drip off the foliage and water the roots of the tree along with the fern bed.

Elle closed her eyes and listened. In the silent forest she could actually hear the heavy drops fall to the ground. This was amazing. This must have been what the Garden of Eden felt like before humans were cast out. Then, as now, mankind had failed to appreciate all the nurturing and unselfish gifts of Mother Earth.

She braced with both hands against a nearby trunk to stabilize herself as she looked skyward. This particular tree had been struck by lightning but survived. A jagged, blackened wound jutted upward, but beyond that, the tree was healthy.

Redwoods were among the most complex plant forms on earth. A single tree might have many re-sprouted trunks so that the crown of a redwood was almost like a self-contained forest. Infant redwoods generally sprouted around the base of an adult tree. The fledgling trees would take in nutrients from the mature tree and form a circle of trees called a fairy ring. What a magical wonderful thing to experience firsthand.

Elle loved trees.

Standing among these stoic giants from another time was awe inspiring.

This has to be what heaven feels like. If there was such a place.

She closed her eyes and listened again to the sounds of the forest. The wind, a bird call, and the distant surf. This brief time to commune with nature had been just what she needed. The urge to have some time alone had been too great to ignore. Everything since that first meeting with Liam had been about *the mission*. Elle needed a moment for herself. Was that too much to ask?

Unsure of the time, she decided to head back to camp. The thick canopy would make it seem darker than it was as the sun began to set. She rotated with the intention of carefully retracing her steps only to discover that she was no longer alone.

An enormous wolf studied her from several feet away. His head low, his eyes shadowed.

Her heart began to race, and she wondered how long the animal had been following her. How stupid she now felt for venturing out alone without any way to defend herself. She'd only been thinking of the plant life she might find, not the animal life. *Stupid, stupid, stupid.*

Elle froze. Should she run? Could wolves smell fear?

She couldn't remember.

"Back slowly away." Jackson, by some miracle, was behind her.

Elle glanced over her shoulder. Jackson was standing a few feet away. Elle wanted to run to her.

"Don't turn your back on it." Jackson motioned for Elle to stay still. "And don't run. A wolf can outrun you."

Elle nodded and began to take slow backward steps toward where Jackson was standing.

The wolf sniffed the air, then ducked his head, his gaze intensely focused on Elle. He took one step, then two. Jackson stepped in front of Elle in a protective stance. She raised her arms, making herself seem larger and then blew a loud whistle, shrilly piercing the stillness of the forest. He bolted, disappearing from view into the dense understory several yards away.

"Are you okay?" At some point, Jackson had drawn her side arm. She was still holding it, pointed at the ground.

"Yes, thank you." She was shaken and the sound of the whistle had completely shattered her quiet communion with the trees. But that was better than becoming wolf food.

"You can't walk into the wilderness without an escort." Jackson's words were stern. "Do you understand?"

"Yes, I'm sorry." She truly was. And grateful that Jackson had been the one to find her. "Would you have shot the animal?"

"Only if there was absolutely no other option." Jackson holstered the weapon. "But then we'd have had to track down the bullet and casing. We leave no trace."

Elle nodded. She felt stupid for wandering off. This wasn't some field trip for core samples. This was much more serious.

"We should head back before it gets any darker." Thankfully, Jackson didn't sound angry.

"How did you even find me?"

"You have a PDT in your wrist, remember?"

"Oh, right." Elle had completely forgotten about it. She rubbed the tiny tracker capsule with her finger. It moved a little under her skin when she touched it.

Jackson motioned for Elle to walk in front.

"That orange micro-fleece vest you're wearing also really stands out. Not exactly military issue." Jackson smiled.

Elle looked down. Nikki had loaned her the garment and she'd packed it as an afterthought. A splash of color to offset the drab military garb. Plus, an extra layer worked nicely under the military jacket she'd been given. It was chilly here and she was glad to have it.

"I never thought a fashion choice might save my life." Elle laughed.

They'd only walked for a few minutes when Wallace met them. "I heard the whistle." He fell in beside Jackson.

"Elle made a friend and when he got a bit too curious, I had to scare him off."

Wallace glanced at Elle.

"It was a wolf."

"A wolf!" Wallace seemed genuinely disappointed that he'd missed it. "I've never seen a wolf."

They were extinct in modern times. They only existed in natural history museum exhibits. This particular fellow was probably a dire wolf, larger than his modern cousins, but not as fast, or as bright, but just as lethal once he captured his prey.

"Let's just be sure we stay close to the fire tonight." Jackson kept up her pace. Elle dropped back to fall in behind her and Wallace. "I'm sure the sound spooked him, but he might be back with friends if he's hungry."

CHAPTER TWENTY

Jackson rubbed her shoulder and then rolled it. She was feeling stiff and tired, but the warmth of the fire was soothing and hard to leave. She could almost imagine this was an expedition trip for fun. Almost. Nunez and Harris were reminders that it wasn't, because she'd never hang out with these two by choice.

"You have a girl back in the now?" Wallace, being the gregarious member of the team, tried to get Harris to open up.

"No." He stirred the fire with a stick.

"A dog?" Wallace was fishing.

"No."

"So, you're a girl-less, dog-less kind of guy." Wallace joked, but Harris didn't seem amused.

"I've got a dog." Nunez had a half-grin on his face. "He eats losers like you for breakfast."

Wallace bristled.

"That's enough small talk," Jackson cut in.

It seemed impossible to draw them out, even in the most congenial setting. Lounging around a campfire could have been a perfect opportunity for team building. She decided that Nunez and Harris were a team of two, or maybe two separate teams of one.

She was ready to call it a night, but she didn't want to be the first.

"I'm going to turn in." Finally, Ted left for the tent he was sharing with Wallace.

"Yeah, I'm with you." Wallace scowled at Nunez.

An awkward silence fell over the four who remained. Jackson wanted to be the last to leave the fire. She studied Nunez and Harris through the flames. Were they really as unlikeable as they seemed? Elle was easygoing, she seemed to take them in stride. Being a woman in the field of science, she was probably used to dealing with male egos.

"Good night, Captain…Dr. Graham." Harris brushed debris and dust from his pants.

"Good night." They answered almost in unison.

Nunez followed Harris with a nod in their direction.

Finally, Elle and Jackson were alone. A tiny amount of tension released its grip on Jackson's shoulders. She wished for different circumstances. In another time, in another place, this would have been incredibly romantic.

The fire danced and crackled, almost transparent against the dark of the primordial forest behind them. Leaves stirred somewhere high above her. A reminder that the grove was darkly and secretly alive. She heard the distant call of an owl.

"Should we?" Jackson tipped her head toward the tent.

"Yes, I'm beat." Elle's face was warmly lit by the fire. "It's hard to leave the fire though. It feels so good. Although, it's also making me very sleepy."

Jackson stood up and offered her hand to Elle.

"Is it okay to leave the fire?" Elle's hand was soft and warm in hers.

"Yeah, we've got a good clean buffer around it. And it'll slowly burn out." Jackson finally released Elle's hand. "Plus, I think it may rain shortly." She looked up as if the sky might tell her something.

The air was cool and damp as they left the warm oasis near the firepit. Jackson unzipped the front of the tent and held the flap for Elle to enter. Elle sat on her sleeping bag so that she could take her shoes off beside the door. Jackson did the same, after she zipped the flap closed. She stowed her weapon at the edge of her thin air mattress on the side farthest from Elle. Then she placed a flashlight on the tent floor between them.

"If you need to go to the latrine during the night, please wake me." Jackson slid down into the bag. She decided under the circumstances to sleep in her clothes.

"Are you sure?"

"Yes, no more solo trips for you." She quirked an eyebrow at Elle.

"Got it." Elle smiled. "Or should I say, yes, Commander."

"I do like the sound of that." She smiled. Jackson was on her back with her eyes closed. She adjusted the position of the inflated pillow. They each had an ultra-thin expedition style air mattress and the pillow was supposed to add comfort, but she wasn't sure it did. They were still sleeping on the ground.

Not too long after they'd settled in, as Jackson had predicted, the rain arrived.

Only the faintest flicker of light from the dying fire glowed across the nylon at the front. The light tapping of raindrops hitting the tent was a nice sound to drift off to. So why wasn't she sleepy? Oh yeah, because a woman she couldn't stop thinking about was lying next to her in a separate sleeping bag. She let out a long slow breath.

"Jackson, are you asleep?" Elle whispered.

"No."

"I can't sleep either."

Jackson rotated her head to see that Elle was lying on her side, facing Jackson. She waited for Elle to say more.

"I think I'm having an existential crisis."

Jackson wasn't sure if Elle was joking or serious.

"Do you ever have that feeling?"

"Maybe, sometimes. Although, I'm not sure exactly what you mean." Jackson tried hard not to think of some things but couldn't always help it. Losing Camille had shaken her world view and her perception of herself in that world. It didn't take much to send her to dark places.

"I have these moments when I worry that I have no idea what I'm doing. Or...or if what I'm doing will have any significant effect on anything." Elle was serious. "Sometimes I feel insignificant in the face of all the challenges."

"The world has big problems." Jackson stated the obvious.

"Civilization *must* shift from simply maintaining our current state toward repair and protection." Elle paused. "Or what we're doing now, the risk we're taking...if society doesn't evolve, then regardless of what we're doing here, nothing will change."

Was Elle trying to convince herself to feel better about the future? She was talking to the wrong person if she was looking for optimism.

"I think we all want our lives to have purpose and meaning." Jackson hesitated. What was she really trying to say? "But you can only really have an impact on what's right in front of you." She couldn't make out Elle's expression in the dark, but she could see that she was propped up on her elbow. "We will all eventually be forgotten, no matter how hard we try to make a difference."

Elle was quiet. Jackson realized her thoughts had gone to that dark place anyway. Then Elle touched her shoulder.

"I'm sorry. I didn't mean to make you think of that." How did Elle know what she was thinking of?

"What do you mean?" Jackson wasn't trying to reveal things to Elle, but she feared she had already.

"Can I sleep next to you?" Elle didn't wait for a response. She wiggled in her sleeping bag until it was against Jackson's.

"Um, sure...yeah, that's fine." She had no idea how to respond to that request.

"Thank you for coming to my rescue today." Elle kissed her lightly on the cheek, then settled back onto her pillow. But she left her arm draped across Jackson on the outside of the sleeping bag.

"You're welcome." Jackson was stiff, trying not to feel things. But her body had a mind all its own where Elle was concerned.

She was afraid to touch Elle or she'd give herself away. She needed to keep her head in the game. This wasn't some college excursion and she wasn't sharing a tent with Elle in the hopes of getting laid. They were mission collaborators, colleagues, friends, and Elle was seeking comfort and some sense of security, that was all.

Jackson lay quietly, listening to the rain and Elle's steady breathing. Elle had quieted and was likely asleep. Jackson closed her eyes and attempted to still her unsettled mind. A nearly impossible task despite the fatigue of the day.

Elle had woken with the sun. She'd slept fitfully, not quite able to get comfortable on the nonexistent air mattress. Or maybe it was her proximity to Jackson. She'd suggested they should be friends, but she probably should have clarified whether that was *with* or *without* benefits. The former was clearly her preference. Maybe once they were back in real time they could sort that out.

Camp coffee tasted pretty good. She'd downed two cups along with a protein bar. After freshening up and brushing her teeth, she was wishing for a shower, but that would have to wait until they returned to the SLST craft. Unless they lingered here for an additional day, in which case, the wide, shallow stream she'd crossed just north of their position, despite the chilly water, would be quite appealing.

She'd grabbed one gallon-sized container and some small specimen jars that she'd placed in her backpack, along with her water bottle. They were here to get phytoplankton, but there was no harm in harvesting other organic matter that might prove helpful for additional research. Elle was inspired to make the most of this expedition.

The previous night's rain made the path to shore slick in spots. She alternated between looking up and focusing on her steps. Ted was in front of her. He'd almost slipped at the steepest part of the trail but caught himself on a rock jutting from the cliff side. Once they reached the sand, they split up. Ted had been oddly quiet all morning, but she assumed he was overwhelmed the same as she was by all that they were seeing in this new, old world.

She was a hundred feet or so north of Ted's position. The day was clear and bright, although chilly. It was still morning, probably not much past nine. She finished filling the gallon tank and affixed a cap and then carried it back to the beach beyond the reach of the undulating surf. Her back was stiff. She stretched in an arc with her hands against her lower back as she scanned the shoreline. Sand dunes carried by nearby rivers were stacked up by coastal winds and stabilized by plants such as beach primrose and beach morning glory.

Dune plants were unique. They had to tolerate salt, partial burial from time to time, and a lack of fresh water. She admired their adaptive tenacity.

Green skeletal remains of giant kelp clumped together at the edge of the surf in spots. Green-brown fronds with long tubular stalks with many crinkly toothed, leaf-like blades, each attached to a stalk by a pear-shaped air bladder. They gave off the strong odor of living things now dead.

Shore birds sang from their perches. She'd seen whimbrels and willets. Nearby, sanderlings probed the sand for small organisms, including burrowing pismo and razor clams. Above the high tide line, she noticed a snowy plover's nest in the open sand. She took a few moments to jot down her observations in a small journal she carried in her pack.

Creatures carried on with the stuff of living all around her.

This could be yesterday, or tomorrow, but not modern Earth. Present day Earth had lost so much diversity of species. Modern Earth had lost so many voices.

Elle was struck again by her own insignificance in the immense march of life.

She bent again to her task. She'd filled the gallon container with sea water and now wanted to place other specimens in the smaller jars. She'd waded out in order to get the best samples. She'd worn water shoes and lightweight pants that she'd rolled above her knees. But they'd still gotten wet from the receding surf. She was waiting for more containers. Jackson and the rest of the team had taken turns ferrying the containers back to base camp two at a time. By Elle's count there were only two more to fill to meet their target. She didn't see anyone returning to the beach yet. It was a steep climb and no doubt better to rest before making the return trip.

In the meantime, she'd work with her smaller glass jars. She squatted near a tidal pool. The tide pools were like miniature seas. They contained sponges and starfish, while sea anemones clung to the glistening rocks. Elle would be content to spend hours on the beach. Being here like this made her feel like a young girl, enlivened by discovery.

CHAPTER TWENTY-ONE

Things were going well. Jackson's legs were feeling the climb from the beach, but they'd made good progress this morning. At the current rate they'd have all the containers filled by noon which would allow them to break camp and sleep at the ship tonight. They were going to easily hit the seventy-two-hour extraction target.

She and Wallace were standing at the back of the ATV. She was taking a long swig from her canteen. The hike made her thirsty.

"I think these are the last two." Wallace checked the caps. He dropped one and bent to retrieve it.

He'd been blocking her line of sight, and when he leaned down she saw Harris aiming a sidearm in their direction.

"Stay down!" She dropped behind the ATV.

But Wallace was already in motion when she yelled. A bullet clipped his shoulder. He spun, dropping the container. He fell sideways. Harris fired again, catching Wallace in the leg before Jackson could pull him safely behind the oversized wheel.

"What the fuck?" Wallace pulled his weapon free from the holster. Red seeped through the cloth of his pants just above his knee.

"It was Harris."

"Asshole!" Wallace grimaced as he tried to peer around the back of the vehicle.

A bullet whizzed past just as he ducked.

"My gun is on the passenger seat." She'd taken it off for the last trip to the beach. Now she regretted the decision. She crawled on her stomach toward the passenger side of the vehicle and felt on the seat for the holster. It was missing.

Jackson's mind raced. Where was Nunez?

She scuttled back as Wallace fired a couple of rounds in Harris's direction.

"He's got my gun." She was pissed at herself for being careless. For trusting someone she hadn't personally vetted for the team. Jackson crouched beside Wallace. "There's no way he's on his own in this."

"Nunez was headed to the beach a minute ago." Wallace winced and gripped his leg.

Jackson could tell they were thinking the same thing.

"You go." Wallace angled for a better firing position. "I'll cover you."

"Let me tie that off first." Jackson took off her belt and tightened it around Wallace's thigh to slow the loss of blood. He grimaced as she cinched it.

"Are you okay?" Stupid, rhetorical question. He was not okay and this was a bad situation. Wallace was wounded, she was unarmed, and the science team was undefended.

"I've got this." He nodded. "You need to go. I can't get there with my leg like this. And if we lose the science team then we lose everything."

Elle!

All she could think of was Elle.

"Okay." Jackson mentally prepared to make a run for it. "You stay frosty, Wallace." She put her hand on his uninjured shoulder and set her canteen on the ground next to him. "You're a much better shot than this gun for hire. You know that, right?"

He nodded.

"Go kick some ass, Captain." He braced his arm and waited for her to give him the signal.

She'd have tree cover only for the first part of her sprint, then the tree line would transition to shrubs and rocks before reaching the path to the cliff and finally, the beach trail. She'd be completely exposed at that point. If Nunez was in on this ambush, which she had to assume he was, then he had a good head start. He'd have heard the gunfire so she'd already lost the element of surprise.

Jackson took a deep breath, nodded at Wallace, and bolted from her position. A tree splintered from gunshot as she dove behind it. She didn't stop, she couldn't stop. Her focus became singular. She sprinted from tree to tree as Wallace returned fire to offer her cover. Another bullet came close, striking a branch just above her head as she sprinted over the uneven ground.

The price of doing what Jackson did was high. She'd shut down parts of herself, a biological, physiological response to missions where things didn't go as planned. Where decisions had to be made, where people got hurt, where force was necessary in order to defend the team. She would do anything to protect the people she cared about.

At some point in her career as a soldier, she'd come to the realization that conflict was much more about love than hate. In the moment of reckoning, you harnessed everything you ever loved, everything you ever cared about—those were the things that propelled you forward, those were the things you fought for. Not the entire world, just one little part of it.

Jackson was at a dead run when a bullet came from her left. She'd surprised Nunez by catching up with him just before exiting the tree line. He was close. He fired again just as she lunged at his midsection. They both went down with a thump and tumbled. His pistol hit the dirt, and while still on the ground, she kicked it out of his reach. He swung at her landing a right hook to her jaw. The blow was like a sledgehammer to the side of her head. She saw stars.

He swung again, with his left fist, and she tumbled out of range and scrambled to her feet. They faced off. The gun lay in the dirt behind Jackson, but she didn't think she could get to it before he stopped her.

More shots sounded from the direction of base camp.

"That's Harris going down." Jackson sidestepped, keeping her knees bent so that she could react more quickly. "What the fuck is going on, Nunez?"

She wasn't hoping for some monologue of villainy, she just wanted answers. None of this made any damn sense.

"I'd say your pilot just bought it," Nunez taunted her.

"And how's that gonna work out for you? How do we fly a ship with no pilot?"

"Wallace isn't the only pilot, Jarhead."

"Wrong branch of the service, asshole." So, either Harris or Nunez was a pilot. That was news. But still, why derail the mission? What could they possibly hope to gain? Unless…unless, they weren't the ones calling the shots. These guys weren't mental giants for sure. Someone else had put all of this in play.

Nunez went for her, catching Jackson around the waist. She hit the ground hard. He was on top of her now. He tried to punch her in the face, but she dodged, angled her head sharply, and his fist hit the hard-packed ground. She struck him in the throat but not hard enough to dislodge his position. He outweighed her and she was struggling to regain control of the fight. She lurched beneath him using every muscle in her legs as torque. She tried to rotate and twist out from under him. He lost his balance for just a second, and she was able to use that small imbalance to roll with him. She kicked free and reached for the gun, but he caught her leg and dragged her back. She kicked him twice in the face. Blood gushed from his nose, but she couldn't break free.

He dragged her farther and yanked her to her feet by the front of her shirt.

"You're such an arrogant bitch."

Her toes barely touched the ground, making it hard to regain her footing. She braced against him with her elbow digging into his chest. In such close combat her choices were limited. He drew back one arm to land another punch and she seized the opportunity. She lunged, breaking his nose with her forehead.

He let go and she dove for the gun. But he regrouped, even angrier now. He grabbed for her, blood gushing from his smashed nose.

He had her ankle. She kicked at him with her other foot.

Jackson stretched for the weapon.

Her fingernails scraped at the ground.

She was so close.

Just a little more.

Just a little more.

He tried to twist her foot in an attempt to force her to roll onto her back. He was on her again. Fuck, he was heavy. He had her in a choke hold. Blood from his face dripped onto hers. She wedged her arms between his and braced against his elbows to break the hold. As she gasped for air she only had one thought in her head.

Elle.

Adrenaline and rage surged in her chest. This was not the end. There was no way she was giving this asshole control over her destiny, her life. She wedged the heel of her hand beneath his chin and applied pressure. When that didn't work, she swung for his broken and bloody nose. That did it. He recoiled and uttered some combination of a growl and a gurgle. She punched him in the throat and wriggled out from under him while he tried to regroup.

She lunged for the gun.

He grabbed the back of her T-shirt and yanked her up from the ground, but she already had the weapon in her hand.

Elle was startled by the sound of gunshots. They reverberated off the rocky cliff above her. It was hard to know for sure where the shots were coming from. Something must have happened at base camp. She was in shallow water near one of the tidal pools. She gathered her things with the intention of hustling up the trail to see what was wrong. But when she looked up, Ted was standing at the water's edge holding a gun.

She blinked, hoping she was seeing things, but Ted was still there. His hand shook and he steadied it by gripping the sidearm with both hands. He held the weapon out in front of him as if Elle were a threat. But she wasn't a threat. Was he hallucinating? He hadn't been quite himself since they'd made the jump the previous day.

"Ted, it's me. What are you doing?" She was standing knee-deep in water, still holding the collection of specimen jars.

"I'm sorry, Elle."

"What's there to be sorry about? Put the gun down, Ted. Everything is going to be okay. You're okay." She bent to set the jars on a flat rock at the edge of the pool she'd been sampling from.

"Don't move!"

"I'm not moving." She held up one hand. "I'm just putting these down so that I don't drop them."

"I'm sorry, Elle." He repeated the apology and sounded as if he truly meant it.

"Ted, whatever is going on, we're in this together. I'm not your enemy." She took a step in his direction.

"We're not in this together." He took a step back, keeping the gun in front of him. She was afraid he might shoot her by accident. "There's nothing you can do."

"Okay, okay." She wanted to calm him down.

More distant gunshots. Ted glanced over his shoulder toward the trail and then back. Her heart rate ratcheted up. Where was Jackson? What was happening?

"They can do things. They can make things happen if you don't do what they want."

"Who is they, Ted? What are you talking about?"

"They wrecked my car." A tear slid down his cheek. He wiped at it with his shoulder.

"Who, Ted? Who wrecked your car?"

"The AI driver never fails unless someone wants it to. They were sending me a message, Elle." His voice faltered. "I have no choice. I have to do this."

"And if you do this, then what happens?" She still didn't know what this was, but maybe if she could keep him talking she could find out.

"If I don't do this, they derail the surgery, the transplant for Alden."

"Your son, Alden?"

"They promised, Elle." He sniffed and shook his head. "I do this for them and they make sure Alden gets a new heart and lungs. That's the deal." He took a breath. "I have no choice."

"Who is they?" She understood now why he was desperate, but she needed more information.

"Don't pretend you don't know." He was getting angry.

"Ted, I really don't know."

"Liam."

"Liam? But why?" Could this be true? This made no sense. The mission was funded by BIOME *for* BIOME. "Why would BIOME sabotage their own expedition?"

"Not BIOME." He shook his head. "Liam works for other people, people who stand to make a lot of money off this expedition...from the samples we bring back."

"But—"

"Don't be so naive, Elle."

"But why?" She couldn't stop the question.

"Greed...selfishness...It's always the same reason, isn't it?"

"Ted, think about what you're doing." Another gunshot, this one sounded closer, but she still didn't see anyone descend the trail. No one was coming to save her this time.

"I've already thought about it."

"Ted, you might save your son, temporarily, but if we don't do what we set out to do here and reseed the oceans we're all dead. The world is dead. Don't you get that?"

"There's nothing I can do." But for an instant he seemed to consider it.

"You can make the choice to do the right thing, Ted. You have free will in this."

"People certainly have a will, but is it free?"

"Yes, it is." Elle's feet were numb from standing in the cold surf. "People make choices all the time. We are free to choose."

The tide was coming in. Each wave washed a little farther. The water swirled around Ted's feet. He was lost in thought and didn't avoid the rippling shallow wave.

"I'm sorry, Elle. But we've talked enough. There's nothing either of us can do to change reality. The world is a horrible place and we each have to figure out our own way to survive it." He pointed the handgun at her with renewed resolve. "You're a good person. Just know that this isn't easy. But I have to do this to save my son."

Her eyes widened to the sky for an instant. Was this the last light she would ever see? A sharp rush of panic constricted her chest. She covered her face with her hands. And with the darkness had only one thought—Jackson. *Please let Jackson be okay.*

"Good-bye, Elle."

She still covered her face and didn't respond.

The gun fired.

She flinched but felt nothing.

Had he missed?

She lowered her hands and opened her eyes to see Jackson, splashing through the knee-deep water, rushing toward her. Ted was lying on the beach. The surf lapped at his unmoving form. Jackson swept Elle up into a hug, lifting her out of the water.

"Are you hurt?" Jackson set her down and held her face in her hands.

"I'm okay." Elle's heart still raced. "But you're hurt."

There was blood on Jackson's face and her T-shirt had smudges of dirt.

"No, I'm fine, but I'm worried about Wallace. He was wounded and I had to leave him."

"Why did you leave him?" The answer seemed obvious the instant she uttered it.

"I had to make sure you were safe." Jackson drew her into another embrace.

Elle sank into Jackson. Relief tumbled over her in successive waves.

"I think I've lost the feeling in my feet." She stumbled and Jackson caught her.

Jackson kept her arm around Elle's waist as they waded to shore.

"Here, sit down." Jackson helped her to a spot near the trail where a few large rocks jutted from the sand.

Jackson knelt and removed the water shoes.

"Your feet are ice cold." She rubbed them briskly between her hands. "Hang on."

Jackson walked to where Ted had fallen and dragged him up and away from the surf. She retrieved his gun and came back to where Elle was sitting.

"I've checked the cartridge and the safety is off. If anyone but me or Wallace comes down that path you just point and shoot." Jackson put the gun in her hand.

She stared at it. Guns weren't her thing at all.

"Where are you going?" Her teeth chattered; she was probably in shock.

"I have to go back for Wallace." There was urgency in Jackson's voice.

There'd been no more distant gunshots. Elle wasn't sure what that meant. She involuntarily shivered, from shock or the cool air, she wasn't sure which.

"Hey, you're going to be okay." Jackson swept her palms up and down Elle's arms to warm her. "Just sit tight."

She stood and checked the ammunition in her gun. She shoved the magazine back into the handle.

"I don't want to stay here. I want to go with you." Elle got to her feet.

"No, if there's more shooting I don't want you becoming a target." Jackson was firm.

Elle nodded and then watched Jackson sprint up the trail.

She sat and tried to make sense of all that Ted had revealed. Liam was someone she admired, someone she trusted. Was it really possible that he'd worked against her on this? Why had he even selected her for the mission if he'd planned for her to fail?

Maybe she was supposed to succeed, but only in the acquisition of the samples. Liam knew how much this meant to her; she'd spent her entire career on this research. He had to know she'd go to any length to succeed. She was his guarantee of mission success. Ted was blackmailed into delivering the samples, but she must have been the only person Liam trusted to choose the right spot and verify the organisms were viable.

He had used her.

He'd used her and then planned to discard her. And not only her, Jackson and Wallace as well. Shock and sadness gave way to anger.

She'd sunk her toes in the warm, brown sand until the feeling began to return. She tugged on her soggy shoes and started the climb to base camp. Whatever awaited Jackson there, Elle didn't want her to face it alone. They were in this together now.

CHAPTER TWENTY-TWO

Jackson jogged all the way from the beach. She was winded when she reached the tree line. She slowed her pace and tried to calm her breathing as she approached base camp. Nothing was moving. The scene was eerily quiet. With her weapon drawn, she slipped from tree to tree until she was close enough to get eyes on Wallace. He was where she'd left him. His back was against the oversized tire with his legs extended in front.

She scanned the area for Harris.

Finally, she saw him, facedown not too far from Wallace. She checked for a pulse. Harris was dead.

Jackson moved swiftly to Wallace's position. He was still breathing, but he was gasping for air. He'd taken a third bullet in the chest and he'd lost a lot of blood from his leg wound. Red-brown ooze spread on the ground under him.

"Hey, man. Hang in there." She knelt beside him. He didn't look good at all.

"Is everything…" He coughed and drew a shaky breath. "Elle and Ted?"

"Elle is safe. Ted was part of this." She tried to offer him some water, but he couldn't choke it down. "Ted didn't make it."

"Nunez?"

"He's gone." She frowned. "That bastard tried to kill me."

"You finish this, Cap." His words were raspy, barely more than a whisper. He was fading. "You see this through."

"Don't worry, Wallace. I'll finish this. You can count on that."

His head lolled to one side and she tried to prop him up.

"Wallace, stay with me. Wallace?"

But he was gone.

Jackson sank back, letting her hand holding the canteen drop to the ground. This whole situation was royally fucked up. And she still had no idea why or for what purpose.

Footsteps behind her caused her to pivot on one knee, weapon drawn.

"I'm sorry, I didn't mean to surprise you." Elle held her hands up. She still had Ted's gun with her. "I…I didn't want to…I was worried you might need me. I was afraid Wallace might need help."

"Wallace didn't make it." Jackson holstered the weapon and stood up.

"I can't believe this. Ted, he—" The knot in her throat choked the words.

"Hey, we're okay." Jackson removed the pistol from Elle's loose grip and drew her into a one-armed hug. "We're okay now."

Elle took a shuddering breath.

"We're going to be okay." She said it again.

Elle wasn't sure whom Jackson was trying to convince, but still, the words soothed her. She was grateful for Jackson's calm strength.

"We're alone." The words sounded far away in her own head. Had she actually spoken or simply thought them?

The immensity of the primeval world seemed suddenly overwhelming.

"Yeah, and we can't stay here." Jackson surveyed the camp. "There's too much blood. Your wolf friend will be back and he'll bring others with him."

"I didn't even think of that." Elle watched Jackson pace. "What should we do? We can't leave the bodies here either."

Jackson's *leave no trace* lecture was on point, even now, even more so.

"We can take a stretcher and carry Ted up from the beach. We should work fast." Jackson searched through first aid gear in the nearest trailer. "The scent of blood will bring too many unwanted creatures in our direction. There are big cats here too, right?"

"Yes." Elle nodded.

"Come on." Jackson had the collapsible stretcher under one arm as she started back toward the beach.

❖

Jackson wanted to know what Elle was thinking, what she was feeling as they moved Ted to the stretcher. As a soldier, Jackson had experienced the loss of comrades in the line of duty before, but this was different. Elle was a civilian and her research partner, her friend, had tried to shoot her. That was betrayal on a level Jackson had thankfully never had to experience.

Elle stepped away to retrieve her backpack and other things she'd left earlier. There was also a gallon of seawater. She set it in the sand beside the stretcher.

"We'll come back for that." Jackson riffled through Ted's pack. She found what she was hoping for, a small towel. She used it to cover his face, tucking it beneath his head.

"Thank you." Elle's words were soft, quiet. She reached for the large container again.

"Elle, leave it."

She had a confused expression.

"We'll come back for it because we have two other containers to fill." Jackson figured they'd have a hard enough time carrying Ted without the additional weight.

"We're going to fill all the tanks?" Elle slipped the straps of her small pack over her shoulders.

"Hell yes, we are." Jackson faced her. "If we don't then Wallace gave his life for nothing. Not to mention all the people we left behind who are counting on us."

Elle nodded. She was shaken, Jackson could see it. But they had a lot to deal with at the moment and she needed Elle to pull it together.

"Listen, focus on the tasks for now." Jackson put her hand on Elle's shoulder. "We'll deal with our feelings later, okay?" Jackson cupped her cheek. "Act now, feel later."

"Okay…yes, you're right…I'm sorry."

"Don't be sorry. There's nothing to be sorry about." Jackson grabbed the handles on one end of the stretcher. "Ready?"

Elle nodded. They hoisted Ted and made the slow climb up the steep trail. Jackson was in back, in the downhill position, so that she could bear the brunt of Ted's weight as they climbed.

Once they were back at camp, Jackson retrieved a body bag for Ted. There was always the chance that something unforeseen could befall a team in the field, so they had prepared for every scenario, or tried to. That preparation involved the loss of a team member. They had bags that could be vacuum sealed for transport. Each would be contained within one of the black bags and then placed in their assigned g-tube for the return flight.

Nunez was the most difficult to retrieve. For one thing, he was extremely heavy. Additionally, he was in the open, away from camp. By the time they got back to him vultures were circling. The huge black wings cast moving shadows on the ground.

"How did Nunez die?" Elle stood, looking down at his body, which was facedown.

"I shot him." Jackson glanced up at the dark-winged scavengers.

"Did he…" Elle didn't finish the question.

"Yeah, he tried to kill me." Jackson readied the black plastic bag for Nunez. "And then I'm pretty sure he was on his way to make sure Ted had taken care of you."

"I still can't believe it." Elle swept her fingers through her hair and looked out at the churning sea.

The wind had picked up and the water was choppy.

"I believe it only because I lived it." Jackson knelt beside the body.

She'd driven one of the ATVs, pulling a trailer to pick up Nunez. After his body was bagged, they half dragged, half lifted him onto the trailer.

"Stay here. I'll go get that container from the beach." Jackson started toward the cliff.

"No, I'll go. You look exhausted."

"You're exhausted too." Jackson studied her.

"Yes, but I didn't have to survive hand-to-hand combat the way you probably did."

Jackson hadn't described what had happened, but maybe she didn't have to. She was fairly sure her face was bruised. Her cheek and her eye socket throbbed from the punches Nunez had landed. Her ribs were definitely sore too. Once she stopped moving she'd probably collapse. But she needed to get them to safety before that happened.

"Let's just fill the last two and take everything back in one trip." Jackson swiped the last two empty containers from the back of the ATV and followed Elle.

CHAPTER TWENTY-THREE

Elle's fingers shook as she struggled to affix the cap to the last container. She released the plastic jug to bob in the water as she zipped her vest. The wind off the ocean had seriously picked up. It was midafternoon and the morning's warmth was gone. The air carried a damp chill that cut right through her clothing, amplifying her fatigue.

The walk up the steep grade to the ATV warmed her a little, but not enough. She needed to add a layer of clothing to what she was wearing and change out of the damp trousers, still wet from the knees down.

Elle slipped into the tent once they were back at camp and changed pants. She pulled on a sweatshirt and then put the vest back on. She handed a light jacket to Jackson.

"You should put this on."

Jackson was only wearing a T-shirt. Adrenaline was probably keeping her warm, but Elle knew the minute Jackson stopped moving she'd chill.

"Thanks." Jackson didn't argue with her.

"What's next?" Elle was so spent she just wanted someone to tell her what to do.

"We'll break camp and drive everything back to the ship." Jackson braced her hands on her hips. "Have you ever driven one of these before?" She tipped her head toward the nearest ATV.

"Um…no."

"This will be easy." Jackson opened the vehicle door. "I'll show you. Then you just follow me and go where I go, okay?"

Elle nodded.

"We'll take it slow."

"How can we go back?" Elle asked

"We just retrace our route from yesterday." Jackson leaned against the open door.

That wasn't what she'd meant, but she was too tired to explain it just now. She was still sorting it all out in her head anyway. If Liam was behind all that had happened, then they couldn't just return to the substation as if everything was normal. There was no way in hell she was going to deliver the samples right to his doorstep, not after all of this. There had to be another way.

Jackson consumed a full canteen of water during the drive back to the ship. They hadn't had any food since early morning, and she wanted both of them to eat something because they had more work to do before they could stop for the day. She needed Elle to keep her strength up.

The sleek, silver orb of the SLST was like a beacon. She spotted it while they were still fairly far way. The foreign object stood out like an alien life form on the grassy meadow.

Jackson typed in a security code that opened the rear cargo hatch remotely from the ATV console. There was enough room to drive both light-duty ATVs and trailers into the bay side by side. She pulled in first and then waved Elle in. The tight space didn't leave much room for offloading. Jackson stepped down from the driver's side and walked around the front of the vehicle to face Elle.

Elle didn't get out. She maintained her grip on the steering wheel and rested her forehead against it. Jackson watched her through the windshield. When she didn't move, Jackson touched her shoulder.

"Just take one step at a time, okay?" She rested her palm on Elle's back.

Finally, Elle raised up. She looked at Jackson and nodded, still not speaking.

"I don't think I have the strength to do anything else."

"I know, I hear you." Jackson rubbed the stubble on top of her head a few times. She was exhausted too. "We need to rest and eat. Not necessarily in that order." She also wanted a shower. "Come on, I'll help you."

Elle accepted Jackson's hand as she climbed out of the ATV. Jackson closed the hatch behind them as they entered the main part of the ship. They walked through the gravity lounge where the vacant tubes stood open, toward the control center. The galley was on the left. Jackson stopped and motioned to the right.

"There are two crew compartments here that we can use." She dropped the small duffel she'd carried. "You can shower first. Just know that because of limited carrying capacity, the water will shut off after five minutes. The timer will chime to give you a one-minute warning before the water cuts off."

Elle tried to focus on Jackson's words. She was taking some small comfort in the mundane detail of how much hot water she was allotted. Talking about a shower, thinking about fresh clothing, the normalcy of those things was so abstract at the moment. She must be in shock. She shivered and then hugged herself.

"I'll get your bag from the ATV."

She was grateful to Jackson for this small kindness because she didn't think she could go back in the chamber with the bodies of their crewmates.

After a minute, Jackson rejoined her and showed her how to operate the shower. It was a tiny, narrow square space with non-intuitive fixtures. Without Jackson's help she'd probably have stood there for quite some time just trying to figure out how to turn it on. The technicians had no doubt gone over all of this during the introduction in the simulator, but she now had no memory of it. Her head was a jumble of thoughts, none of them having to do with basic self-care needs like bathing, or eating, or sleeping.

After showering, Jackson set Elle up with a cup of coffee in the galley. She held the warm cup between her hands and stared into the inky liquid without sampling it. She'd have sworn only an instant had elapsed before Jackson rejoined her, but probably ten minutes had passed.

"You know, I meant for you to actually drink that." Jackson made a cup for herself and then opened several metal cabinets. She'd open one, without finding what she was looking for, and then move on to the next. "We need to eat something too. Do you think you could?"

Elle nodded and took a sip of the coffee without looking at Jackson. She had no appetite, but she knew Jackson was right. They needed food; her system was running on fumes.

"How does chicken teriyaki sound?" Jackson held a ration packet in her hand. "I mean, it'll probably taste like mush, but…"

"That sounds fine." Nothing was going to sound edible. Might as well just pick something.

Jackson added hot water from the dispenser and divided the contents of the pack into two serving bowls. Elle tried to choke down a few bites. She had a lump in her throat that just wouldn't dislodge. No matter how many times she swallowed.

"Yesterday…yesterday, everything was different. Today the world is upside down, cancerous at the root." Elle stared at the tabletop.

"Hey, you're supposed to be the optimistic one."

"Am I?" She looked up to meet Jackson's gaze. "How do you do this?"

"Do what?"

"This." Elle swung her arm in an arc. "Death, betrayal…mission failure."

"Death happens, unfortunately." Jackson paused. "And if it's all right with you, I'm not quite ready to declare mission failure."

Elle realized what she'd said. Jackson certainly was familiar with loss. She regretted her word choice, but how could this *not* be a failure?

"I'm sorry, but you can't possibly consider this particular expedition a success."

"There are varying degrees of success." Jackson ignored her sarcasm. "Did Ted say anything to you?"

"Yes, he said quite a lot, in fact." Elle realized that she hadn't had a chance to share anything that Ted had revealed to her.

"Well, maybe now's a good time to fill me in, because I got nothing from Nunez or Harris."

"I'm really sorry about Wallace." She sincerely was and felt bad about not saying it sooner. The entire day had been so surreal that her emotions weren't at all in sync with her brain, or her words.

"He was a good guy." She cleared her throat. Elle couldn't tell if Jackson was upset or angry or a mixture of both. "He didn't deserve to go down like that."

Elle gave them both a minute to come up for air before she launched in.

"Ted basically told me that Liam set this whole thing up."

"Really?" That bit of news obviously surprised Jackson.

"Let me see if I can remember everything…" She tried to focus despite the fatigue. "He kept talking about *they*. *They* wrecked his car, *they* threatened him, *they* could get his son an organ transplant, but only if he did this…Only if he helped them." She'd been staring at her unsavory bowl of freeze-dried chicken. She looked up, making eye contact with Jackson. "And then he said that it was actually Liam who was calling the shots."

"That just doesn't sound right."

"I know, so I pushed Ted to help me understand why. Why would Liam do this?" She tried to visualize the conversation in her head. "He said greed, selfishness…so, it's got to be about money."

"If we took the specimens back as planned, then BIOME would utilize them and no single person would make a profit from the discovery."

"But if one person controlled the release of the phytoplankton and held it back until the situation was much worse, then they could charge governments anything they wanted for the samples to reseed the oceans." This still sounded like some comic book scheme for world domination. Was Liam really diabolical enough to sell everyone out? "I'm sure there's a black market for biological material like this. I mean, that's what happened with rare and extinct animals."

"That's a cruel business for sure, but those guys weren't trying to hold the entire planet hostage for cash."

"I know." Elle covered her face with her hands. "I'm going to need to think this through when my head is clearer…maybe tomorrow. It's just so hard for me to believe."

"We have to believe it. Regardless of how painful it is to face a betrayal as huge as this." Jackson sounded pissed. "Four people died today. That's pretty serious collateral damage."

"Obviously, the plan was to shoot three of us. Half the team." Elle was supposed to be one of them, and then Wallace, and Jackson.

"I can't imagine Ted would have made it back." Jackson sank back in her chair with her arms stretched out on the table in front of her, palms down. "My guess is the science team knew too much."

Elle didn't respond. Her intuition told her that Jackson was probably right.

"My question to you, Dr. Graham, is are we going to let these bastards get away with it?"

"No, Commander. Not while I'm still standing."

"Good." Jackson nodded. "We're on the same page."

Elle finished the last spoonful of dinner and downed a cup of water.

"I set up the sleeping bags in the crew compartment. We both need rest." Jackson stood up. "We can figure out our plan tomorrow."

Chapter Twenty-four

The small bath area separated the two crew cabins. Standing between the two rooms, Elle could see Jackson had set up a sleeping bag in each room. That discovery heaped even more disappointment on the shittiest day ever.

"Can't we sleep in the same room tonight?" The question wasn't supposed to sound needy, but she was afraid it did.

"Um, sure, I…" Jackson fumbled her words. "I just didn't want to assume."

"A psychotic private security team just tried to take out our entire team, we're surrounded by infinite wilderness, and currently we're the only two humans on the entire continent. Please, by all means, assume."

"Good point." Jackson retrieved Elle's sleeping bag.

"And please, don't toy with me." Elle shook her head. "Zip them together. I'm not sleeping alone. Not tonight."

Jackson did as she was directed and then returned to Elle.

"Better?"

"Much…thank you." Elle smiled.

Jackson held Elle's face in her hands tenderly and ran her thumb across Elle's cheek. As if in slow motion, the space between them began to shrink. Like the slowly collapsing orbit of a celestial body, she sank into Jackson. Their lips met and she kissed Jackson. And then Jackson was kissing her back.

As certain as she was now of the non-linear nature of time, the melting of the polar ice caps, and the spinning of the Earth—their meeting seemed just as inevitable.

"Hey, what's going on?" Jackson stroked her hair.

"I don't want to be alone right now." She hated to be demanding. But after all that had happened, she hated even more to be dishonest. "Is that okay?"

Jackson kissed her forehead but didn't speak.

Was she more afraid of the future or what she was feeling right now for Jackson?

"What do you need?" Jackson asked as if she really wanted to know.

"I want you to make love to me as if you care for me." Elle swallowed. "Not as if I'm some stranger you met at the Green Club, but someone you truly desire."

"That won't be hard." Jackson kissed her gently.

"I want to believe you." If tomorrow was the end. If the whole thing went badly, then she wanted tonight to feel as if it were the real thing.

"I always tell the truth." Jackson's statement was reassuring.

"Do you?"

"Yes."

They had methodically undressed as they talked. Elle was still wearing her bra and underwear, having discarded the awful military cargo pants. Jackson was in white, Y-front briefs. Jackson's fingers swept slowly down Elle's arms giving her goose bumps.

"What truth do you want to share with me right now?" Elle asked softly.

Jackson smiled, as if she were about to reveal some deep secret.

"The truth is, I don't really want to be friends." She slipped one of the bra straps down and kissed Elle's shoulder. "Does that make me a terrible person?"

"No, I don't really want to be friends either." Elle's words came out breathy, almost like a moan. Jackson was kissing her neck and caressing her nipple through her bra.

Elle felt the side of the bed at the back of her legs and eased onto it. She unfastened her bra as Jackson followed her backward crawl until they were snuggled into the joined sleeping bags, facing each other. Elle's breasts brushed against the firm points of Jackson's. She closed her eyes and took a deep breath in an attempt to slow her heartbeat.

This wasn't the first time she'd been in bed with Jackson, but somehow, it felt different. Possibly because they knew so much more about each other. Possibly because she'd forgotten how unbelievable Jackson's body was. Possibly because everything was laced with urgency. Almost losing your life made every moment and every detail of living precious.

She had the urge to trail her fingertip across Jackson's shoulder and down her arm to commit to memory the muscles of her bicep and forearm. And then there were her strong hands. Those beautiful, strong hands. She brushed the back of her fingers up Jackson's stomach. The contact sent a jolt of electricity to the throbbing place between her legs.

"Can I take these off?" Jackson slipped her fingers beneath the waist of her panties.

"Yes, please." She kissed Jackson while Jackson got rid of the last barriers of clothing between them.

They lay facing each other, their legs intertwined. Jackson drew Elle close, kissing her languidly, as if they had all the time in the world. Maybe they did.

"What do you need?" Elle asked Jackson the same question.

"I think all I need right now is this…you." She held Elle closely in her arms.

From deep inside her body, from the cord of her spine, the nerves spiderwebbed outward, to the muscles across her ribs. The tingling sensation traveled up Elle's back and then settled as tightness in her stomach before rising to her chest. She tucked her head under Jackson's chin. She wasn't sure if she'd wanted to make love, or simply be held. She was exhausted and the warmth of Jackson's body was soothing her, lulling her into letting go.

As much as she wanted to be swept along by her intense desire, exhaustion weighed her down, and she dozed off in the solace of Jackson's embrace.

CHAPTER TWENTY-FIVE

Jackson woke first. Her arm beneath Elle's head was numb. Elle's back was pressed against her chest. She gently dislodged her arm. It tingled as the blood flow returned. She wasn't sure of the time. They'd fallen asleep so suddenly and completely that she wasn't sure she'd even shifted her position all night.

Elle's breathing was slow and steady. She was still asleep. Jackson unzipped her side of the sleeping bag and padded barefoot to the bathroom. After relieving herself, she stood at the sink and studied her face in the mirror. The harsh fluorescent glow was fairly unflattering even on a good day, but this morning was not a good day. She touched the bruises around her right eye. She looked as if she'd been in a boxing match and lost.

She filled the sink with cold water and sank her face into it. Ice would have been better, but this would have to do. After a few minutes of soaking repeatedly, she reached for a towel. She'd taken her watch off before showering and left it on the small shelf above the sink. It was still very early. Even in the deep past, she couldn't sleep late.

In the dark room, she searched through discarded clothing for her T-shirt, underwear, and pants. She'd considered climbing back in bed with Elle, but that would only lead to other things. She was surprised they hadn't made love, but at the same time she wasn't. By the time they'd crawled into bed her limbs had turned to rubbery mush from exhaustion. Probably both of them were feeling emotionally spent and raw; she knew she was. So, it was probably best that all they'd done was hold each other and sleep. Just that simple act of comfort had been incredibly satisfying for Jackson.

She'd said she didn't want to be friends, but the truth was, Jackson genuinely liked Elle. Liked her in a way that she hadn't liked any woman in a very long time. Last night, holding Elle, she'd been completely present. She was with Elle and thinking only of her. That was a first. She'd met women she was attracted to, she'd sleep with them, and in every instance immediately compare them to Camille. She and Elle had fallen asleep in each other's arms and she hadn't thought of Camille until this morning, and then only to note that she hadn't thought of her. This was strange new territory.

Was it possible that she was finally moving on? Could there be a more inopportune time to have this realization? Now that the world was ending...now was the moment she was going to fall in love again?

Fall in love?

Where did that come from?

Jackson rummaged in the kitchen and made coffee while she mulled all this over. They were in one of the worst situations she'd ever been in and yet, she was actually in a good mood. Maybe she was really losing it. She laughed and shook her head.

"What's so funny?"

She turned to see Elle in a rumpled T-shirt standing in the doorway to the galley. Elle had put on her underwear, but no pants. Elle had great legs, long and toned. Jackson sipped her coffee as she leaned against the back counter of the small galley and enjoyed the view.

"I was wondering to myself if I was cracking up."

"Ooh, that's too much honesty before coffee." Elle squinted at her. She lifted the cup from Jackson's hand and took a few sips. "Where's yours?" She shuffled to a chair, taking Jackson's coffee with her.

"It's good to know that even in a disaster, you maintain your sense of humor."

"Was I being funny?" Elle quirked an eyebrow as she unabashedly drank Jackson's coffee.

This whole morning-after encounter felt so charmingly normal that Jackson had to force herself to remember where they were and what lay ahead. She turned back to the console and made a second cup of coffee, then joined Elle at the table.

"Thank you for last night." Elle was serious. "I'm sorry if I was too needy."

"I was feeling the need for closeness too. The need to feel something...normal." Jackson slouched in her chair. "No need to thank me."

Elle smiled thinly, as if her brain was just now waking up to their new reality.

"That bruise looks bad." Elle leaned forward with her elbows on the table. "How are you feeling?"

"Sore, but I'm okay. You?"

Elle simply nodded. It was impossible to articulate how she was feeling. She'd focus on physical things for the moment. The coffee was warm and satisfying, although she was a little cold. She left the galley to change into cargo pants. Jackson watched her come and go.

"I was feeling a little chilly." She sat back down facing Jackson.

The SLST was sort of like an oversized Airstream trailer. That would have been the way she'd described it. The curved walls and ceiling were appealing, the shape of the long narrow ship felt familiar somehow and foreign at the same time. Her grandfather had owned a vintage Airstream. When gas was no longer affordable, he'd parked it on a lot in the foothills of the Sierras and constructed a biodome around the trailer. She'd spent many days in her childhood hanging out there. Looking back, she always credited that early exposure to a small oasis in the wild for her love of nature and botany.

"Where did you just go?"

"Sorry, childhood flashback." She'd zoned out for a moment without meaning to.

"A good one?"

"Yes." Elle smiled. "Vacations with my grandparents in their vintage Airstream trailer." She couldn't help surveying the room. "This ship reminds me of a tricked-out Airstream."

"Yeah, I guess it does sort of have that feel." Jackson mimicked her review of the space by looking at the ceiling and around.

"Tell me something about yourself." Elle sipped her coffee.

"Like what?"

"Did you have a happy childhood?" Elle hesitated. "I'm just realizing there are things about you I'd like to know."

"I suppose so. Maybe not as happy as yours?"

"Why do you say that?" Elle furrowed her brow.

"You just seem so…normal…well-adjusted…optimistic." Jackson tilted her head as if she were reading some list from inside her mind.

Elle laughed.

"I think you can take optimistic off that list." Elle studied Jackson. "What's normal anyway?"

They were quiet for a moment. It seemed obvious Jackson wasn't going to volunteer details unless Elle asked.

"Do you have any siblings?"

"Yes, a brother."

"Are you going to make me pull information from you? Will you just please talk to me?" Elle leaned forward. "Pretend we're friends and we want to get to know each other."

"Even though we've both declared we don't want to be friends." Jackson's statement was playful.

"Yes, despite that."

Jackson took a deep breath.

"Okay, I have a brother, he got involved with a rough crowd. He was in prison for a little while on drug charges. He's out now and working on a protein farm in Southern California." Jackson paused. "We're not really close. He hates the military."

"Parents?"

"I don't really remember my mom. She left my dad when I was pretty young." Jackson had a far-off look in her eyes, as if she was remembering things she hadn't thought about in a long time. "My dad was a good guy. He did his best. We just never had much. I joined the military in order to attend college and ultimately become a pilot. The Air Force was my way out."

"And then at some point you joined the Space Force?"

"Yeah." Jackson took a swig of her coffee. "What about you? You have a sister, right?"

"How did you know?"

"Just a good guess from the photo I saw at your place."

"Yes, she's younger than me by a couple of years. Her name is Olivia. She lives in the Midwest with her husband. She's not into science at all. She's an accountant."

For some reason that amused Jackson.

"My mom and dad also live in the Midwest. My dad is a lawyer and my mom teaches English at a university near where they live."

"Wow, super normal."

"Yes, I suppose." She worried that *normal* was code for *boring*.

"So, you grew up in the Midwest then?"

"Yep, just outside of Chicago. I moved out to California after grad school."

"I suppose that explains part of it."

"What?"

"That intangible thing that makes you so likeable." Jackson grinned. "I've always liked people from the middle states."

"Thanks, I think." Elle was amused by Jackson's personality assessment.

They were quiet, each lost in her own thoughts, until Jackson spoke. "I have an idea." Jackson leaned forward with an earnest expression.

"That sounds promising." It seemed sharing time was over. Elle still had a million questions, but she'd table them for later.

"First, can you tell me how the phytoplankton multiply? I mean, do they need to be delivered in some special way to the ocean when we get back?"

Jackson was suddenly more serious, all business.

"When growing conditions are right, phytoplankton multiply quickly through various means of asexual reproduction." Elle paused, collecting her thoughts. "The simplicity of plankton enables them to reproduce easily and quickly. Fast-growing dinoflagellates typically divide through binary fission."

"Whatever that means." Jackson's words were laced with sarcasm.

"Sorry, dinoflagellates are basically single-celled eukaryotes—algae."

"Wouldn't it be easier to just say algae?"

"No, not really." Elle was amused by the question. "And fission, in biology, is the division of a single entity into two or more parts. And then regeneration of those parts into separate entities resembling the original."

"Asexual reproduction. Okay, I get it. Phytoplankton are like microscopic marine rabbits who divide and multiply without assistance as long as the sea water is available."

"Well, if that makes it easier to understand, then yes."

"Okay, then I think my plan might work." Jackson was serious again. "I think we could swap the containers."

"Explain."

"I can purge one of the water tanks on the ship. We could store the sea water samples in that empty tank and put fresh water into the gallon sample containers."

"What good would that do?"

"I can alter the trajectory of the re-entry so that we land in the ocean."

"But I thought the slingshot only traveled through time, returning to the same location?" Elle tried to remember the details from the brief training she'd had before departure. "Won't we return to the same place we departed from?"

"It is possible to change the re-entry coordinates. It's a little risky, but I'm fairly certain I can alter our course so that we splash down in the ocean." Jackson paused. "Do you trust me?"

"Yes." At this point, Elle would literally follow Jackson anywhere.

"In a water landing, the ship should automatically purge the water tanks and take on air to keep the ship from sinking."

"Purging the harvested phytoplankton into the sea." Elle's heart raced. This was a genius idea. "Once in the water, the phytoplankton would do their thing."

"And then we deliver the sample containers just like we're supposed to."

"Only once they're at the lab, Liam will know he's basically got tap water with nothing in it."

"Yes."

"Jackson, can you really make this work?"

"I'm an engineer, remember? And a pilot."

"This is a terrific plan. This might actually work." Elle extended her hand across the table and Jackson took it. Elle squeezed lightly. "We could actually see this through and achieve what we set out to do."

"Yes." Jackson finished her coffee. "We'll be groggy when we land. I'll figure out a way to get a coded message to Nikki. We'll need someone on our side, watching our back."

Elle was optimistic, for the first time since her encounter with Ted at the beach. She was feeling as if they really might be able to turn this whole thing around.

"Are you hungry?"

"Probably." Elle sipped loudly. "My stomach isn't awake enough to know for sure."

"Well, either way, we should eat." Jackson stood and checked packets of food as she talked. "We've got a lot of work ahead of us and we're gonna need to keep our strength up."

Chapter Twenty-six

After breakfast, the first task was securing the bodies in their assigned gravity tubes. The body bags were oddly dehumanizing. Jackson had to focus on each task while she pushed back the memories that the bags brought up for her. Wallace was the last crewmember put in place. Jackson strapped him in and then had to lean against the tube structure for a minute with her eyes closed.

"Are you okay?" Elle placed her hand on Jackson's back.

Jackson nodded but kept her eyes closed for a few more seconds.

"No, you're not. What's going on?" Elle's question was filled with concern.

Jackson straightened and took a deep breath.

"This, the black bags, they remind me of the…the day Camille died." She met Elle's gaze.

She sometimes talked with friends about Camille. About missing her, about things she remembered. But she never talked about the Tyvek suits or the body bags or the fact that she never got to say good-bye. The entire contagion site had been locked down. The dead were bagged and numbered unceremoniously. The whole scene was brutal, and she just couldn't shake it.

"I'm so sorry." Elle wrapped her arms around Jackson's waist and hugged her tightly.

She slowly returned the embrace, a little afraid that contact between them would bring tears. This was not the time for tears, but tears didn't always follow direction.

"Thank you." She didn't know what else to say.

"It must be terrible to have that memory haunt you." Elle's words were muffled, quiet, since her cheek was pressed against Jackson's shirt. "It's okay to talk about it."

"There's nothing to say." But she knew that wasn't true. She touched the screen to lower the glass door of Wallace's tube.

"Why don't we take a break?"

"No, I'm fine. Really." Jackson knew she sounded defensive.

"I don't think that's true and I wish you felt safe enough with me to be honest." Elle wasn't buying it.

"It has nothing to do with you."

"Except, I'm the one that's here and I would really like to know you, Jackson." She placed her hands on Jackson's forearms for emphasis. "Will you talk to me?"

Jackson swallowed. This was the part she was never very good at—vulnerability. Every ounce of training she had was in contrast to this, and that training had served her well, in most ways. Elle was looking at her, waiting for something. She might as well start with the truth.

"Elle, I'm not very good at this."

"Which part?" Elle's fingers lightly squeezed her arm.

"The talking part. The sharing."

"Just start small."

Jackson rubbed her face and stepped away from Elle, out of her reach. She had her back to Elle when she started talking.

"The day Camille left for LA I asked her not to go." Jackson dropped her head and sighed, still not facing Elle. She braced her hands on her hips. "I begged her not to go."

Elle was quiet and made no move to touch her.

"I had a bad feeling and I didn't want her to take the assignment." Jackson turned toward Elle, but kept a few feet of space between them, not an easy feat in the narrow compartment. "But that was her job, to go where outbreaks happened to try to minimize the spread."

She rubbed the stubble on top of her head briskly with her fingers, as if that would dislodge the mental image.

"She thought she could save the world, even if that meant sacrificing herself." Jackson frowned. "Maybe I'm just selfish. Maybe I wasn't willing to share her with the world. I mean, we had a life too."

Elle hugged herself and kept quiet. Her expression was warm. Her eyes telegraphed empathy. Maybe she'd lost people too. Maybe Elle really did understand. It was all coming back to her now; she couldn't stop.

"The thing that I regret most is what I said to her when she left. I begged her to stay, and when she wouldn't I got angry, I said hurtful things to her." Her words came out raspy from the lump rising in her throat. "I actually said she was selfish. I called *her* selfish. I shouted at her as she was leaving."

Jackson swiped roughly at a tear with her hand. The tears made her angry.

"I shouted at her. I said she was selfish. When in reality, Camille was the least selfish person I've ever met. She was—" A sob choked off the words.

Elle was in her arms again, holding her as she fought the tears.

"It's okay. She knew you didn't mean it."

"I never got to make it right. I never got to tell her how amazing she was." Jackson took a big shuddering breath. "I never got to tell her that she was the brave one. Much braver than I am."

"Jackson, listen to me." Elle held her face in her hands. "I am certain that what Camille thought of at the end was only how much she loved you and of the life you shared, not some stupid thing you said because you were hurting." She wiped at a tear with her thumb. "Look at me."

Jackson tried, but Elle's caring gaze was only making the hurt rise to the surface.

"She loved you, Jackson." Elle paused. "And she knew that you loved her."

"How can you be so sure?"

"Because I know you."

Elle tugged her down until their lips met. Salt from her tears mingled as Elle's tongue teased hers. The kiss deepened and she gave in to it. She clung to Elle, drawing her close, holding her tightly.

"Oh, Elle." She pressed her damp cheek to Elle's.

"I'm here, Jackson. I'm here." Her lips brushed the outside edge of Jackson's ear. "Please let me in."

Jackson felt something break away inside. Some tethered weight she'd been anchored to. She inhaled sharply, deeply, and squeezed her eyes shut. She held on to Elle as if letting go might mean floating away, losing herself. She cried softly, her shoulders shaken by sobs as she allowed herself to be held.

CHAPTER TWENTY-SEVEN

Elle stared at the dispenser as it filled the first, then second cup with coffee. It was late afternoon. They had spent the bulk of the day moving the seawater samples to one of the main tanks on the ship. And then afterword, rinsing and filling the empty gallon containers with freshwater from one of the other tanks. The bulk of the work had only taken a couple of hours, but it involved a lot of trips from the cargo area up into the infrastructure of the ship, into the network of crawl spaces overhead.

Her arms felt like jelly from lifting gallons of water over her head and up to where Jackson was perched on the scaffold.

After all the heavy lifting, she took a brisk shower while Jackson worked on altering their return flight. She'd needed the per volume weight of the sea water to make the calculations for re-entry, adjusting for the weight calibration of the ship since now the sea water was in the tank instead of where it was supposed to be. Which made the tail of the craft lighter than anticipated. It wasn't about the total weight, because that was the same, it had to do with distribution and balance. At least that's how Jackson had explained it and her tired brain had tried to keep up.

Coffee seemed in order, so she'd set about figuring out how to make it.

Elle walked down the slim, tapered corridor to the pilot's position. Jackson's broad shoulders were visible on either side of the slender aviator's chair. If it was possible, in their current scenario, Jackson actually seemed relaxed. Some of the tension she'd carried in her shoulders was gone. Elle leaned past her to set a cup of coffee on the console for her. Jackson was typing on a keypad and didn't look away from the readout nearest where she was seated. She was facing a bank of screens, angled to mimic the curved surface at the nose of the ship.

"How's it going?" Elle stood behind Jackson, sipped her coffee, and tried to make sense of what was on the screen, but she couldn't. GPS coordinates maybe? But also, lots of other readouts that she couldn't decipher.

"Things are good here." Jackson reached for the coffee and partially swiveled in the chair. "I've altered our re-entry trajectory so that we splashdown in the Pacific, not too far from base." She paused while she took a drink. "Then the ship does the hard part for us by purging the water tanks and taking on air."

"And then our tiny passengers swim free and multiply."

"That's the plan." Jackson returned to her original position. "Now, I just need to get a message to Nikki." She started typing. "I'll place it in the outgoing message center so that as soon as we're in satellite range she'll get it."

"What are you going to say?" Elle wondered what Jackson might say that wouldn't trigger red flags when intercepted.

"Take a look." Jackson pointed at the typed email on the screen.

Nik, we're back a little later than planned. Remember that great trek to Jakarta we did? Jusuf was a terrific host. Let's have a do-over to celebrate mission completion. Maybe we could meet up after re-entry with a cooler of beer. But no pressure if you've made other plans. See you soon, buddy.—JD

"That seems like a totally normal message." Elle wasn't following. "I don't see how this is going to help us out."

"Well, the first red flag to her will be that I called her 'Nik,' which I never do because she doesn't like it and I've admitted that we're late. I'm never late, unless there's a problem. Then there's this part about Jakarta and Jusuf." Jackson sipped her coffee as she studied the screen. "The city government of Jakarta is completely corrupt, in one of the most corrupt countries on the planet. The leadership there basically sold the soul of their country to make money off palm oil. They ruined vast swaths of native habitats in order to plant more palms and cash out."

"Oh, I see." Elle was beginning to understand.

"And Jusuf was our contact there for a black op four years ago. He was a double agent. He completely sold us out. We almost didn't make it back."

"And the part about the cooler with beer?"

"I never drink beer."

"How will she know that we need her when the ship splashes down?"

"Because I told her there was no pressure." Jackson grinned. "She'll know the opposite is true. When you run ops with someone long enough, you develop codes so that you can communicate openly about secret things."

"I hope she's there when we come out of the gravity tubes."

"She will be, you can count on Nikki." Jackson hit send and the message cycled in the outgoing folder on the screen. "She'll be there."

"We'll just sit tight, all tucked in until the extraction team fishes us out."

"And by then it'll be too late for Liam. The samples will be free-range at that point."

"Exactly." Jackson slouched back in her chair and angled her head as if she were examining some curious thing. "Departure time isn't until zero-eight-hundred tomorrow."

Plenty of time to fret and worry about whether their plan would actually work and what to do to stave off disaster if it didn't.

"There's one more thing we need to take care of." Jackson rotated in the chair. "Do you feel up to taking a drive?"

CHAPTER TWENTY-EIGHT

Jackson gripped the wheel of the ATV as it crawled through thick understory. They backtracked toward the coast. Taking care of the fallen members of their team and breaking camp had stretched the limits of Elle's physical strength, and Jackson's, for that matter. But she knew, in order to leave a clean site, they had to go back.

Semi-automatic pistols used a single firing chamber that remained fixed in a constant linear position. After the trigger was pulled and the round fired, the recoil of the handgun automatically ejected the shell casing. In her head, she'd done the math about how many shots had been fired. The only casings she'd retrieved were the one from the beach and the shot she fired at Nunez on the trail. By her count, they needed to retrieve at least twelve casings from base camp and the surrounding area. She knew her count probably wasn't perfect. There was no way to be sure how many shots Harris and Wallace exchanged while she was engaged with Nunez. If she got lucky, the casings would be localized to one or two areas from where the shots were fired.

Base camp was cloaked in coastal fog when they arrived. The scene evoked the perfect visual for spooky woodland creatures, setting upon unprepared travelers. She hoisted one of the metal detectors from the back of the ATV and handed it to Elle.

"Do you remember approximately where we found Harris and Wallace?" Jackson reached for the second device.

"Yes, I think so."

Jackson switched on the detector for Elle.

"Just do slow sweeps until you get a positive signal."

"Where will you be?"

"There were a couple of shots at the trail head I need to look for." She had a momentary flashback of Nunez firing across her shoulder as she exited the tree line. Jackson fished a silver whistle on a long nylon string from her pocket and held it out to Elle. "And if you see any of your wolf pals, blow this. It'll scare them for sure, and I'll come running."

"Thank you." Elle hung the whistle around her neck with one hand.

Jackson headed down the rough path toward the beach. When she reached the tree line, she tried her best to retrace the path she'd taken. She found the tree splintered by Nunez's first shot and then walked toward the point of origin. The shell ended up being pretty easy to locate beneath a bit of leaf debris. There was one other shot fired a few yards away, the casing should be somewhere in the tall dry grass. She swept the plate sized sensor slowly in an arc as she walked. The device pinged and she knelt to search for the small metal casing.

She stowed both of them in her pocket and stood, facing the light breeze that brought fog in from the Pacific. It was as if she were standing in the midst of a cloud. The air was moist and heavy and smelled of seawater.

Jackson took a cleansing breath. This was the moment of calm before the storm. Re-entry would mean a military inquiry into what went down and what went wrong. She wondered how all of that would play out. She hadn't voiced any of those concerns to Elle yet. She wasn't sure Elle was even aware of what they'd be returning to. Dealing with Liam was only one part of what they'd face after splashdown.

The dark shape of a bird materialized in the fog and banked overhead.

Lucky bastard.

The past was a beautiful place.

Elle's search was successful. Her fingers were dirty from digging around to find the empty casings. This was a morbid task, but she was grateful that Jackson had remembered it. Her attention to detail was impressive. Elle hadn't even thought of it. A dozen casings clinked in the deep pocket of her cargo pants. She paused and looked skyward.

She just couldn't get enough of the trees in this place, in this time. Northern California was a land of endless rivers and mountains where the tallest trees in the world reigned over a forest of unparalleled diversity. A bioregion of rare plants, trees, and animals extended from where she stood, up over the Trinity Alps and into Oregon.

Elle longed to stay here—to explore and experience the wildness that once was everywhere and now was nearly nowhere.

She heard the rhythmic bellow of a frog and was reminded of something her grandmother had said. "When all the frogs were gone, we should have known." Elle had been only a child and hadn't understood, but now she did. She realized she never heard bullfrogs or treefrogs in the wild any longer and the world was worse off for the loss.

Footsteps caused her to turn. Jackson took long strides in her direction.

"Hey, listen." She caught Jackson's hand. "Listen for there."

"Wow, a frog."

"Isn't it amazing?"

They stood quietly, like wide-eyed children. They held hands and listened to the chorus of sounds around them—birds, frogs, and more birds. So many birds amid the vast, swaying canopy. Like a green sea of trees.

"We should probably get going." Jackson squeezed her hand lightly. "It'll be sundown in a couple of hours."

The fog made the hour seem later than it was. Elle definitely wanted to be back aboard ship before dark. That one close, personal encounter with the dire wolf had been enough to remind her of her lowly position on the food chain.

Elle savored the return trip.

She tilted her head back against the seat and strained to see the tops of the trees as Jackson wound around them. Elle was certain that on dark, noisy nights in San Francisco, she'd remember this drive and long for the solace of wild spaces.

CHAPTER TWENTY-NINE

Dinner was yet another freeze-dried culinary disaster. Elle was amazed that someone had gone to the trouble to give each meal a name, when in fact they all tasted exactly the same. A more accurate naming convention might have been brown mush with noodles and sauce. She could discern no taste difference between packets labeled marinara and packets labeled teriyaki. In fact, *brown mush* covered most of what they'd eaten except for breakfast which did bear some slight resemblance to oatmeal only in that it was a light brown.

Elle decided to shower after dinner. Jackson had taken one just before her. Elle pressed clumps of wet hair between a towel as she crossed barefoot to the galley. She'd thrown on a T-shirt and underwear and nothing else. Cohabiting in close quarters had created a level of comfort between them, a small bit of familiarity. But that still hadn't completely dislodged the hummingbirds in her stomach that sometimes swarmed when Jackson touched her.

Jackson was staring off into space. She held a small flask between her hands.

"You've been holding out on me."

"What?" Jackson blinked.

"Don't you know when to offer a girl a drink?"

"Oh, sorry." Jackson smiled and held the flask out to her.

Elle sat across from Jackson and took a few sips. The liquor was warm as it slid down. She handed the flask back.

"What were you thinking about just now?" Not that she necessarily thought Jackson would tell her, but she couldn't help asking. She suspected there was a lot that Jackson didn't share, although, she'd been slowly getting glimpses of what lay beneath the surface.

"I was trying to anticipate our return." Jackson sounded serious.

"What do you mean?" Elle suspected she meant more than just the return trip.

"When things go sideways like this, there's always a military inquiry into what went wrong." Jackson sipped from the flask. "I'm just trying to imagine how that will go."

"Won't we just tell the truth?"

"Yes, but then what?" Jackson offered her the flask and she took it.

"Are you worried that Liam will somehow be able to cover his involvement? Or that he'll counter our story in some way?"

"I don't know."

"You acted in self-defense. You saved my life." For the first time, Elle realized that this whole situation might have a very different outcome for Jackson. That thought scared her.

"Let's hope that's how the inquiry counsel sees it." Jackson smiled thinly.

They were silent for a moment.

"Have you thought about how you'll handle things when you see Liam?" asked Jackson.

Punching him in the face had a nice ring to it but wasn't really her style.

"I suppose I'll have to wait and see how much he reveals to me first." She wondered if he'd come clean or pretend he'd had no involvement in what had gone down. "It's hard to anticipate every possible scenario."

"Yeah." Jackson nodded.

It was late by the time they finished the small flask of whiskey and retired for the night. The last night of the expedition. The last night in the wilderness. The last night in deep time.

Elle slipped into the joined sleeping bags and snuggled next to Jackson as if this was how they slept all the time. A darkness had shadowed Jackson's eyes all night and she wanted more than anything to lift it. If they were going to return to the unknown, to likely separation during some official inquiry, then tonight they should relish the bed they shared.

She propped on one elbow and caressed Jackson's face, then she kissed her. Elle focused on distracting Jackson from dark places. She slid her leg on top of Jackson's. Jackson gripped her thigh, tugging Elle tightly against her body.

Elle stopped kissing Jackson. She raised up and swept her T-shirt off over her still-damp hair. She lowered herself, strategically placing her breasts within reach. Jackson had her hand inside Elle's underwear, her fingers pressed into Elle's ass, as Jackson explored her breasts with her mouth.

Jackson rotated their position. Before she settled on top of Elle, she removed her shirt too. The skin on skin contact was making Elle hot for more. Beneath Jackson, she wriggled out of her underwear, pushing them all the way off with her toes. Jackson did the same with her briefs.

Jackson was between her legs now, her rock-hard abs pressed against Elle's center. She rocked against Jackson as they kissed feverishly, as if starved for each other. Then, suddenly, Jackson pulled back. She braced above Elle, her biceps flexed, taut, as if she were about to launch herself and flee. Her expression made Elle's heart hurt. She slid her fingers tenderly up Jackson's arms until she reached her shoulders and then the back of her head. She tugged Jackson downward.

"It's okay, baby." She held Jackson's face in her hands. "It's okay to feel this way."

"Elle, I…" Jackson didn't finish. She regarded Elle with a soulful expression.

Elle kissed her softly on the cheek and then feathered light kisses all over her face before Jackson relaxed, sinking into her again. Jackson kissed her deeply as she caressed Elle's body. Jackson stroked her teasingly and then slipped inside. She arched against Jackson's hand.

Jackson thrust slowly as if she were savoring even the slightest contact between them. Her mouth was at Elle's neck, hot against her skin. Elle applied pressure with her hands against Jackson's ass as she rode Jackson's hand. Jackson was driving her crazy.

"Faster, you can go faster," she whispered against Jackson's cheek.

Jackson obliged. She was getting so close when Jackson slowed her movements again.

Jackson wanted to savor this time with Elle. She didn't want to rush their last night together. She searched Elle's face, Elle's gaze was intense. She hovered above her, knowing Elle wanted more. But so did she. She took Elle's hand and pressed it between her legs.

"Are you sure?" Elle asked, her eyes searched Jackson's face for confirmation.

"I'm sure." Jackson groaned when she felt Elle slip inside. She kissed Elle, savoring their connection. "I want to come with you."

She'd readjusted so that Elle's thigh was between hers and she began to once again thrust slowly and then faster. She rode Elle's hand and thigh as she focused on making Elle come. It was a complicated dance. She'd sense Elle crest and then lose focus on her own orgasm. She decided to focus on Elle. She used her thumb to tease Elle's clit as she thrust inside her.

"Yes, yes…Jackson…don't stop." Elle gripped Jackson's arm with her free hand.

She was rocking beneath Jackson, pushing her higher. Jackson climbed with Elle. She was lost now, they arched against each other, clinging to each other tightly. Jackson's orgasm coursed through her. She tensed and gasped for air as she tumbled with it. Beneath her, Elle's body was rigid and then limp. She collapsed on top of Elle, breathing hard.

"Elle, I've wanted you so badly…all day…every day." She was breathless. It was hard to form her thoughts into words.

"Yes, baby…me too." Her head rested on Elle's shoulder. Elle pressed her lips to Jackson's forehead.

Jackson relished the feel of Elle's body beneath hers. She possessively slid her hand up and down Elle's breast and over her ribs, down to her hip. She was nearly capsized by the realization that she needed Elle, she needed all of her. And not just in this moment, but for as long as she could have her. Emotion overwhelmed her, she swallowed it down. She shifted on top of Elle, caressed Elle's lower lip with her thumb before slipping it into Elle's mouth. She wanted to swallow Elle whole, until it was impossible to tell where she ended and where Elle began.

She covered Elle's mouth and kissed her.

Elle sensed a shift in intensity from Jackson. Her touch, her mouth, desire pulsed off her. Elle could feel it in her chest. Jackson's thumb had been in her mouth and then her tongue. Jackson slid down Elle's body, exploring with her mouth as she moved, until she was between

Elle's legs. Elle gripped the fabric on either side, in an attempt to hang on. Jackson was bringing her to the brink again. Just as she was about to come, Jackson rolled her onto her stomach and slipped inside her from behind. Jackson pressed her wet center against Elle's ass as she pumped inside her.

"Yes, yes…" The words came out raspy. Her face was against the bed.

She'd never experienced sex like this. She'd never had a lover who took control the way Jackson had. And despite the fact that Jackson could completely overpower her, she felt safe, cared for, and needed. Jackson needed her. Her heart soared.

Jackson was coming. She pressed hard against Elle, she stopped thrusting but kept her fingers deep inside. Against Elle she stiffened, trembled, and then sank on top of her. Elle had been so close, but she hadn't made it all the way to orgasm. She let Jackson rest for a moment, the rise and fall of her breathing firm against her back. Then she raised up from beneath her, rolling Jackson onto her back.

Elle took Jackson's fingers into her mouth and sucked them, then she slid them between her legs. She lowered her mouth to meet Jackson's.

"Is this okay?" She began to move on top of Jackson.

Jackson nodded, her eyes heavy-lidded with desire. She cupped Elle's breast with one hand while Elle rode the other, bracing her arms on Jackson's shoulders.

"You're so beautiful."

Jackson was mesmerized, watching Elle above her.

It only took a few minutes, rocking on top of her, for Elle to climax. Elle tightened around her fingers, threw her head back, and cried out. Jackson rose to meet her, cradled her with one arm, and pumped inside her until she begged Jackson to stop.

Together, they collapsed back onto the bed.

What just happened? Jackson's heart thumped in her chest as if it were trying to escape.

She was falling for this woman.

Who was she kidding, she'd already fallen. Was it mutual?

"What are you thinking?" Elle's question was soft, non-demanding, but it still made Jackson nervous.

"What if I told you I wasn't thinking anything?"

"I wouldn't believe you. I can feel you thinking." Elle caressed with her fingertips down the center of Jackson's chest.

Okay, time to show up. What did she have to lose by being honest? She stalled, kissing Elle's forehead as her head was on Jackson's shoulder.

"I haven't been with anyone the way I was just with you...in a long time." Jackson's arm was around Elle's shoulder. She made small circles with her finger against Elle's arm. "It felt really good to be with you." She paused, this was hard to explain. "To be with you completely."

"I've never been with anyone the way I've been with you." Elle nuzzled into Jackson's neck. "I feel like I can be myself with you. I'm not afraid to need you." She raised up on one elbow to look at Jackson. "I think you like to be needed."

"I do." She stroked Elle's cheek. "I like looking out for you."

"Promise me something."

"Anything." And she meant it.

"When we get back, promise me that we'll be together like this." Elle searched her face. "When all this is behind us and we can just be us again, promise me you'll come to me."

"Elle, I'm not letting you go, I promise."

Elle sank back onto Jackson's shoulder, and she held her close. She hoped she'd get the chance to keep that promise, more than Elle could possibly know.

CHAPTER THIRTY

Elle kissed Jackson one more time. A lingering kiss that almost felt like a good-bye kiss. This wasn't good-bye, she reminded herself. This was temporary separation.

"It's time."

Elle nodded. Jackson offered a hand to help her climb into the gravity bed. She knew that Jackson was right, but still, she wanted to linger. She'd tried to mimic Jackson's stoic attitude about the return trip, but she struggled to do so. When she thought of what had almost happened, when she thought about what Liam had tried to do to her, and Jackson, and even Ted—anger swelled inside.

Elle looked up at Jackson from her prone position in the gravity tube. Jackson reached across her and clipped the safety belts into place. This was it. Somehow, Elle was much more nervous for this return trip. She was more afraid to go back to the place she knew than she'd been to travel into the complete unknown. That was a depressing thought. The only bright spot in the looming future was that Jackson would be there when she arrived.

"You're going to be okay." Jackson braced her arms on the side of the tube's frame. Had Jackson read her thoughts? "We're going to be okay."

"I know." She didn't actually, but she didn't want to add to Jackson's stress.

"I'll see you on the other side."

She opened her mouth so that Jackson could place the mouthguard. Then Jackson lowered the glass hatch until Elle heard it click into the locked position.

She'd worried that there was no one to make sure Jackson was properly strapped in, but Jackson had assured her that she had five minutes to get into her tube once she initiated the ion drive. A five-minute window didn't seem like enough time and yet felt like an eternity as she waited for the vibration to begin to build beneath her. Shadowed movement was visible at the edge of her field of vision. She squeezed her eyes shut and ran her tongue over the mouthguard.

As before, the shuddering slowly increased until it became intense and then the pressure. Knowing what to expect didn't make anything easier. Then suddenly, she was suspended, having broken free from gravity, from time, from self—wisps, strands of light filtered into her vision.

Elle was confused. Was she asleep or awake?

How long had she been here? Had they arrived?

Dull sounds of pounding now, and maybe voices.

Jackson!

Where was Jackson?

Her vision cleared. Nikki's face was above hers. Hands worked at the straps that confined her. A wave of nausea threatened. She was going to be sick. Nikki managed to anticipate her need. A trashcan or something was right where she needed it, when she needed it.

"Take it easy." Nikki supported her as she leaned halfway out of the tube. "You're safe."

Elle flopped back to the bed. Her eyes couldn't seem to adjust to the light.

"Where's…where is Jackson?" The look on Nikki's face frightened her. She gripped Nikki's arm. "What's wrong?"

Elle caught a glimpse of Jackson being carried on a stretcher, there was blood on her face and shoulder.

"It was just a rough ride, that's all. She'll be okay."

"Damn her. She told me she could handle everything by herself." Elle tried to get to her feet and almost toppled. Nikki caught her.

"Yeah, that sounds about right. Hey, take a minute to get your land legs back and we'll meet her in the infirmary."

Panic climbed from her chest and lodged in her throat, closing her airway. Jackson was hurt and she couldn't stand the thought of not being with her.

The deck pitched beneath her feet. Oh right, they'd made a water landing. She and Nikki exchanged a knowing look. Her brain was coming back online. Nikki handed her a bottle of water and she took big gulps.

"Slow down." Nikki took the bottle from her. "Hey, Elle, look at me."

Elle swallowed.

"Remember what I said about Jackson?" Nikki paused. "She knows what she's doing."

She had to believe Nikki was right. The fact that Nikki was here meant that Jackson's coded message had gotten through.

"What's the status of the ship?" Elle braced against the open grav tube as the floor tipped again.

"Don't worry, we won't sink. The ship automatically purged the water tanks and then took on air to keep it afloat until the extraction team arrived." Nikki held her arm as they walked toward the cargo compartment. "We'll go up through the roof hatch. There's a navy ship waiting."

Optimism returned. So far, Jackson's plan had worked. But she was anxious to see Jackson and know that she was okay. Nikki shadowed her up the ladder and then helped her navigate the narrow passageways once they were aboard ship. The infirmary was below deck. Elle was feeling claustrophobic and a little seasick, but she tried her best to beat it back. She was frantic with worry by the time she finally reached Jackson. Nikki draped a blanket around Elle's shoulders as she took a seat near the bed.

"Thank you."

Elle took Jackson's limp hand and held on to it.

A medic opened each of Jackson's eyes and examined her pupils with a small light. Then he began to explore the gash at her temple, just inside her hairline. He was still attempting to clean the wound when Jackson began to stir. She jerked awake and tried to sit up. The medic had to press her shoulders against the bed to keep her from rolling off. She blinked, realizing where she was. Then reached to touch her head. She seemed to slowly realize Elle was holding her other hand. Elle stood up so that Jackson could see her without raising her head.

"Hey, you're back, you're okay." The blow to her head, combined with the passage through the gateway had to be disorienting.

"How's the ship?"

"Everything went according to plan." Elle didn't want to say anything specific.

"Yeah, nice soft water landing there, Cap." Nikki stood at the foot of the bed.

Jackson was still wearing the gravity suit and boots. The medic had unzipped it to examine the blood on her shoulder, but all if it seemed to be coming from the gash on her head.

"The team will get all the gear and the samples unloaded and get you guys back to base. You just rest easy, okay?" Nikki put her hand on Jackson's leg, just above her boot.

"We lost Wallace." Jackson focused on Nikki.

"I know." Nikki's gaze was direct. "I also know you did everything you could to ensure the safety of the team."

Jackson winced as the medic dressed the wound.

"Stay with Elle." Jackson was talking to Nikki as if Elle wasn't there.

"I'm okay, Jackson."

"Just stay close to Nikki. Will you do that for me?"

"Thank goodness you're all right." Out of nowhere, Liam appeared in the doorway.

Elle wanted to launch into him right away. Jackson squeezed her hand, a reminder to wait for the right moment. As far as Liam was concerned, his plan had still worked, although, with a different crew than he'd had in mind. The samples were back, and if he played dumb he could still pull this off. At least that's what Elle assumed he was thinking. He was in for a rude surprise the moment he tested the water inside the containers they'd brought back and discovered they contained nothing.

"When I heard about Ted, I was concerned."

I'll bet you were. Concerned for your own agenda. Elle was afraid to say very much. She'd never been very good at subterfuge. She would have made a terrible spy.

"I'm fine. You didn't have to make the trip." She was sure he could tell she was pissed.

Despite the fact that she tried to sound neutral.

"I'll go make sure the samples are secure for the ride back to the BIOME lab." He turned to leave, but then looked back. "You've done a great job here, Elle."

She knew he didn't mean it, and she couldn't wait for him to get the results back on those samples.

"I'll check in later." It almost sounded like a threat, but she was sure Liam didn't notice.

"Take your time." Then he was gone.

Nikki gave her a *what's going on* look. She shook her head. A signal that she'd fill Nikki in later. Once she was sure that Jackson was back on her feet.

"Commander, you need to let someone know if you begin to feel dizzy or lightheaded. Or if you begin to have any problems with your vision." The medic removed his gloves and tossed them into a waste bin. "That was a nasty bump, but I don't think you'll need stitches."

"Thank you." Jackson's words were raspy.

"Can we get her some water?" Elle asked.

The medic helped her sip from a straw. She coughed and took a few more sips before sinking back to the pillow. She looked at Elle.

"Hey, I'm okay here. You should go...get some rest...I'll come find you."

"Are you serious?" Elle stood up. "I'm not leaving here without you. And by the way, we're on a boat. So, we're all going together."

"I guess you two have a lot to fill me in on." Nikki crossed her arms and looked from one to the other, smiling.

"Yeah, one mission together and she thinks she can boss me around." Jackson quirked an eyebrow and then winced because it hurt.

"Sarcasm doesn't pay does it?" Elle couldn't help smiling.

Chapter Thirty-one

The Navy vessel docked at a military port in San Francisco, and then the crew and samples were shuttled north to the base via helicopter. Time travel, boat travel, air travel—when they reached the base, Elle was certain she never wanted to travel again. The experience of traversing the gateway left her exhausted and woozy. And that was *without* a head injury.

Jackson wanted to jump right into things with Major Riley, but Elle had intervened. Nikki had been there to back her up. Together they convinced Jackson to take a night off. The shit would inevitably hit the fan the minute the samples were tested. Elle tried her best to anticipate how Liam would react and she honestly couldn't.

Elle wanted to leave the base. She wanted to eat normal food, wear normal clothes, hell, she even missed the bad coffee from the breakroom at BIOME.

Oh yeah, then she remembered, she could never go back there again. There was no way she could work for Liam, and she was pretty sure he'd never give up his post as the director. That was a depressing thought.

"I'm going to go get some clean clothes and then I'll come back." She and Nikki had escorted Jackson to her quarters to make sure she was okay.

"Stay…and as soon as Nikki is back she can go with you." Jackson was reclined on the bed, resting, but trying not to sleep until Nikki returned with some food. "It's not every day I can talk Nikki into providing room service."

"If I don't go now then I'm going to be sleeping in these clothes." Weariness was making it hard for her to think. "I'll be back before Nikki."

Elle dipped down and kissed Jackson before leaving. She had to think for a moment about how to get back to her room from Jackson's. Oh yes, head toward the mess hall and then turn left. She was thrilled to see the clothes she'd arrived in laundered and folded at the foot of her bunk. She'd never been so happy to see a pair of pants in her life.

The dorm rooms on this side, the non-military side of the base, seemed very quiet. As she thought back she realized, Harris, Nunez, and Ted had been the only others besides herself assigned to this wing. The entire area was a little too dark, with only the lights in the corridor illuminated. The tiny hairs on the back of her neck began to tingle and she wished now that she'd waited for Nikki. This was silly, she was inside a high security facility. What was there to be afraid of? She was being ridiculous. She shook her head.

When she looked up, Liam was blocking the doorway. He was uncharacteristically casual, which was odd. She'd never seen him not wearing a suit and here he was wearing a gray T-shirt under a dark windbreaker with faded jeans. If she'd passed him in the street she might not have recognized him. This was yet another new perspective on the man she thought she knew.

"Liam." She said his name, but there was no one else around to hear it.

"Funny thing about those containers." He scraped a shred of loose paint off the door-frame with his fingernail without looking at her. "They're empty."

"What are you talking about?" Yes, she was in a high security facility and she'd forgotten for a moment to be afraid of her own damn team.

"I worked really hard to get the funding for that expedition approved. I staked my reputation, my life, on the success of that expedition only to discover that for all my effort I've got fifteen gallons of tap water to show for it." He took a step into the room and she took a step back.

"There must be a mistake." She was stalling. She really wasn't ready to have this discussion with him and she certainly didn't want to have it alone.

"You could have had part of this."

"Really? Because that's not the story I heard from Ted." She was too exhausted to play dumb, and besides, he was pissing her off.

He moved toward her. She clutched the clean clothing to her chest as if it were a shield and took another step away from him. The room was small. Soon there would be nowhere to go unless she could get past Liam and out the door.

"Ted was weak, obviously. It was you I wanted to partner with all along." He rubbed the back of his neck. She didn't believe him.

"Except I'd have never agreed to shoot another member of the team." She hesitated. "For what? Just for money?"

"I underestimated you, Elle." He was talking to her but looking at the floor. His voice sounded strained, angry. "You could have been part of something really big, but now you've ruined everything."

"Actually, I'm pretty sure I've only ruined you." It was hard to temper the fury and resentment rising in her chest. "I might just have saved the world for everyone else."

He glared at her. The muscle along his jaw tightened.

"I think my work here is done." She was finished with this conversation and she was too tired to allow herself to be bullied. "Now, if you'll excuse me."

He lurched in front of her, blocking the door with his outstretched arm.

"You know, I've spent my whole life trying to save the world." He braced his shoulder against the doorframe and crossed his arms. "I thought science could make a difference, I thought people really wanted what we had to offer…a better world, a healthier world."

"Liam—"

"Governments only care about short-term gains. No one wants to truly change things. We're witnesses to our own extinction and no one even gives a shit." He advanced on her again. "And you know what? I don't care anymore either." He pointed something at her. In the dimly lit room she realized it was a small handgun. "You, Dr. Eliza Graham, have ruined everything."

"Liam, calm down. I don't really understand what you're talking about." He was scaring her now and she backed away from him.

"Where are the real samples?"

"What?"

"Your research was conclusive. There's no way you returned without the specimens you went back to collect." He rubbed the sidearm against his temple as if the weapon might help him think.

She reminded herself that he didn't know the *real* samples were already in the ocean. He was assuming she still had them in her possession somehow.

"Liam, I know you're upset—"

"How stupid do you think I am?" He invaded her personal space.

"I don't think you're stupid, Liam. Please put the gun down."

"Where are they? Where are the samples? There is no way in hell you didn't find what you were looking for. I know you, Elle. You're never wrong. And if you think you can keep them from me, you're sadly mistaken." He grabbed her, pressing the gun to her jaw. She squeezed her eyes shut. "I can do this with you or without you. Your choice."

"It's too late." Her words sounded small and far away as if she were lost somewhere.

"What do you mean, it's too late?"

"You'll never get the samples." She opened her eyes. "You're right, I did what I set out to do."

He uttered something that sounded like a growl. He grabbed her hair and yanked her head back. The nose of the gun pressed painfully into her skin. If he was going to shoot her, if this was it, then she wanted him to know that he hadn't won. This time, the good guys won.

"Drop the gun."

She opened her eyes to see Jackson with a pistol trained on Liam. Nikki was with her. Nikki swiftly moved to flank him.

"There's nowhere to go, Liam. Put the gun down." Jackson stepped closer. "It's over...Let her go."

Liam stiffened, no doubt considering his options. Elle used that tiny moment of opportunity to twist out of his grasp and quickly moved behind Jackson.

"Easy." Nikki stepped closer, with her sidearm trained on Liam. "Put down your weapon."

Liam lowered the gun, almost in slow motion.

Elle realized she'd had a death grip on her folded clothes. When she relaxed her arms, she discovered her hands were shaking. Liam was facedown on the floor now, with his hands behind his head. Nikki radioed for a security team, and within seconds they descended. The room was a flurry of activity.

"Come on, they can get your statement later." Jackson ushered Elle away from the scene, back in the direction of her quarters.

Once they were in Jackson's room, Elle sank to the edge of the bed with her face in her hands. She was spent.

"How did you know to come after me?"

"A hunch." Jackson touched her shoulder. "I shouldn't have let you go alone in the first place."

"I can't get my mind around what just happened."

"He's not the person you thought he was." Jackson sounded sympathetic. "That's a hard thing to discover."

Liam, the Liam she thought she'd known, was dead—or never existed. She hadn't experienced betrayal like this before and she wasn't sure how to deal with it. Was she a terrible judge of character? How had she been so blind?

"I suppose on some level, I didn't completely believe Ted. Although, at the same time, why would he have lied."

"Listen, this was going to come to a head one way or another. At least this way, Liam tipped his hand and he's now in custody." Jackson knelt in front of her, invading her line of sight. "This is good for us."

"Is it?" Elle hoped so.

"Yes." Jackson stood and extended her hand to Elle. "Take a shower and wash this day away." She kissed Elle. "And then come to bed because I'm not leaving your side for the rest of the night."

"Promise?"

"I promise."

"How does your head feel?" She touched Jackson's face on the side with the bandage.

"Oh, I'd forgotten it already." Jackson placed her fingers over Elle's.

Jackson stood in the center of the room as she walked to the shower. "I'll be waiting for you."

The hot shower was just what she needed. No five-minute limit and the steam cleared her lungs and hydrated her skin. She toweled off and walked barefoot into the dark room. The light from the bathroom cast a rectangular highlight onto the concrete floor, cool beneath her feet. It was easy to lose the time of day in this underground bunker, in a room with no windows. She suspected it was still early evening, but her body considered it well past midnight.

She dropped the towel and slid under the covers next to Jackson. At first, she thought Jackson might already be asleep, but she wasn't. Jackson drew Elle's head to her shoulder and hugged her against her body. Jackson wasn't wearing any clothes either. The warmth, the firmness of her body against Elle's was soothing and exhilarating at the same time. She felt safe in Jackson's arms. She had the sensation that nothing could harm her as long as she was with Jackson.

"I'm sorry my hair is still damp."

"I don't mind." Jackson's fingers brushed across her hip.

"You saved me again today."

The sound of Elle's voice was like a caress, gentle and comforting. Jackson had been thinking a lot about who had saved whom and she wasn't sure Elle was right. When she'd first met Elle, she'd been adrift. She'd been lonely and forlorn and searching—she didn't even know for what. Elle had plucked her from the depths of hopelessness. And when Elle was in her arms she felt renewed, practically optimistic. Her heart was full, and keeping it contained was like trying to hold back the tide.

"Elle, I need to tell you something."

"Yes?"

Jackson was quiet, gathering her thoughts.

"You've changed me...or I should say, meeting you has inspired me to change." Jackson hesitated, not exactly sure how to say what she wanted to say. "When I lost Camille, I was certain I'd lost everything. I couldn't find my way back. Sure, I was going through the motions of living, barely, but I wasn't really living." Her voice cracked. She swallowed and pressed on. "I didn't know how much I needed you and I know, initially, I even tried to push you away."

"Jackson, you don't have to explain yourself—"

"But I do." Jackson propped up on one elbow so that she could see Elle's face. "Elle, *you* actually saved me. *You* came to my rescue."

"Thank you for saying that, but I'm pretty sure we rescued each other." Elle caressed Jackson's face. "And I want you to know that you don't have to forget Camille, or be afraid to talk about her. She was a big part of your life that you should always remember with fondness."

"Thank you." Jackson sank on top of Elle, sliding her thigh between Elle's as she shifted her position. "Thank you, from the deepest part of my heart."

She kissed Elle, deeply, unhurriedly, hoping that Elle could feel what she was feeling through the intimate exchange.

"There's something I need to say to you too." Elle spoke softly against Jackson's mouth.

Jackson pulled back, giving Elle her full attention.

"I'm in love with you, Captain Jackson Drake." Elle smiled. "Utterly and completely."

Jackson's heart drummed loudly in her chest. She let Elle's words wash over her.

"I'm in love with you too, Dr. Eliza Graham." She smiled and then kissed Elle.

"I'm so glad." Elle adjusted so that Jackson was firmly between her legs. "Because that whole *being friends* thing just wasn't going to work for me. I have no idea why I suggested it in the first place."

Jackson laughed. She feathered kisses down Elle's neck, until Elle began to squirm beneath her.

"Please make love to me," whispered Elle. "Make me forget everything about this day, except you."

Jackson caressed Elle with tender devotion, as if Elle was the most precious thing on Earth. And in truth, as far as Jackson was concerned, she was.

CHAPTER THIRTY-TWO

In the days that followed, Elle learned that a military court of inquiry was not a judicial tribunal. It was instituted solely for the purpose of investigation, to assist the commanding officer, in this case, Major Riley, in determining whether or not any further proceeding, executive or judicial, should be pursued. The proceedings determined that Jackson's swift and clear actions had salvaged the prime directive of the mission. Despite the loss of life, the mission objective had been achieved, thanks to the alternative plan Jackson and Elle had devised. Liam's role in undermining the objective was still under investigation but, given his assault against Elle, he had been arrested and was awaiting trial.

Jackson offered to drive Elle to the BIOME lab to gather some small personal items and a few notebooks she didn't want to lose track of. Her old office seemed surreal to her now. The ice cores contained the dead remnants of a world she'd actually had the chance to experience. It would be hard to go back to her life as it existed before the jump. She made a sweep through her office, grabbing a sweater she'd forgotten, her favorite coffee mug, some photos, a rubber T-rex—the important things. She placed everything in a small box she'd taken from the recycling bin.

She started down the hall but lingered at the door to Ted's office. The images of Ted's final moments on the beach were slowly being overwritten by all that they had shared before that day. She didn't want to remember him from that one flawed action. They'd been collaborators until that fateful hour, and she'd never have pinpointed the exact date without his data to cross-reference against hers. So, she rationalized, in the end, Ted had contributed to the solution. He just got trapped and couldn't find a way out.

It would take some time to know for sure if the reintroduced phytoplankton would reset ocean acidity and oxygen levels. The tiny plankton would need weeks to colonize their new habitat.

She left her key card with security on her way out. She smiled when she saw Jackson leaning against a sedan with the Space Force insignia on the door. Damn, she looked good. Jackson made a simple oxford shirt look sexy. Jackson straightened and met Elle halfway across the courtyard.

It was hard to be back where the sky was gray with smog and the sound of birds were almost nonexistent.

"Here, let me help you with that." Jackson took the cardboard box from her as they walked toward the car.

"Thanks."

The sun was low, casting long shadows across the concrete quad in front of the BIOME Institute.

"So, how'd it go in there?" Jackson opened the trunk and settled the box inside.

"Well, I just quit my job."

"What a relief." Jackson closed the trunk. "I heard your boss was a real asshole."

"Yeah, the worst."

Jackson opened the passenger door.

"Well, Dr. Graham, now what?" Jackson leaned against the doorframe, waiting for Elle to get in. "What does the woman who just saved the world do for an encore?"

"Take her girlfriend out for Thai food?" Elle grinned up at Jackson as she settled onto the passenger seat.

"Girlfriend, huh?"

"And don't forget it."

Jackson laughed.

"Listen, are you sure you're okay?" Jackson was still standing in the open door.

"I'm fine...truly, I am." Elle nodded. "I'm ready for my next adventure."

Jackson watched Elle through the windshield as she rounded the front of the car and then sank into the driver's seat. She waited for Elle to click her seat belt into place. Every time she looked at Elle her heart soared. How was it possible that one human could make another human feel so good?

The BIOME building was just north of the city. She merged into heavy traffic, heading south toward the Golden Gate Bridge.

"What if, instead of going out for dinner, we ate in?" Jackson gave Elle a sideways glance.

"Sure. I could cook something."

"I was thinking I'd cook for you."

"You cook?" Elle's question was playful. "A commander and a chef. How lucky am I?"

"Don't get too excited…I was just thinking something simple, like pasta with sauce."

Elle's phone buzzed before she could respond. She fished in her bag for it.

"Sorry, do you mind if I get this?" Elle held the phone up before answering.

"Sure, go ahead."

Jackson relaxed in the seat as the AI driver took control of the car. She scrolled through messages on her phone while Elle talked.

"Hello." Elle listened. "Yes, thank you for calling, Major Riley." She looked over at Jackson. "I'd be happy to discuss this further." Another pause. "Tomorrow at ten would be perfect."

Elle was nodding and smiling.

"Yes, and thank you again. I'll see you tomorrow." Elle clicked off. She had a contagious, gleeful expression when she turned to Jackson.

"Well?" Jackson prodded. "What was that all about?"

"It seems there's an opening for a lead scientist in the SLST program."

"Elle, that's terrific." Jackson reached for her hand. "They'd be crazy not to recruit you."

"I admit, unemployment wasn't where I saw myself at this point in my career, you know, having just saved the world and all that."

Jackson laughed.

"And she's so humble, too." She squeezed Elle's hand.

"A girl has to work with what she's got."

Traffic converged to squeeze a sea of cars onto the two southbound lanes of the bridge. The top of the red-orange struts stretched upward into the grayness of the sky. She was looking ahead at the traffic and the outline of the smog shrouded city when the steering wheel jerked. The car made a hard right onto the access road just before the bridge.

"Why are we turning?"

"I'm not sure." Jackson grabbed the wheel and attempted to switch the car back to manual driving mode. "The system has locked me out."

"What?" There was understandable concern in Elle's question.

"What the fuck? Something is jamming the signal." The car picked up speed and banked right up the steep grade. Jackson checked the mirror; they were being followed by a dark SUV with tinted windows.

"Jackson, what's going on?" Elle rotated in her seat. She'd noticed the SUV also.

Jackson hit the door lock, but it wouldn't engage.

The brakes locked, and she lurched forward against the seat belt as the car came to a hard stop. Doors opened and four men got out of the vehicle behind them and approached the car. Jackson was unarmed but got out and faced the approaching strangers. Her heart pounded. She clenched and unclenched her fists.

"Get back in the car." One of the men spoke to her.

She quickly cataloged the men as they approached. Two had semi-automatic rifles; the other two wore sidearms clipped on their belts. They were dressed in all black and wore masks over the lower part of their faces.

"What the fuck is going on?" One of the men opened the passenger door and reached for Elle. "Hey! Take your hands off her."

Elle struggled with the man as he yanked her from the car. Jackson took a step toward them, prepared to come to Elle's defense, but she was met with immediate resistance. Two of the guys grabbed her by the arms and dragged her back toward the driver's side door. She wrestled, broke free, and landed a punch. But that only incited aggressive retaliation from her captors. A hard blow to her ribs and she was on the ground. A boot to her stomach knocked the air from her lungs. She fought to get up, fought to get a glimpse of Elle. Where was she?

"Jackson!" Elle screamed her name. "Stop! You're hurting her!"

Hearing Elle's voice caused a surge of adrenaline. Jackson grabbed the foot of the nearest man and rolled, taking him with her and toppling him to the ground. But the advantage was short-lived. The second guy pressed a knee to her chest and struck her with the butt of his gun. Her head banged against the hard surface of the road, her vision dimmed, and then she had the sensation of being dragged before darkness overwhelmed her system.

"What are you doing? What do you want?" Elle squirmed, but the men were too strong. They wouldn't answer her and they wouldn't release her.

She struggled to see Jackson who'd fallen to the ground behind the driver's side door. She caught a glimpse of Jackson being hoisted into the car. One of the men reached inside the car and then slammed the door. Why wasn't Jackson moving? Why didn't she get out of the car?

"Stop! Let me go!" Elle kicked at the shins of her captor. Her blows were insignificant. He ignored her and shoved her onto the back seat.

She was terrified.

Through the windshield she could see the other two men pushing the car toward the steep drop-off. It kept rolling as if in slow motion as the two men turned to walk toward the SUV.

"No! Please, don't do this!" Elle was frantic. She tried to free herself, but the two men got into the car, one on either side. They were huge and immovable.

She watched the taillights of the car disappear over the crest of the cliff. The two men walked back to the SUV and got in. Elle was afraid she was going to be sick. Then nausea was replaced by rage. She started beating the beefy shoulder of the man next to her with her fists.

"Hold her still." The man in the passenger seat rotated. He had something in his hand.

Her arms were pinned, and the second man pressed her legs to the seat as the guy reached over the console from the front seat with a syringe. The needle stung and then warmth spread from the point of entry in her thigh. Dizziness swarmed, her tongue was thick, her mouth dry, she tried to speak, but no words came. Her body sagged against the seat. She was at the mercy of these men. Her last thought as consciousness fled, was of Jackson.

CHAPTER THIRTY-THREE

Jackson had the sensation of floating, of swimming. She shivered and blinked. Her head ached, her ribs ached, and it took her a moment to realize that her legs were in water. She jolted up but banged her head on the steering wheel. The car was upside down and partially submerged.

She had no memory of how she'd ended up here, or even where here was. The last thing she remembered was the scuffle on the road and two guys grabbing Elle. *Elle!*

Jackson slid on her stomach along the roof of the car, squeezing past the headrests of the two front seats. The rear of the car was dry. Her duffel was still there. Where was her phone? She frantically searched. Miraculously, it had landed in a dry spot. She found it wedged in the narrow space between the back seat and the door. She searched through recent numbers. Her fingers were shaking so badly that she had a difficult time hitting the call button.

"Nikki." Her throat was so dry that speaking caused a coughing fit.

"Jackson?"

"Nikki, I need your help." Jackson tried to calm down. Panic wasn't going to help anyone. "Some guys grabbed Elle."

"What?"

"Our car was forced off onto the service road just before the bridge." Jackson tried to check her position. "I think I'm at the shore, somewhere near the foot of the bridge. I can hear traffic."

"I'm on my way."

"Bring the tracker. I still have my PTD and so does Elle." Thank God for small favors.

Jackson clicked off and stowed the phone in her pocket. She checked the doors. The roof of the vehicle was against the ground making it impossible to open the doors. The doorframes were probably bent from the inverted weight of the car. She crawled back to the waterlogged front seat and opened the console in the dash. Various items spilled out, splashing into the murky water. She felt around until she found what she was looking for. A hammer with a sharp point meant for just this purpose—breaking a window in the off chance your car became submerged in water.

Within minutes, Jackson crawled out the rear side window, careful to avoid the confetti of glass on the ground. She crawled to a spot on the dry grass, dragging the duffel behind her. She searched in the bag for an inhaler and took two hits. Her lungs felt instantly soothed. Too much unprotected time in the open made her lungs ache. She squinted at the sky trying to decipher the time of day.

Hang on, Elle. We're coming.

Elle woke with a jolt.

She was lying on her side on a thin cot in a dimly lit room. There were no windows, but there was a metal door in one wall with a small rectangular opening rather than a window. She sat up, swinging her feet to the floor. The sudden repositioning made her head swim. She pressed her fingers to her temple. A low wattage light came on overhead. She blinked into the glare.

The door opened and a man in a suit walked in. He dragged a chair from across the room and placed it a few feet away. He took a seat, facing Elle.

He looked more like a banker than a gangster. His fine clothing seemed an odd contrast to the dinginess of the room. His gaze was intense and made her skin crawl. His jacket was dark and so was the dress shirt and tie underneath, making it hard to tell where one ended and the other began. He was probably Liam's age, with close-cropped gray hair.

She waited for him to speak.

"We have a problem, Dr. Graham."

She didn't respond.

"You see, we've leveraged ourselves against the future sale of phytoplankton." He paused. "And now, it seems, we're empty-handed."

Still, she said nothing.

"You're going to explain to me what happened."

"What do you mean?"

"I find it impossible to believe that you came back with nothing." He dusted some tiny bit of fuzz from the sleeve of his suit jacket. "I think…no, I know, that you're a very smart woman. And when you found out what was happening, you found an alternative way to transport samples."

"You're mistaken, we—"

"No one is coming to save you, Dr. Graham." His eyes were shadowed. "I'm your best hope of survival here. You help me and I help you."

These people had to be the *they* that Ted had alluded to. Ted, Harris, and Nunez were all dead. And if Jackson hadn't surprised Harris and then overtaken Nunez, Elle would be dead too. In desperation, Liam had been willing to shoot her. Now she had some idea why. Liam wasn't pulling the strings, he was simply the front man. There was no way this guy was her savior. He was right. She was smart. Too smart to fall for these lies.

"Where are we?"

"This is how things work." He paused, his voice unnervingly calm. "You tell me something and then I tell you something. That's how we're going to play this game."

His patronizing tone fanned her anger.

"Your men drugged me and brought me here against my will." An image of Jackson being hoisted into the car flashed through her mind threatening to upend her. She needed to stay focused and remain calm. "Why would I trust you?"

"You have no other choice." He didn't apologize or make excuses for his methods.

He stood and slid the chair closer, then sat down.

"Now, let's begin again."

The door opened and a creepy looking man walked into the room carrying a small case under his arm. He was wearing gray slacks and a white oxford shirt buttoned all the way to the top, but without a tie. He wore dark framed glasses and had short, unruly brown hair. His back was toward them. He unzipped the case and let it fall open on the narrow table against the far wall. Then he turned to face them. His hands were casually clasped in front. He seemed to be waiting for further instruction. This was quickly turning into a scene from a horror movie.

"You will tell us everything, Dr. Graham." He motioned toward the other man. "Or my associate will force you to tell us everything. We'll let you choose."

A cold chill ran up her spine and tears threatened her precarious composure.

The anguish of not knowing what had happened to Jackson further threatened to capsize her fragile state. She'd somehow wrongly, naively imagined that bad things only happened to bad people. But it seemed that there was no guarantee from the universe of the existence of some moral order to the world. It seemed now the world was indifferent to individual destiny. The good were swept along with the evil, both hurtling toward the inevitable demise of the planet.

What did it matter now if she told him the truth, or not? She assumed she was dead either way. Jackson was probably dead already too. A world without Jackson was a world she had no interest in continuing to inhabit.

CHAPTER THIRTY-FOUR

Jackson climbed the embankment to the edge of the service road to wait for Nikki. There was nothing she could do except wait and the waiting was making her crazy.

If anything happened to Elle she knew she wouldn't survive it. Meeting Elle had been like looking through a window and getting a glimpse of a better world. Everything looked different since they'd made their return jump. Everything felt different with Elle. She wasn't ready to let that go.

She saw the car approach and paced at the side of the road.

Nikki pulled to a stop and opened the door.

"Don't get out." Jackson held up her hand and rounded the SUV to the passenger side. "You drive. I'll read the tracker."

Nikki handed her the device when she got in.

"Jackson, you look like hell. Are you sure you don't need a medic?" Nikki reached in the back and then offered Jackson a small towel.

"What's that for?"

"Your head." Nikki motioned with the towel.

Jackson touched the place where the bandage had been. It was long gone and the cut had reopened. Her fingers were red when she looked at them. She accepted the towel and pressed it to her temple.

"I don't need a medic. Just go, just go now."

Nikki did a three-point turn and drove back the way she'd come.

The tracking device rebooted and Jackson set it to search for Elle's signal. Her heart beat painfully fast until a flashing blue dot appeared on the GPS screen. Finally, a fucking break.

"South, go south." She pointed and Nikki turned right and hit the gas.

"Liam is dead."

"What?" Jackson wasn't sure she'd heard correctly.

"Liam is dead." Nikki glanced over. "He was being transferred to await a hearing. There was an ambush. Liam and the two guards with him were gunned down."

"Fuck." Jackson's mind raced. "Liam's dead and someone kidnapped Elle. There's got to be a connection. I just don't know what it is yet."

"It makes sense."

"What do you mean?" Jackson's eyes had been glued to the tracking screen. "Turn left here."

"There was no way Liam was the only one in on this, right? There was just no way."

"Yeah." She felt stupid. How had she let this happen? How the fuck had this happened?

"We'll get her back, Jackson."

Jackson nodded, but doubt and worry crowded her mind.

"Jackson, look at me." Nikki grabbed her arm. "We're going to get her back."

"Did you call this in?" Jackson wasn't waiting on backup, but it would be nice to know if it was on the way.

"Yeah, I called it in right after I spoke to you."

"Good."

❖

Twenty heart-pounding minutes later, Nikki slowed and parked in an alley. They were close. Elle was somewhere nearby in one of these abandoned factory buildings. Water was halfway up the tires when they parked. Jackson's pants were still wet from earlier. She sloshed from the SUV to the back side of the nearest concrete building. This had once been an industrial park and was now being slowly reclaimed by the sea. A couple of the structures were on a slight rise so they were practically an island, surrounded by shallow tidal seep.

Jackson checked the magazine and jammed it back in. She'd put an extra full clip in her pocket. She adjusted the straps of the Kevlar vest over her damp T-shirt and then switched the tracking device to silent mode. Nikki was at her shoulder.

"It looks like she's in that one." Jackson motioned toward one of the two structures not standing in water.

She eased to the corner of the building and surveyed the empty street. The air quality was crap down here. This wasn't going to work. She'd be coughing her head off and give their position away. As if reading her thoughts, Nikki trotted back to the vehicle and returned with masks with side mounted re-breathers.

"Thanks."

"I've got your back."

Jackson paused before slipping on the headgear and looked at Nikki.

"Thank you."

"Hey, you'd do the same for me." Nikki touched her shoulder.

Jackson nodded. She was too choked up to speak. The stakes were too high.

"Listen, this is what we do. We've got this." Nikki slid the visor down over her face.

Jackson appreciated the pep talk. That was usually her job. And maybe this time she was the one who needed it.

Using hand signals to communicate, they silently and methodically worked their way through random rubble along the broken pavement until they reached the entrance to the building. Only when they got close did Jackson spot the SUV that had taken Elle. It was parked on the first floor of the building. Someone had driven it right through a huge opening where a wall must have once existed. There was no one on this first floor, but that didn't mean they wouldn't run into resistance once they entered the building.

Jackson took a moment to settle. She closed her eyes and took a deep, slow breath.

She needed to focus. And she needed to tamp down her anger. She needed to be cool and tactical. Elle needed her and she wasn't about to let her down.

Nikki signaled toward a dark stairwell ahead and to the right. Jackson nodded.

Showtime.

They descended cautiously into the belly of the beast.

CHAPTER THIRTY-FIVE

The drugs were kicking in. They had tied Elle to the chair to keep her from sliding out of it. She'd been stalling, hoping for a miracle. The thin man had given her sodium thiopental. The drug slowed the speed at which her body was sending messages from her spinal cord to her brain. As a result, it was going to become more difficult to perform high-functioning tasks, the concentration needed to think up a plausible lie, for example.

She had the sense that she was somewhere between consciousness and nodding off.

The man who'd first come to the room clapped his hands loudly.

"Wake up, Dr. Graham." He sat in a chair facing her.

"Please let me go."

"Tell me what I want to know first." He tipped her head back with a finger under her chin. "Where are the samples you harvested?"

"In the ocean."

"I know they came from the ocean. Where are they now?" He slapped her, jolting her back to the moment. "Stay with me! There's no way you would go through everything you went through to come back empty-handed. Where are they?"

"We put them back in the ocean."

"You gave her too much. She's not making any sense." He was angry with the thin man.

There was a loud pop, and then a second and third in rapid succession. Elle squinted beneath the bright, overhead light. Her head was pounding. She wiggled her fingers which had fallen asleep. The ropes were stinging her wrists.

"What the fuck is going on?" The angry man stood up, knocking his chair over.

Someone else was in the room now. Another loud blast. Was that gunfire?

Jackson got a glimpse of Elle through the narrow opening in the door. She plowed into the room in a rush, Nikki was right behind her. They surprised the two men, one of whom lunged at her. He reached inside his jacket for a weapon, but she was on him before he was able to take aim. She committed all her weight into charging him. She caught him in the gut with her shoulder and they both went down. His sidearm slid across the floor and under the bed. She straddled him and struck him twice with her pistol. He didn't move.

Behind her, Nikki had pinned the second man to the floor. She was on a radio now. The cavalry had arrived and was following the trail of bodies to their location. She and Nikki had taken out the four guys who'd forced her off the road.

Jackson registered everything despite her focus on Elle. Jackson rushed to her. She brushed Elle's hair away from her face to get a better look. Elle didn't seem herself; her head lolled so Jackson held onto her.

"Baby, talk to me. Are you hurt?" She worked the ropes loose, and when she did Elle practically slid into her arms.

"Jackson?" Elle touched Jackson's face. "Are you real? Am I dreaming?"

"Yes, sweet girl…this is a bad dream, but it's over now." Jackson sank to the floor cradling Elle in her arms. She drew Elle to her chest and held her. "It's over now. Everything is going to be okay."

A medic was at her side within minutes. He checked Elle's pulse and her pupils. Jackson reluctantly released Elle so that the emergency medical team could get her onto a stretcher.

"We've got her now, Commander." One of the men spoke to her. "She's in good hands."

On some level, Jackson knew he was telling her the truth, but it didn't matter. She didn't want to let Elle out of her sight. Jackson swiveled, looking for Nikki. From across the room, Nikki met her gaze.

"Go." Nikki motioned for her to leave. "You go, we've got this."

The two men had been handcuffed and a handful of soldiers were in the room now to assist with the captured assailants.

Jackson nodded and strode to the door. She followed the stretcher upstairs and climbed into the back of the ambulance. She held Elle's hand. Elle blinked and then smiled at her.

"You came to my rescue again." Her voice was weak.

"I'll always come to your rescue." Jackson raised Elle's fingers to her lips and held them there. Relief flooded her system. Elle was alive. Elle was safe. Nothing else mattered.

CHAPTER THIRTY-SIX

Elle held a forkful of noodles aloft to allow them to cool. It had been two days since the incident, and she was finally getting to cash in on the pasta dinner she'd been promised. Across from her, Jackson swirled noodles using her fork and a spoon.

"I never mastered that." Elle was amused by the mouthful Jackson had just managed.

Jackson chewed and swallowed.

"I have skills."

"No one doubts that." Elle laughed. "Most certainly not me."

So much had happened in the past two days. So much had been revealed.

Liam had not acted alone. He was simply the tip of the spear for Emosyne, one of the largest polluters of air, water, and climate on the planet. Emosyne Industries dumped more pollutants into the nation's waterways than US Electric and American Paper combined.

They'd seen the writing on the wall because they'd been the ones who put it there.

What better way to cash out than to sell the cure for the problem they'd helped create in the first place. They basically bought BIOME's leadership with dark money, and in return, Liam was to deliver the harvested phytoplankton. They would grow it, store it, and then sell it for a huge profit to nations all around the world.

It was an exploitive opportunity too big to pass up, like buying up water rights in Third World countries.

"What deep thoughts are you thinking over there?" Jackson's question coaxed her back to the moment.

"I was just thinking how I was working for the devil without even realizing it."

"You don't know that."

"They funded this mission, I'm sure they funded lots of the research at BIOME, including mine."

How had their lucrative blend of pollution, speculation, and law-bending been allowed to continue? Their dirty money had even been one of the primary funders for climate denial. How could Liam have been so completely turned?

"I can't stop thinking about Liam. About what changed for him." Elle genuinely struggled to understand why he'd acted as he had.

"Maybe he just lost hope." Jackson reached across the table and covered Elle's hand with hers. "It happens to all of us."

Elle rotated her hand to entwine their fingers. She dislodged the negative thoughts. Elle wanted to focus on Jackson and on getting back to a normal life.

"I'm sorry, I just can't stop turning over every detail in my head, looking for what's underneath."

"I know how you science types are." Jackson smiled. "Always looking for answers."

Elle squeezed her hand lightly.

"At least something good has come out of all of this."

"You mean, besides meeting me?" Jackson twirled more noodles with her free hand.

"Yes, besides that." Elle laughed and returned her attention to her plate for a moment. "Ted's son will get the surgery. BIOME's board came through for him. They were probably in need of some good PR. I spoke to Ted's wife, Anna, yesterday." Anna had no idea what had truly happened during the mission. And as far as Elle was involved, she never would.

"That's great news."

"Yes, it is."

Elle couldn't finish the large serving of pasta, and after a few more bites she surrendered. She rested her elbows on the table, sipped wine, and watched Jackson finish eating. Jackson poured more wine for each of them. She smiled at Elle over the lip of her glass as she drank.

In a million years, she'd never have thought they would be sitting having dinner at her apartment. After their first encounter at the Green Club, Elle had been so sure she'd never see Jackson again. So much had happened since that first night. Elle didn't even feel as if she were the same person she'd been that night. And Jackson had certainly changed.

Jackson picked up their plates and set them in the sink. She sloshed a little water on them but stopped when Elle encircled her waist.

"Let's leave everything until tomorrow." She stood on her tiptoes and kissed the back of Jackson's neck.

"Oh wait, I almost forgot...I have something for you." Elle went to retrieve it from her bag in the bedroom and then returned holding the small gift in her hand.

She held out the small, shallow package to Jackson. It was a simple brown gift box with a blue ribbon. Jackson tugged the ribbon free and lifted the lid. Nestled in a bed of tissue paper was a wooden, hand-hewn slingshot with a heart carved into the handle.

Jackson laughed and then kissed her.

"It's perfect, just like you."

"It's a small token of the thing that brought us together."

"Elle, I never thought I could feel this way." Jackson grew serious. "I thought there was a part of me that would be forever stuck in the past, unable to truly feel...like this, again." Jackson's voice broke. "And then I thought I'd lost you."

Elle took the package from her and wrapped her arms around Jackson's neck. Feathering kisses along her cheek.

"I thought I'd lost you too. It was the single worst moment of my life." Elle rested her cheek against Jackson's shoulder as Jackson encircled her with her arms. "I don't ever want to let you go."

"Then don't," Jackson whispered into her hair.

Elle led Jackson to the bedroom where they helped each other undress. Jackson still had bruises on her cheek. Elle touched her face. Such a handsome face.

Jackson felt almost as if she was now living in one long, beautiful daydream. She took in every detail of Elle's gorgeous body before she let herself be tugged onto the bed. She spooned next to Elle under the lightweight blanket and kissed her slowly, deeply. If Jackson allowed her mind to think of what had almost happened, that she'd almost lost Elle, she'd get the worst sinking sensation deep in her gut. She'd been in that dark place before; she knew it well. She clung to Elle for a moment, waiting for the desperate feeling to pass. She closed her eyes and pressed her face into Elle's neck.

"Hey, what's going on?" Elle tenderly caressed her face.

"Sometimes, sometimes I can't help thinking...what if I hadn't been able to find you."

"But you did." Elle kissed her cheek. "Don't go to that dark place. Stay here with me."

Jackson sighed. How did Elle know?

"I'm here." Jackson softly declared. "I am with you and I'm not going anywhere."

Jackson shifted on top of Elle, braced above her so that she could see Elle's face.

She was about to take another jump. And this next jump was a complete leap of faith.

"Elle."

"Yes?" Elle let her hands drift from Jackson's face to her shoulders.

Elle's delicate fingers sent shivers down Jackson's back. She adjusted so that her hips were between Elle's legs. She wanted to be as close as possible for what she needed to say.

"Elle, will you marry me?"

It was true that they hadn't known each other for very long, and at the same time, they'd known each other for a thousand years. All Jackson was sure of was that she didn't want one more day to pass without Elle in it. She wanted all the hours of all the days filled with Elle.

Elle didn't answer right away. She closed her eyes and a slow, playful smile gradually spread across her face. Jackson's heart pounded in her chest and in her ears.

"Ask me again."

"Right now?"

"Yes, I just want to hear it one more time." Elle opened her eyes and smiled up at her.

"Eliza Graham, will you marry me?"

"Yes." Elle drew her down until their lips met. "Yes, yes, yes."

Elle's whispered response calmed the churning sea of emotion within Jackson. She sank into the softness of Elle's body, savoring the closeness and acceptance. Warmth cascaded over her.

"I love you." They'd said it in unison and then laughed.

Jackson felt a surge of happiness, no—contentment. She was no longer stranded with no hope of rescue. Elle had saved her.

The world had changed. Her world had changed, forever.

EPILOGUE

For decades, the oceans had served as a crucial buffer against global warming, soaking up roughly a quarter of the carbon dioxide that humans emitted from power plants, factories, and cars, and absorbing most of the excess heat trapped on Earth by carbon dioxide and other greenhouse gases. Without that protection, the land was heating much more rapidly. But the transplanted colony of ancient phytoplankton proved reversal was possible.

Three months after the initial tank purge, oxygen readings had improved in the seawater surrounding San Francisco. Acidification levels had also improved. Transplanting the green microscopic marine scrubbers had worked. It was working. Things would continue to improve in the coming months.

Plans were underway to harvest plankton from the nearby Pacific for transplant into other key aquatic locations around the globe. This greening of the oceans had become one of the largest multinational collaborations in Earth's history. Finally, world leaders acknowledged that Earth was an ocean world, run and regulated by a single sea. A sea that had been pushed to the brink, an ocean system on life support.

Memory sometimes created its own story. Elle hoped that this would not be one of those instances. People needed to remember how close they'd come to utter collapse. She hoped people would never forget that humanity was just a single part of one big habitat—Earth.

Elle looked up from the tablet and smiled. She'd been taking a few minutes to run through the last bit of data before liftoff.

"Everything looks good." She handed the tablet back to Saro.

Saro nodded and stepped aside, making room for the core members of the team to assemble. Jackson was about to give her speech, the one she always gave before missions. The speech about facing your fears, about pushing through fear for the sake of the team. Elle loved this talk and she loved the woman giving it.

They were jumping back ten thousand years to harvest Pacific salmon from the past and transport them to the future. With the oceans actively healing, it was time to address the rivers.

There was a documented link between salmon nutrients and overall ecosystem health. By going out into the ocean, feeding and storing nutrients, then returning to their stream of origin to spawn and die, salmon enriched the river habitats. Salmon were a keystone species for repairing rivers and watershed ecosystems.

"Okay, people. Set your watches back ten thousand years." Jackson clapped her hands together. "Wheels up in fifteen minutes. Everyone to your assigned grav tubes."

Nikki shook hands with Jackson as she strode to the ship.

"See you on the other side, Commander." Nikki gave a little wave as she stepped through the portal.

Jackson stood on deck and watched the rest of the crew file in as Saro's band of technicians scurried about with last-minute preparations.

"Well, if it isn't Dr. Graham, the new head of our science division." Jackson grinned.

"Hello, Commander." Elle stood close to Jackson, intentionally invading her personal space. "I'm mission ready and reporting for duty."

"Past, present, future…I don't care where I am, as long as I'm with you." Jackson zipped the front of her flight suit.

"Just remember, Commander, in the future, you promised me a *real* honeymoon." Elle walked toward the Slingshot, with a sway in her hips.

Jackson caught up to her, capturing her hand, entwining her fingers with Elle's just as they boarded the Slingshot. She was almost giddy, like a kid about to set out on some grand new adventure.

"Dr. Graham, any future with you in it is looking very bright indeed."

The End

About the Author

Missouri Vaun spent a large part of her childhood in southern Mississippi, before attending high school in North Carolina and college in Tennessee. Strong connections to her roots in the rural south have been a grounding force throughout her life. Vaun spent twelve years finding her voice working as a journalist in places as disparate as Chicago, Atlanta, and Jackson, Mississippi, all along filing away characters and their stories. Her novels are heartfelt, earthy, and speak of loyalty and our responsibility to others. She and her wife currently live in northern California.

Books Available from Bold Strokes Books

Best Practice by Carsen Taite. When attorney Grace Maldonado agrees to mentor her best friend's little sister, she's prepared to confront Perry's rebellious nature, but she isn't prepared to fall in love. Legal Affairs: one law firm, three best friends, three chances to fall in love. (978-1-63555-361-1)

Home by Kris Bryant. Natalie and Sarah discover that anything is possible when love takes the long way home. (978-1-63555-853-1)

Keeper by Sydney Quinne. With a new charge under her reluctant wing—feisty, highly intelligent math wizard Isabelle Templeton—Keeper Andy Bouchard has to prevent a murder or die trying. (978-1-63555-852-4)

One More Chance by Ali Vali. Harry Bastantes planned a future with Desi Thompson until the day Desi disappeared without a word, only to walk back into her life sixteen years later. (978-1-63555-536-3)

Renegade's War by Gun Brooke. Freedom fighter Aurelia DeCallum regrets saving the woman called Blue. She fears it will jeopardize her mission, and secretly, Blue might end up breaking Aurelia's heart. (978-1-63555-484-7)

The Other Women by Erin Zak. What happens in Vegas should stay in Vegas, but what do you do when the love you find in Vegas changes your life forever? (978-1-63555-741-1)

The Sea Within by Missouri Vaun. Time is running out for Dr. Elle Graham to convince Captain Jackson Drake that the only thing that can save future Earth resides in the past, and rescue her broken heart in the process. (978-1-63555-568-4)

To Sleep With Reindeer by Justine Saracen. In Norway under Nazi occupation, Marrit, an Indigenous woman; and Kirsten, a Norwegian resister, join forces to stop the development of an atomic weapon. (978-1-63555-735-0)

Twice Shy by Aurora Rey. Having an ex with benefits isn't all it's cracked up to be. Will Amanda Russo learn that lesson in time to take a chance on love with Quinn Sullivan? (978-1-63555-737-4)

Z-Town by Eden Darry. Forced to work together to stay alive, Meg and Lane must find the centuries-old treasure before the zombies find them first. (978-1-63555-743-5)

Bet Against Me by Fiona Riley. In the high stakes luxury real estate market, everything has a price, and as rival Realtors Trina Lee and Kendall Yates find out, that means their hearts and souls, too. (978-1-63555-729-9)

Broken Reign by Sam Ledel. Together on an epic journey in search of a mysterious cure, a princess and a village outcast must overcome life-threatening challenges and their own prejudice if they want to survive. (978-1-63555-739-8)

Just One Taste by CJ Birch. For Lauren, it only took one taste to start trusting in love again. (978-1-63555-772-5)

Lady of Stone by Barbara Ann Wright. Sparks fly as a magical emergency forces a noble embarrassed by her ability to submit to a low-born teacher who resents everything about her. (978-1-63555-607-0)

Last Resort by Angie Williams. Katie and Rhys are about to find out what happens when you meet the girl of your dreams but you aren't looking for a happily ever after. (978-1-63555-774-9)

Longing for You by Jenny Frame. When Debrek housekeeper Katie Brekman is attacked amid a burgeoning vampire-witch war, Alexis Villiers must go against everything her clan believes in to save her. (978-1-63555-658-2)

Money Creek by Anne Laughlin. Clare Lehane is a troubled lawyer from Chicago who tries to make her way in a rural town full of secrets and deceptions. (978-1-63555-795-4)

Passion's Sweet Surrender by Ronica Black. Cam and Blake are unable to deny their passion for each other, but surrendering to love is a whole different matter. (978-1-63555-703-9)

The Holiday Detour by Jane Kolven. It will take everything going wrong to make Dana and Charlie see how right they are for each other. (978-1-63555-720-6)

Too Hot to Ride by Andrews & Austin. World famous cutting horse champion and industry legend Jane Barrow is knockdown sexy in the way she moves, talks, and rides, and Rae Starr is determined not to get involved with this womanizing gambler. (978-1-63555-776-3)

A Love that Leads to Home by Ronica Black. For Carla Sims and Janice Carpenter, home isn't about location, it's where your heart is. (978-1-63555-675-9)

Blades of Bluegrass by D. Jackson Leigh. A US Army occupational therapist must rehab a bitter veteran who is a ticking political time bomb the military is desperate to disarm. (978-1-63555-637-7)

Guarding Hearts by Jaycie Morrison. As treachery and temptation threaten the women of the Women's Army Corps, who will risk it all for love? (978-1-63555-806-7)

Hopeless Romantic by Georgia Beers. Can a jaded wedding planner and an optimistic divorce attorney possibly find a future together? (978-1-63555-650-6)

Hopes and Dreams by PJ Trebelhorn. Movie theater manager Riley Warren is forced to face her high school crush and tormentor, wealthy socialite Victoria Thayer, at their twentieth reunion. (978-1-63555-670-4)

In the Cards by Kimberly Cooper Griffin. Daria and Phaedra are about to discover that love finds a way, especially when powers outside their control are at play. (978-1-63555-717-6)

Moon Fever by Ileandra Young. SPEAR agent Danika Karson must clear her werewolf friend of multiple false charges while teaching her vampire girlfriend to resist the blood mania brought on by a full moon. (978-1-63555-603-2)

Quake City by St John Karp. Can Andre find his best friend Amy before the night devolves into a nightmare of broken hearts, malevolent drag queens, and spontaneous human combustion? Or has it always happened this way, every night, at Aunty Bob's Quake City Club? (978-1-63555-723-7)

Serenity by Jesse J. Thoma. For Kit Marsden, there are many things in life she cannot change. Serenity is in the acceptance. (978-1-63555-713-8)

Sylver and Gold by Michelle Larkin. Working feverishly to find a killer before he strikes again, Boston Homicide Detective Reid Sylver and rookie cop London Gold are blindsided by their chemistry and developing attraction. (978-1-63555-611-7)

Trade Secrets by Kathleen Knowles. In Silicon Valley, love and business are a volatile mix for clinical lab scientist Tony Leung and venture capitalist Sheila Graham. (978-1-63555-642-1)

Death Overdue by David S. Pederson. Did Heath turn to murder in an alcohol induced haze to solve the problem of his blackmailer, or was it someone else who brought about a death overdue? (978-1-63555-711-4)

Entangled by Melissa Brayden. Becca Crawford is the perfect person to head up the Jade Hotel, if only the captivating owner of the local vineyard would get on board with her plan and stop badmouthing the hotel to everyone in town. (978-1-63555-709-1)

First Do No Harm by Emily Smith. Pierce and Cassidy are about to discover that when it comes to love, sometimes you have to risk it all to have it all. (978-1-63555-699-5)

Kiss Me Every Day by Dena Blake. For Wynn Evans, wishing for a do-over with Carly Jamison was a long shot, actually getting one was a game changer. (978-1-63555-551-6)

Olivia by Genevieve McCluer. In this lesbian Shakespeare adaptation with vampires, Olivia is a centuries old vampire who must fight a strange figure from her past if she wants a chance at happiness. (978-1-63555-701-5)

One Woman's Treasure by Jean Copeland. Daphne's search for discarded antiques and treasures leads to an embarrassing misunderstanding, and ultimately, the opportunity for the romance of a lifetime with Nina. (978-1-63555-652-0)

Silver Ravens by Jane Fletcher. Lori has lost her girlfriend, her home, and her job. Things don't improve when she's kidnapped and taken to fairyland. (978-1-63555-631-5)

Still Not Over You by Jenny Frame, Carsen Taite, Ali Vali. Old flames die hard in these tales of a second chance at love with the ex you're still not over. Stories by award winning authors Jenny Frame, Carsen Taite, and Ali Vali. (978-1-63555-516-5)

Storm Lines by Jessica L. Webb. Devon is a psychologist who likes rules. Marley is a cop who doesn't. They don't always agree, but both fight to protect a girl immersed in a street drug ring. (978-1-63555-626-1)

The Politics of Love by Jen Jensen. Is it possible to love across the political divide in a hostile world? Conservative Shelley Whitmore and liberal Rand Thomas are about to find out. (978-1-63555-693-3)

All the Paths to You by Morgan Lee Miller. High school sweethearts Quinn Hughes and Kennedy Reed reconnect five years after they break up and realize that their chemistry is all but over. (978-1-63555-662-9)

Arrested Pleasures by Nanisi Barrett D'Arnuck. When charged with a crime she didn't commit, Katherine Lowe faces the question: Which is harder, going to prison or falling in love? (978-1-63555-684-1)

Bonded Love by Renee Roman. Carpenter Blaze Carter suffers an injury that shatters her dreams, and ER nurse Trinity Greene hopes to show her that sometimes love is worth fighting for. (978-1-63555-530-1)

Convergence by Jane C. Esther. With life as they know it on the line, can Aerin McLeary and Olivia Ando's love survive an otherworldly threat to humankind? (978-1-63555-488-5)

Coyote Blues by Karen F. Williams. Riley Dawson, psychotherapist and shape-shifter, has her world turned upside down when Fiona Bell, her one true love, returns. (978-1-63555-558-5)

Drawn by Carsen Taite. Will the clues lead Detective Claire Hanlon to the killer terrorizing Dallas, or will she merely lose her heart to person of interest, urban artist Riley Flynn? (978-1-63555-644-5)

Every Summer Day by Lee Patton. Meant to celebrate every summer day, Luke's journal instead chronicles a love affair as fast-moving and possibly as fatal as his brother's brain tumor. (978-1-63555-706-0)

Lucky by Kris Bryant. Was Serena Evans's luck really about winning the lottery, or is she about to get even luckier in love? (978-1-63555-510-3)

The Last Days of Autumn by Donna K. Ford. Autumn and Caroline question the fairness of life, the cruelty of loss, and what it means to love as they navigate the complicated minefield of relationships, grief, and life-altering illness. (978-1-63555-672-8)

Three Alarm Response by Erin Dutton. In the midst of tragedy, can these first responders find love and healing? Three stories of courage, bravery, and passion. (978-1-63555-592-9)

Veterinary Partner by Nancy Wheelton. Callie and Lauren are determined to keep their hearts safe but find that taking a chance on love is the safest option of all. (978-1-63555-666-7)